Kara's breath hitched in her throat

Sitting there, Lucas looked dark, sexy and a little bit rumpled. He looked gorgeous, really, and despite all of her best intentions, her heart kicked into high gear. Her stomach fluttered even as her mouth went desert dry. Trying to get some moisture back, she rubbed her lips together. Licked them. And felt Lucas stiffen against her even as a deep, rumbling growl started in his chest.

"Kara." It was a warning, and a blatant one at that, and she felt it sizzle along every nerve ending she had. Drowning now in the scent and sight and sound of him, she reached up and rested her hand against his cut-glass jaw. Stroked her thumb over his dark stubble and lost herself in the dark pools of his eyes.

"Kara." He whispered her name this time, his hand coming up to cup her own face. "What are you doing?"

Dear Reader,

Every once in a while, if she's very lucky, an author gets the chance to write a series of books that really speaks to her. For me, these three Harlequin Superromance books about doctors who work in Africa—*From the Beginning,* February 2012, *Healing Dr. Alexander,* May 2012 and this one—is that series. *About the Baby* was the most difficult of the three to write, I have to say. Partly because my hero, Dr. Lucas Montgomery, is an all-around great guy (I usually specialize in writing bad boys) and partly because I have to say good-bye to six characters who I really like and admire.

When I was in college, I always thought I would graduate then join the Peace Corps or another such group that did humanitarian work in places that desperately need help. Though I knew my parents would not be overly excited to let me go off to a part of the world that was constantly war and disaster torn, I never doubted that one day I would do it.

Well, life has a way of taking paths you never intend. When I left college I went straight into grad school where I fell in love with a wonderful man (from Africa, by the way), got married and had a baby all before I finished my master's degree. Needless to say, I've never made it to Africa for more than a three-week visit. And while I have since volunteered my time here in America for numerous women's and children's organizations, there's a part of me that still feels like I should have gone to Africa, should have tried to help. It is this part of myself that I tapped into when I wrote *About the Baby,* and when I conceived of this trilogy.

Thanks so much for giving *About the Baby* a try. I hope you enjoy reading it as much as I enjoyed writing it. I love hearing from my readers either at my email tracy@tracywolff.com or at my blog, www.tracywolff.blogspot.com. If you get the chance, please stop by and say hello!

Happy reading!

Tracy Wolff

About the Baby

TRACY WOLFF

HARLEQUIN®
entertain, enrich, inspire™

Recycling programs
for this product may
not exist in your area.

ISBN-13: 978-0-373-71816-0

ABOUT THE BABY

ABOUT THE AUTHOR

Tracy Wolff collects books, English degrees and lipsticks, and has been known to forget where—and sometimes who—she is when immersed in a great novel. At six, she wrote her first short story—something with a rainbow and a prince—and at seven, she ventured into the wonderful world of girls' lit with her first Judy Blume novel. By ten, she'd read everything in the young-adult and classics sections of her local bookstore, so in desperation her mom started her on romance novels. And from the first page of the first book, Tracy knew she'd found her lifelong love. Tracy lives in Texas with her husband and three sons, where she pens romance novels and teaches writing at her local community college.

Books by Tracy Wolff

HARLEQUIN SUPERROMANCE

Other titles by this author available in ebook format.

To my mom,

the most amazing woman I know.

Acknowledgement

Thank you, Wanda, for your never-ending patience with me as I struggle to get things right, usually at the last possible minute. I really appreciate your support.

CHAPTER ONE

April

"CAN I BUY YOU A DRINK?"

Dr. Lucas Montgomery turned with a frown, annoyed at having his few minutes of hard-won solitude disturbed. The annoyance turned to something else entirely, however, at his first glimpse of the leggy redhead with the killer curves and impish smile. She was holding out a glass of champagne, her green eyes twinkling in the dim courtyard lights of the hotel terrace.

"The champagne's free," he told her.

"And yet you're not drinking any." She gestured slightly with the glass. "Come on. Live a little."

Raising an eyebrow at her teasing, he reached for the champagne flute and kept his gaze locked with hers as he downed the effervescent liquid in one swig.

"Shall I get you another?" she asked dryly as he set the glass on top of a stone ledge.

"Shouldn't that be my line?"

"Perhaps, but I haven't finished my drink yet." She held up the nearly full glass for his inspection.

"I won't hold that against you," he answered with a smile. He couldn't help it—he really liked looking at her. Clasping her free hand in his, he murmured, "Dance with me."

Her lips twisted in contemplation and when she didn't immediately answer, he slipped the glass of champagne from her hand and set it next to his empty one.

"Come on," he urged. Wrapping his right arm around her waist, he pulled her against him and started to glide over the redbrick patio.

"You want to dance here?" She paused for a moment, refusing to budge as she considered.

"What's wrong with here? Live a little," he mimicked, certain the dare would get to her.

She laughed then, a husky, full-bodied sound that made him laugh along with her. "Nothing's wrong with here. I just didn't realize terrace dancing was one of your specialties."

It wasn't, but he had a feeling it was right up her alley. And when she stopped resisting and allowed him to propel her out of the shadows and into the small pool of light cast by the old-fashioned globe lantern, he knew he was right.

They were close enough to the ballroom to hear the music, and for long seconds neither of them talked as they moved together under the heavy branches of a centuries-old magnolia tree. With her heels on, she was only a couple inches shorter than his own height of six foot four.

He liked the way she fit against him. When the song ended, she tried to step away, but he held on. She indulged him for a moment, eyes closed and head resting against his shoulder. Then, with a sigh, she stepped away. He let her go, but when she tugged a little in an effort to free her hand, he refused to relinquish it. "How was Africa?" he asked softly.

"Same as always." While the reply was flippant, the sadness that moved behind her eyes was anything but. "Beautiful, but nightmarish."

"Did you get everything taken care of?"

"As much as we could. Cholera isn't something to play around with. We managed to vaccinate nine refugee camps as well as educate them on prevention measures and the handling of blood and tissue samples. It's not enough, but at least this outbreak is under control. But I'm sure it will pop up again soon and then we'll be right back where we were two months ago."

His stomach clenched a little at the thought of Kara going up against such a miserable illness, but he made himself ignore it. After all, it wasn't the first time she'd taken on a deadly disease and it sure as hell wasn't going to be the last. She was an epidemiologist for the Center for Disease Control. Traveling to hot spots around the world and figuring out where and how the outbreak happened was her job—and her calling.

Concern about his best friend's safety might keep him up some nights, but he was the only one. An adventurer through and through, Kara rarely worried about herself. She relished the thrill of running a virus to ground, as well as helping the people who so much of the world preferred to forget.

He understood her drive, her need to make the world a better place. He'd done his stint in For the

Children, one of the leading organizations that brought doctors into developing nations, and in doing so had seen just how desperately people needed help.

But, unlike Kara, he hadn't been able to hack it long-term. He'd gotten out early, had chosen to start a low-income clinic in the poorest area of Atlanta instead. Not because he didn't believe in helping those who couldn't help themselves, but because he knew that staying in Africa, witnessing the soul-deep suffering, would eventually kill him—as it nearly had his clinic partners, Amanda Hart and Jack Alexander.

Together the three of them dealt with everything at their clinic, from gunshot wounds to diagnosing cancer. And while there never seemed to be enough time, enough money, enough *anything,* at least here he could see that he was making a difference. When he'd been in Ethiopia it had felt like everything he'd done had been barely a drop in a leaky bucket.

Though he knew Kara didn't feel the same way about her time in Africa, he couldn't help asking, "You sure you're okay?"

"I'm fine. A little tired is all," she admitted with a grimace. "I got in late last night and my body's clock is all messed up."

"So what are you doing here? You should be home sleeping."

"Well, that was the plan. But earlier, I called the clinic to see if you could do lunch today but you had scheduled appointments right through your lunch hour, as usual. Your receptionist told me about this benefit event. And since I know how much you *love* these things, I figured it was my duty as your oldest and dearest friend to dust off my dancing shoes and suffer right along with you."

"Have I mentioned lately that you are a terrific best friend?"

"A time or two." She pretended to buff her nails on her dress. "But it's a sentiment that bears repeating."

"No doubt." He draped an arm around her shoulders, gave her a quick squeeze. "And I very much appreciate your sacrifice."

"And well you should. I've been in Somalia for the last seven weeks, running around in hiking boots and tennis shoes. Squeezing my feet into these heels—" she held up one slender foot encased in a pair of red-sequined stilettos "—has been absolute torture."

"I don't deserve you," he said with a grin.

"Well, that's obvious. But since you've got me, at least until the next crisis rears its ugly head, what do you say we blow this pop stand and go find something more interesting to do—after I sit down for five minutes."

"I can't leave. I'm one of the hosts," he said as he cupped a hand around her elbow and escorted her to the closest stone bench.

She sat, gratefully, and kicked off her right shoe so she could rub her toes. "Which is why you're hiding out on the patio? Because you're so concerned about your hosting duties?"

"I'm taking a break. I wanted a breather before I had to start making the rounds to say good-night to everyone."

"So take a longer break. I was just in the ball-room. It's well after midnight and the party has al-ready started to break up. Amanda, Jack and your mother have everything under control."

"No doubt. But Amanda threatened me with many, *many* painful things if I stepped out of line tonight. Not to mention what my mother said she would do if I embarrassed her. Somehow I think ducking out right before I'm supposed to position myself near the door and thank everyone for the copious amounts of money they've spent here tonight definitely falls into both categories."

"Okay, I can understand your fear of your mother's wrath. She can be scary when she gets going. But don't tell me you're afraid of a pregnant woman?"

"Damn right I am. Amanda's mean," he said with affection, so Kara would know he was teasing.

"I have to admit, I wondered how she got you here. Normally it's impossible to get you to attend a big charity event, even if it is for your own clinic."

Lucas shook his head. "I'm not even sure how we ended up *having* a big charity event, to be honest with you. One second I'm complaining about how hard it's been to pry funding out of the government and our regular donors—at a time when we need it most. The next thing I know Amanda's dialing her husband to see if his cable news network might like to sponsor a ball to raise money. She got Jack's girlfriend, So-phie, involved along with my mom and sisters, and here we are."

"Nobody throws a party like your mom and sisters."

"Isn't that the truth?" He heard the harsh edge of sarcasm in his voice, and tried to smooth it out. "They throw magnificent parties."

The knowing look Kara sent him told him he hadn't quite managed it. That was the problem with best friends—they'd been around long enough to know your dirty family laundry whether you liked it or not.

"I think they've done a wonderful job," she told him. "The ballroom looks gorgeous and the turnout is huge. You guys are going to make a bundle for the clinic."

"I hope so. Amanda's worked so hard on it that I'd hate to see it fail." Especially since she'd spent all her free time organizing the benefit when she should have been concentrating on her new marriage to Simon and impending motherhood.

"It won't fail," Kara reassured him. "You guys are amazing, and everyone here—especially the ones with deep pockets—has figured that out."

She reached for her champagne and quickly downed it. Then shot him the mischievous look that had first gotten his attention all those years ago. "Last chance to duck out before we head back into the ballroom and get swallowed by the legion of Dr. Montgomery fans. And, as extra incentive, if you leave with me now, I promise to buy you the biggest and best piece of apple pie in Atlanta. There's this great diner right down the street, but they close at one, so if we're going to go, we need to hustle."

Thinking she was joking, he started to refuse a second time. But when he looked at her, really looked at her, he saw. There was something wrong, something in her eyes that said she needed a shoulder to cry on. His had been her shoulder of choice since they'd met in the freshman dorms seventeen years before—and vice versa. It wasn't like he could turn her away and he didn't want to. Kara so rarely needed comforting, or anything else, from him. The fact that she needed it now—that she had so obviously sought him out— worried him enough to have him shifting his priorities.

"So, if we *were* to attempt an escape," he said, kneeling down to slide her shoe back onto her foot, "what do you think our best way out of here is?"

Her eyes lit up. "Really? You want to leave?"

"Darlin', I've wanted to break out of here since two seconds after I arrived. You're just the impetus I've been waiting for."

Obviously afraid he'd change his mind if she let him think about it too long, Kara jumped to her feet. "Let's go, then. I've got the escape route all planned out. Simon has Amanda resting at a table near the ballroom entrance where they can bid everyone goodnight. They're dealing with a steady stream of doctors, socialites and news people alike and they're fielding questions about the baby, so they should be occupied for quite some time.

"Jack and Sophie are dancing—he can't keep his eyes—or his hands—off her. And your mom and sisters, along with their dates, are still holding court in the center of the room." She grabbed his hand, tugging him toward the edge of the terrace. "And can I just say, go Mom! She's with Nicholas Vega, newsman extraordinaire. He's hanging on her every word."

"Of course he is. She's laying on the famous Montgomery charm. Her latest lover got wise and dropped her a couple of weeks ago so she's on the prowl for a new bank account. This benefit is a perfect opportunity for her to close the deal."

Kara laid a hand on his shoulder, and for a second he tensed, expecting her to say the same things his sisters did. That he was being too tough on Candy. That he needed to try to be more understanding. That he should cut her a break once in a while.

But this was Kara, who knew him better than anybody, and all she said was, "Rough couple of months with your mom, huh?"

He snorted. "More like a rough couple of decades, don't you think?"

He knew he sounded cynical, but it was hard to be anything else when it came to his mother. In the years since his dad had died, she'd run through the very significant portfolio he'd left for her and now counted on Lucas or whatever man she was currently dating to take care of her.

After ten years and twice as many rich lovers, he'd given up expecting her to change. Of course, he'd also given up "cutting her a break." If that made him a bastard, then he was willing to live with it—even if his sisters couldn't.

Turning to Kara, he switched the focus back where it belonged. "So, how exactly does this escape plan of yours begin?"

KARA WATCHED AS LUCAS'S eyes went cold and hard at the mention of his mother. Not that she blamed him. Most of the time, she wanted to shake some sense into Candy Montgomery herself and she wasn't even related to the woman. She could only imagine how bad it was for Lucas, control freak extraordinaire and the most dependable man she'd ever met, to be saddled with a mother who not only wouldn't be controlled, but who was completely *un*dependable.

As they scooted around the terrace, she glanced through the ballroom windows and saw his mother doing what she did best—telling an animated story to a gaggle of admirers. She was beautiful and glittery and obviously in her element as the center of attention at a benefit that should be all about her son. Not that anyone who knew her would be surprised.

What was surprising, at least to Kara, was how two people who looked so alike could be such different people. Both Lucas and his mother were absolutely stunning, with classically beautiful faces, piercing blue eyes and dark ebony hair. Lucas wore it too long and his mom wore it in a short, gamine cut that showed off her gorgeous bone structure and ageless skin. And though Lucas, at six foot four, stood about eight inches taller than his mother, they both had long, lean bodies and an innate sense of grace that drew gazes to them wherever they went.

Yet that was where the resemblance ended. Candy Montgomery was simpering, flighty and completely irresponsible. Oh, she was sweet—and as charming as the rest of Lucas's family—but she lived in a dream world. Which would be fine, except for the fact that Lucas's father had taught his son at an early age that he was the responsible one, the one whose job it was to take care of his mom and sisters if anything happened to Lucas, Sr. It was a responsibility he'd taken seriously for the ten years since his father had died, one that required he bail his mom and sisters out of whatever trouble they got themselves into. Which was a significant amount of trouble.

Lucas never complained, and she never brought it up, but after seventeen years of watching his mother and sisters taking financial and emotional advantage of him, Kara wanted to tell them all to grow up. They were adults and it was no longer his job to take care of them. But she refused to give Lucas her opinion on it unless he asked—the last thing she wanted to do was cause him more stress.

Kara saw Candy start to scan the crowd, as if she was looking for someone. It was probably time to show off her son. Kara reached out and shoved Lucas, hard. Completely unprepared for the push, he stumbled back a few steps—just enough to be hidden from view by a giant column, exactly as she'd intended.

"What the hell was that for?" he demanded.

She ducked behind the column with him. "I had to think fast. We were about to be spotted."

"I didn't realize we were actually hiding."

"Of course we're hiding. How else are we supposed to get out of here?" She stuck her head out, looked around. Candy had turned and was walking toward the front of the ballroom—straight for Amanda and Jack but with her back to the window. She grabbed Lucas's hand and tugged him into the shadows of the patio.

"Come on, now's our chance to escape."

Lucas reached out and snagged her hand, his fingers wrapping around her wrist. "You do realize that we aren't mounting a prison break, don't you? We're simply leaving a fundraiser a few minutes early."

She shot him a pitying look. "I will have you know, this is much more complicated than a prison break. After all, in prison, all they do is toss you back in your cell. Here, if we get caught, they might actually kick you out of high society completely."

He snorted. "I couldn't get that lucky."

"Still, why risk it?" Grabbing his hand, she began skulking along the edges of the terrace, sticking to the shadows so that no one could see them.

"You're completely insane," he told her, but he played along, anyway, which was exactly as she'd intended. After all, if he was wrapped up in humoring her, he wasn't brooding about his mommy issues.

Which was a good thing. He was far too good a man to spend his life worrying about things he'd never be able to change. She'd spent too much of the last decade stuck in that catch-22 herself, and there was no way she was going to let her closest friend fall into the same trap.

Finally, they ran out of fence and building to skulk

against and reached an open spot on the terrace. After stepping out of the shadows, she chanced another look in the ballroom and realized that they must have been spotted, because his sisters were headed directly for them.

"Duck," she whispered, bending down so that she was partially hidden by the hedge in front of them. When Lucas just stood there, eyebrows raised incredulously, she grabbed his hand and tugged until he bent down, too.

"*What* are we doing?" he asked again.

"Hiding from your sisters. I think they spotted us."

"It'd be hard to miss us, seeing as how we're acting like maniacs." Despite his words, he didn't seem particularly put out by their actions. "Is there some reason I can't just say good-night to them like a normal person would?"

"No, of course not. Where's the fun in that?"

"Oh, is that what this escape is supposed to be about? Fun?"

"Ha-ha." She elbowed him in the stomach. "We can stand up and go say good-night. But I've got to tell you, your sisters look like women on a mission. If we go talk to them, I don't think we're getting out of here anytime soon."

She watched as he poked his head above the hedge and checked out the way his sisters were storming the terrace. And though the guests had been trickling home for the past half an hour or so, there were still enough people around that they had gathered quite an entourage behind them.

"I think you're right," he finally said.

"So what do you want to do? Stay and talk to them or make a run for it?" She braced herself for the first answer—after all, Lucas didn't know how to shirk responsibility. And though she was disappointed their little game would end, she was just pleased he'd played along with her this long. Lucas didn't have enough fun in his life, and lately, neither had she.

She was so convinced that their little game of hide-and-seek was over that when he said, "Let's make a run for it," it took a few seconds for the words to register.

"Seriously?" she asked him after she managed to close her mouth.

He grinned. "Last one to the lobby is a rotten egg."

CHAPTER TWO

KARA DIDN'T ANSWER HIS challenge right away, though Lucas did see her relax a little in relief. Instead, she crept forward to the edge of the bushes, one small step at a time. But the second she reached the pathway that circled around to the front of the hotel, she was off and running, sprinting down the trail to the hotel's front door.

He was hot on her heels, could have beaten her easily—she *was* in four-inch stilettos, after all. But he was enjoying the view of her long legs and curvy ass in her short, tight red dress too much to rush ahead. She might be his best friend, and off-limits because of it, but he was still a man and it was a hell of a view. Besides, Kara was laughing, the melancholy exhaustion of earlier long gone, and he was definitely willing to finish second if it meant keeping the smile on her face.

"I won!" she exclaimed the second he turned the corner to the valet parking area.

"I noticed."

"So what's my prize?"

"A ride home?" he asked, fishing in his pocket for his valet ticket.

She made a disparaging sound. "That's the best you've got?"

"It kind of is."

"Careful, Lucas, you're getting staid in your old age."

"You are aware that we're exactly the same age," he reminded her, reaching out to yank on one of her flame-red curls.

She kicked off her shoes, scooped them up. "Yeah, but I'm not an old fuddy-duddy."

"I'm not boring." He knew she was just joking, but the accusation stung a little. It hit too close to home, he supposed. It was too similar to what his family told him regularly.

"I never said you were boring," she said, snatching his keys out of his hand and dropping them into her red-beaded clutch. "But I figure we can do better than a ride home. That diner with the apple pie is just up the street. I say we go for it."

She started walking and he found himself following along behind her. That apple pie did sound good—and maybe the chance to relax over dessert would get Kara talking. Because as much as he'd enjoyed being a part of her absurd little getaway, Kara was only ever this crazy when something was very wrong. Through the years, he'd learned there was an inverse correlation between the two. The more upset Kara was, the more lighthearted and silly she'd act. And while he was happy to go along for the ride, at some point she was going to run out of gas and he had every intention of being there for her when she did.

As they walked, Kara bombarded him with questions. *How's the clinic? How's life? How's your family?* He let her get away with the inane small talk, though he knew it was more about keeping the focus on him and off herself than it was about stuff they'd already covered. But sometimes keeping the peace was more important than getting to the bottom of things right away. Life with a histrionic mother and two high-maintenance sisters had taught him that.

Besides, this was Kara. She'd never been able to keep a secret from him in her life and he had no intention of letting her do so now. If he didn't push, she'd eventually loosen up and it would all come spilling out. And if it didn't…well, then he'd push.

Still, though they'd walked together a million times—through the deserted midnight streets of downtown Atlanta as well as a hundred other places—something felt off tonight. Like there was something between them and they weren't quite connecting, though the rhythm of their speech was as relaxed as always.

It made him uncomfortable. He hadn't been able to count on much in his life—more often than not the clinic was one short budget cut away from extinction and since his father had died, he was the one his family turned to for just about everything. But Kara was different. She was the one person he could always count on to be there for him and to be straight with him. He couldn't stand the idea that there was something she wasn't sharing with him, something that was bothering her that she wasn't letting him help with. He'd just made up his mind to ask her what was going on when she stopped in the middle of the sidewalk and looked up at the pocket of midnight sky that wasn't blocked by buildings.

"It's a beautiful night—not too hot or humid yet," she said.

"Seriously?" he asked. "Now we're going to talk about the weather?"

"Not really. I was just making conversation." She never took her eyes from the sky, and finally he glanced up, too, trying to figure out what she found so interesting. But it was the same sky they always saw. "You can't see any stars from here," he finally told her. "The lights are too bright."

She sighed. "I know. I kind of like that."

"Since when? You've been into stargazing as long as I've known you. God knows, we did enough of it in college."

"We did do a lot of it. I used to love driving out to the middle of nowhere with you, staring up at that infinite sky, bursting with possibilities."

"So what's changed?"

"Nothing." She sighed. "Or everything. You know, in Somalia, the sky is so wide-open. It goes on for miles and miles. When I was there, looking at it and feeling completely insignificant, it occurred to me that there's something comforting about only being able to see this little bit of sky. You know what I mean?"

No, he really didn't. He found the whole concept behind her explanation pretty damned depressing, actually. Not to mention it sounded nothing like the take-life-by-the-tail adventurer he knew her to be.

Trying to think over the clang of warning bells going off in the back of his mind, he decided delicacy be damned. He was getting to the bottom of this. "You want to tell me what's going on, Kara?"

"Nothing. Why?"

"You seem…troubled."

She dropped her eyes back to his and smiled stiffly. "I told you, it's the jet lag. I'm just a little off."

If this was a little, he'd hate to see a lot. "Do you want to go home?"

"No!" she answered forcefully, panic flashing before she tamped it down. "The diner's up ahead."

"I'm not really in the mood for pie."

"Now those are words I never thought I'd hear come out of your mouth."

He wanted to shake her, to demand that she tell him what was going on in her head. He knew it wasn't the way to get it out of her, but part of him didn't care. She was hurting and it was his job to make it better. It had always been his job, with everyone in his life. Why couldn't Kara understand that and just let him help?

Frustrated, he ran a hand through his hair before demanding, "Tell me, Kara. Whatever it is, spit it out."

"Spit what out?" She looked confused, but under it all was a shade of panic that set off his own nerves.

"Are you sick?" he asked abruptly.

"What? No."

"Were you hurt in Somalia?"

"Of course not. Why are you asking all these questions?"

"Because you're not talking to me. I want to know what's put that bruised look in your eyes. And don't," he said as she opened her mouth to protest, "pretend that you have no idea what I'm talking about. It will only piss me off."

KARA STARED AT LUCAS, words welling up on her tongue that she had no idea how to say. Not to him when he wouldn't understand. He always knew what he was doing, always had a plan. And once he'd made that plan, he stuck to it. No matter what. How could he understand that she was suddenly, deathly afraid that she couldn't stick to the life plan she'd made for herself? Or worse, that she'd made a mistake ever thinking it was right for her?

No, she couldn't tell him. Not now. She needed more time to figure it out in her own head, more time to decide what her options were before she asked him for his advice. With Lucas, it was always better to have a few backup plans in place before talking to him. Otherwise, he'd just take over and she'd find herself right back where she'd started.

Closing her eyes for a moment to clear her head, she opened them to find Lucas staring straight at her. Since she couldn't meet his eyes, not when she was lying to him, she shifted her gaze behind her—and realized they'd stopped in front of her favorite park. Suddenly the idea of doing something mindless, something just for fun, appealed to her in a way nothing had for a very long time.

Was it absurd? Yes.

Was she going to do it, anyway? Absolutely.

Maybe it would buy her the time she needed to figure out exactly what it was she wanted to say. Because the look in Lucas's eye said he wasn't going to let her get away with evading him for long. Not this time. Not tonight.

"Wanna swing?" she asked him, nodding to the park behind him.

"Swing?" It was like he'd never heard of the word.

"It'll be fun." She walked closer to the locked fence that kept the public out after eleven at night.

"Are you kidding me?" Lucas demanded. "I want to talk about what's going on with you and you want to go play in the sandbox?"

"Swings, not sandbox," she said, tossing her shoes over the fence before grabbing onto the fence and starting to climb. "Try to keep up."

"I would if you weren't completely insane." He paused. "What are you doing?"

"What does it look like I'm doing?" she asked, reaching for the top of the fence and pulling herself up. "I can't leave my shoes here—those are my only pair of Jimmy Choos."

"The park is closed!" he hissed.

"And your point is?"

"My point is, it's *closed*. You can get arrested for trespassing, you know."

"Give me a break. It's a public park." Hiking her

dress up to the tops of her thighs, she climbed over the fence, careful of the iron spikes, then dropped down to the grass below. "Are you coming?" she asked, picking up her heels and pretending she didn't care if he followed her or not.

Lucas sighed heavily and she could all but see his eye roll as he said, "Of course I'm coming. This is downtown Atlanta. God only knows what could happen to you in there."

As he pulled himself up and over the fence in a couple of smooth, well-coordinated movements—much smoother and well-coordinated than her own—she refrained from reminding him that she'd managed to survive on her own in places a lot rougher than Atlanta. But the last thing she wanted was to bring her job into the conversation, not when she'd done everything in her power to avoid talking about it.

He dropped to the ground beside her. "So what do you want to do now?" he demanded, his voice put-upon. But he couldn't hide his grin—or the dimple in his left cheek that only came when he was deeply amused by something.

"We're in a park, Lucas. What do you think I want to do?" She grabbed his hand and took off, running full out down the grassy hill that led to the playground equipment. But about halfway down, she tripped over a sprinkler head. As she stumbled, Lucas tried to stop her fall and somehow they got all tangled up together. They hit the ground, hard, and then they were rolling down the hill, Lucas instinctively wrapping his arms around her to protect her.

They came to a stop against the side of a small gazebo, a few feet from the bottom of the hill. Lucas hit with an *oomph,* though she wasn't sure if that was because he'd born the brunt of the hit or because she had landed on top of him.

Certain she wasn't helping matters, she struggled to climb off him, but was so dizzy from the roll that she ended up straddling him, her head on his chest as she tried to keep the world around her from spinning. She glanced up at Lucas, who had a very disgruntled look on his face—like he couldn't imagine that he had somehow been a part of anything so undignified. The absolute shock, mingled with the sight of his expression, made her throw her head back and giggle like crazy.

Immediately, his hand shot up to the back of her head, his fingers probing her scalp. "Did you hit your head?" he demanded, trying to sit up. Which wasn't easy considering she was stretched out on top of him and laughing like a hyena.

"If you could see your face," she sputtered, "you'd laugh, too."

His left eyebrow rose in that adorably sardonic way of his, which only made her amusement harder to control. Within moments, he joined in and the two of them laughed themselves silly.

This was what she missed the most when she was working on location. Kara rolled onto her back and looked up at the slightly wider expanse of sky above them. She decided it wasn't Chinese takeout or her big feather bed or access to a regular shower that she missed most—though a shower did run a close second. No, what she missed more than anything was Lucas.

Spending time with her other friends and colleagues was never as much fun as spending time with him. Oh, he walked the walk of the rich, Southern gentleman, but inside that smooth, slightly reserved exterior was a wicked sense of humor and an incredible capacity for fun. He didn't show it to many people, and she couldn't help being grateful that she was one of the chosen few he could let down his guard with.

"What now?" he finally asked when their laughter had quieted. "You want to fall off the monkey bars, maybe break your collarbone? Or should we go for something more sedate, like riding the merry-go-round till we puke?"

She reached over, rested a finger against the right corner of his mouth and pressed upward. "You need to smile when you say that stuff. Someone who doesn't know you might think you're serious."

"I am serious. If we try hard enough, maybe we could hang ourselves on the swings."

"Make fun of me all you want," she said, swatting his shoulder. "But you have to admit this is a lot better than that stupid gala."

"So is a root canal, darlin', so don't get too full of yourself."

She went to smack him again but he moved lightning fast and caught her fist in his hand. His face turned serious. "You've been running an awful lot tonight, Kara. It's time to settle down and tell me what it's all about."

Closing her eyes, she tried to block out the concern on his face, but in the end she couldn't do it. Not when he was still holding her hand, his thumb stroking softly across the back of her palm.

"I can't breathe. I just—I can't…" Her breath caught on a sob she could no longer swallow down. It had been sitting there for days and weeks, maybe even months, waiting to escape. She tried to stop it—and the ones that came after it. The last thing Lucas needed was for her to turn into a basket case. Yet, no matter how hard she tried, she couldn't stop the surge inside of her.

"Aw, baby, I didn't mean to make you cry," he murmured, sitting up and pulling her onto his lap.

She went without a struggle, letting him rock her as she sobbed out all her pain and frustration and fear. Her last few trips—to Colombia, Somalia and the Sudan—had been awful. So awful that there was a part of her, despite what she'd told Lucas earlier, that couldn't imagine going back.

Sure, she could map the outbreak of the disease, figure out where it started and why. That helped people in the long run—she understood that. It was why she'd chosen to be an epidemiologist to begin with. But it didn't do anything for people in the short-term and she wasn't sure she could take it anymore, to watch people die terrible deaths in the hope that somehow she could save others two, five, ten years down the road.

Finally, she wore herself out, the crying subsiding to the occasional shudder. "I'm sorry," she whispered

into his tuxedo shirt, ashamed of her loss of control
now that she was coming back to herself. Lucas had
enough on his plate—the last thing she'd wanted to
do was burden him with more.

For long seconds Lucas didn't answer, just stroked
her hair softly. She had pretty much given up on a response when he said, "You don't need to be sorry. Just
tell me what's wrong."

This time she was the one who took long seconds
to answer. And when she finally did find her voice,
the only words that came out were, "I don't even know
where to start."

"Start at the beginning, baby."

She would, except at this point, she had no idea
when that was.

CHAPTER THREE

"I'M THINKING OF LEAVING the CDC."

He knew she was waiting for an exclamation of surprise or denial, and though he was shocked, he made sure not to show it. Instead, he just looked at her, waiting for an explanation.

"You know, I became an epidemiologist because I wanted to help people. I could have taken my medical degree and joined the Peace Corps or For the Children, but I wanted to do more than only treat the victims after the fact. I wanted to track viruses, to figure out how they start so we could prevent outbreaks from happening in the future."

"And you don't want to do that anymore?"

"It's not that I don't want to do that. It's just—" She tried to find a way to explain what she was thinking. "You know, the locals have a phrase down there, one all the relief workers and mercenaries and warlords have adopted in the last few years. *TIA.* Do you know what it means?"

He shook his head.

"This is Africa."

This time when she pulled against his arms, he let

her go. It cost him, though. "I'm guessing that's not a statement of pride?"

Her laugh cut like broken glass. "Not quite. Africa is…Africa. No matter what happens, no matter who tries to help or hurt, nothing really changes under the surface. One revolutionary group seizes control and another rises up to fight them. One drought ends and another natural disaster starts. One horrific virus goes dormant and another one takes its place. It's a damn nightmare, one I've been caught in for ten years now."

"I'm so sorry." It was inadequate, but he had no idea what else he was supposed to say.

She didn't answer, simply shrugged, shivered. Though he knew her trembling had more to do with her memories than it did the breeze in the night air, he slipped out of his jacket and draped it around her shoulders, anyway.

"Einstein defined insanity as doing the same thing over and over again but expecting a different result," she finally continued. "I wonder what he would say about our policies in Africa. I wonder what he would say about me. I do the same tests, run the same research, teach the same classes. It doesn't make a damn bit of difference. There will always be war, always be poverty. And there sure as hell will always be disease."

She stood, walked over to the man-made pond at the center of the park. Looked out over the dark, rippling water for long seconds. Even as he wondered what it was she was seeing out there, she added, "On the plus side, I don't have to worry about losing my job anytime soon. Unless, or course, I totally flip out."

"Are you worried about that happening?"

"Sorry—did I make the doctor nervous?" She glanced at him. "I'm fine, Lucas. No nervous breakdowns or splits from reality in my future."

Her voice dropped and he had to strain to hear as she muttered to herself, "No matter how much I wish there was."

The aside was one more blaring signal of her disillusionment. It was painful to listen to, especially when he remembered the wide-eyed girl she'd once been, determined to make a difference and ready to take on the whole world to do it. Usually he could still find that idealistic girl under the pain and cynicism that came with ten years of public health work, but tonight she was MIA. All he could see when he looked at Kara now was the horror that came from taking on disaster after disaster—and losing, again and again and again.

Not that he blamed her for being tired or angry or heartsick. It had been years since he'd set foot in Africa—he'd made the choice to put all his efforts and resources into his clinic instead—but that didn't mean he didn't remember the utter hopelessness and heartbreaking beauty of the people and the place. The two years he'd spent there, fresh out of medical school, had been the best and worst of his life. He'd often wondered how Kara held it together so well. Now he knew—she didn't. She just looked like she did.

It was the last thing he wanted for her.

"I'm sorry, Kara," he repeated, knowing even as he did that it was a useless sentiment.

She shook her head. "It is what it is."

"What it is, sucks."

"Yeah." She started to shrug it off, but even in the dim light of the park, he could see when she decided not to. There was a change to her face, an opening of it that he hadn't even realized was missing until he saw it happen. "It hurts. The children—" Her voice broke. "This time was bad, Lucas. It was really, really bad."

"I know, baby."

"You don't know. You can't know what it's like." She rubbed a hand over her face. "Because the sickness isn't the worst part. I can deal with the death, deal with the pain of not being able to save everyone, as long as I have the chance to try. But lately, I haven't even been allowed to try."

"You're right," he said with a shake of his head. "I don't understand."

She laughed, a harsh, painful sound that hurt to listen to. "Yeah, neither do I. I mean, we're a scientific organization, right? It's our job to control disease— shit, it's in our name and our mission statement, so why is it so hard to get people who aren't doctors or scientists to understand?"

"What people?"

"Politicians. Accountants." She shook her head. "I shouldn't be back yet. There's still way too much to do in Somalia. Education efforts are just beginning— the conditions at most of the refugee camps practically *breed* cholera and there's nothing I can do about it.

"You know, when I started at the CDC, the team leaders had more control. They said when an epidemic was contained. They said when it was time to go home.

Now, politicians tell us what to do. What to say, where to go, how long before we have to get out...

"I'm one of the best damn epidemiologists in the world and I know I haven't found the roots of this outbreak. Just like I know that, while our efforts are making a difference in Somalia, I needed another six to eight weeks to really make sure the education was working, that the conditions were changing.

"A week ago, I was in the hardest hit area of Somalia, fighting that damn disease and convinced that I actually had a shot at beating it. But then my boss called and here I am. The government has decided that it doesn't want us in Somalia right now, because of some political problem I don't know about or even care about. I tried to explain that this had nothing to do with politics, that we were really getting a handle on things and just needed a little more time. It didn't matter. I was on a plane headed home a few days later. While cholera is loosely contained in Somalia, it will make a comeback in less than three months. I guarantee it. And when it does, it will have spread beyond Somalia's borders and be ten times harder to contain than if we had just been allowed to finish our jobs in the first place.

"I'm so sick of putting bandages on festering wounds instead of actually fixing the problem. I mean, I know politics are a necessary evil. But sometimes, human decency has to exist outside of them, right? Because if we can't do our jobs, then these viruses are going to keep spreading and keep killing people,

people who wouldn't have to die if I could just finish what I started."

She turned away from the pond and walked along its edge in her bare feet. "That's what I can't take. Not the deaths we couldn't prevent, but the thousands of deaths we can prevent and are being told not to. I can't help people, can't do my job, if they won't let me. And if I can't help people, why am I doing this job? Why am I putting myself through the pain and the risk and the abysmal conditions if nothing I do is going to matter?"

She looked at him then and he realized she was waiting for an answer. Too damn bad he didn't have a clue what to tell her. What she was talking about was one of the reasons he'd gotten out of the game, one of the reasons he ran his own clinic now. There was no one around to tell him he couldn't treat people who couldn't pay. No one to tell him he had to stop caring for a patient that needed his help.

"The CDC isn't the only game in town, you know. You have other options."

"That's exactly what I've been thinking about. The thing is, I love my job. I'm really good at what I do."

"Then they should let you do it."

She smiled sadly. "Yeah."

"When are you supposed to go back into the field?"

"Who knows? Two days, two months? Whenever the next epidemic hits."

Everything inside him rebelled at her diving back in so soon. "You can't do that," he said. It was dangerous and she was obviously exhausted. "You need some downtime, a chance to get your perspective back. You need to rest for a while, decide what you want to do."

"Oh, really?" She turned on him. "Is that what I need? To go on vacation and regain some perspective? And here I thought what I needed was to find a way to keep people from dying."

"You're not God, you know. There's only so much you can do."

"Which is why we're having this conversation. I'm trying to decide if I can keep helping the way that I am, or if I need to walk away from the CDC and find another avenue where I can do my job. I suppose I could always track the flu for the Department of Public Health."

While her statement had enough sarcasm to insure he understood her contempt for tracking the flu, he didn't think it was that bad of an idea. At least until she got some distance from Africa and the CDC and could make a reasonable, logical decision. He didn't say that, though, refusing to get drawn into an argument that neither of them would win. She didn't say anything either and an awkward silence stretched long and taut between them, their easy camaraderie disappearing in the face of her hurt and anger.

He let her stew for a few minutes, and tried to compose an apology in his head, even though he hadn't said anything wrong. Now was not the time to antagonize her, when she needed a sounding board and a friend.

But as he opened his mouth, she dove in first, blurting out, "I'm sorry, Lucas. There's no reason for me to take my crappy mood out on you. I guess I should have stayed home and popped a sleeping pill instead of surprising you."

"I'm glad you didn't." Even if his inability to do anything for her was killing him. He was a doctor, for God's sake. Shouldn't he be able to fix this? Fix her?

"You know what's sad?" she said after a minute. "I think you mean that."

"I do mean it."

"I know. But just because you're my best friend doesn't mean you have to put up with all this maudlin shit."

"It isn't maudlin if it's how you're really feeling."

"Sure it is—the two aren't mutually exclusive, you know."

She sat down on the grass, pulling her knees up to her chest and wrapping her arms around them. The innate defensiveness, the wariness, of the position struck him. Made him sad. So that when he sat down beside her, he made sure to give her plenty of personal space.

For the first time in a very long time, he was unsure of what to do, what to say. Still, he had to try—for both their sakes.

"The Department of Public Health isn't your only choice here, you know. As you yourself acknowledged, you're one of the leading field epidemiologists in the world. You can write your own ticket at some university here. Hell, if we're being honest, you know you can write your own ticket at the CDC. You don't have to let them send you all over the world. You can stay here, work in America. There's a lot going on here that isn't the flu— tuberculosis, the resurgence of hep C, new strains of MRSA. Disease is disease, but at least it's not like it is over there. When you're here, it doesn't hurt the same way."

Kara was already shaking her head, as he'd known she would. This was an old argument between them, one that neither of them ever truly won. "If not me, then who, Lucas? I *am* good at my job. Damn good. Besides, the CDC has already lost two of their most experienced epidemiologists this year. If I punk out, how many more people are going to die because the person they send isn't as thorough as I am?"

"How long before *you* die?" he countered.

She shrugged off his concern. "I'm careful."

"That isn't what I meant and you know it. I haven't said anything because you always put up no-trespassing signs, but I've been able to see what this job is doing to you for a while now." Every trip Kara went on she came back a little more tired, a little more distant, and each time it took longer for her to bounce back. She left a piece of herself in every country she went to, a piece of her heart—a piece of her very soul. The things she had managed to hang on to were joined together so precariously that he often wondered how long it would take before she fell apart completely. He wrapped an arm around her shoulders and pulled her into a loose embrace. Part of him expected her to fight—Kara was fiercely independent and she'd already shared more of herself tonight than she usually did—but she didn't. Instead, she wrapped an arm around his waist, laid her head on his chest.

As she did, his body stirred to life, despite the circumstances. Cursing silently, he did his best to ignore his very inappropriate arousal in the hopes that it would go away if he didn't acknowledge it. After all, the last thing she needed was to feel like her best friend was putting the moves on her when she was at her most vulnerable.

Of course, it didn't work—it never did with her—which just pissed Lucas off more. But Kara was everything he admired in a woman—strong, self-sufficient, involved, intelligent, kind. He might know intellectually that being stuck in the friend zone was exactly where he wanted to be, but sometimes convincing his body of that fact was a lot more difficult.

Embarrassed and more than a little annoyed at his lack of control, he started to pull away from her.

Kara made a low, humming sound of protest and her arm tightened around him.

"Not yet," she said, tilting her head up to look at him with eyes made luminous by tears and the dim lights of the park. "Don't pull away yet."

KARA COULD FEEL LUCAS's discomfort. His body had stiffened against hers and she knew she should let him go. She'd already cried on him, yelled at him and dumped her problems in his lap. Now she was clinging to him like he was the only thing standing between her and insanity. No wonder he was uncomfortable.

Needy much?

Still, she wasn't quite ready to let go of him. Being near Lucas, absorbing his warmth and feeling the steady beat of his heart comforted her in a way nothing had in a very long time. Squeezing even closer, she closed her eyes and tried to block out the fears and memories clamoring inside of her.

She focused on Lucas instead, on the gentle rise and fall of his chest as he breathed.

On the warm, delicious scent of him, like a pine forest on a bright, sunny day.

On the feel of his muscled body against her, so big and capable and comforting.

When she was with him, she felt safe in a way she never really had before. She'd been on her own a long time—her mother had died the summer before she met Lucas—and she was more than capable of taking care of herself. Still, there was something nice about knowing, really knowing, that Lucas had her back.

Oh, she'd never ask him for anything important— the last thing she wanted was to be a burden to him— but still, it was nice to know that someone was there if she needed something. Nice to know that *he* was there.

Turning her head a little, she glanced up at Lucas through her lashes. She didn't know what she expected—maybe that he'd be looking out at the park, maybe that he'd be deep in thought. Maybe that he'd just be relaxing and enjoying sitting here as much as she was. But when she looked up, she found him staring at her, his jaw clenched tight and his eyes glittering like sapphires.

Her breath hitched in her throat. Sitting there, he looked dark, sexy and just a little bit rumpled. Basically like his normal, gorgeous self, and while that had never fazed her before, something about this particular moment had her heart kicking into high gear. Her stomach fluttered even as her mouth went desert dry. Trying to get some moisture back, she rubbed her lips together. Licked them. And felt Lucas stiffen against her even as a deep, rumbling growl started in his chest.

"Kara." It was a warning, and a blatant one at that, and she felt it sizzle along every nerve ending she had. Drowning now in the scent and sight and sound of him, she reached up and rested her hand against his cut-glass jaw. Stroked her thumb over his dark stubble and lost herself in the pools of his eyes.

"Kara." He whispered her name this time, his hand coming up to cup her own face. "What are you doing?"

She shook her head. She had no idea what she was doing and she didn't want to know. For this moment, this instant, she just wanted to feel something other than the despair that was her constant companion. Wrapping her other hand around the back of his neck, she pulled him slowly, inexorably closer.

He didn't fight her, didn't shrug her off, didn't make a joke like she half expected him to. Like she'd been half afraid he would. Instead, he watched her, eyes wide-open as they closed the distance between their mouths one small centimeter at a time.

And then, when her whole body was trembling in anticipation, he kissed her.

CHAPTER FOUR

IF SOMEONE HAD ASKED HER if she'd ever planned on kissing Lucas, she would have told them—quite truthfully—that she never had. If that same person had asked her if she'd ever *thought* about kissing him, she would have lied like a rug and told them the same thing. But nothing she had ever thought about in passing, nothing she had ever imagined, could have prepared her for the jolt that went through her as Lucas brushed her lips with his.

It was a quick kiss, just a passing press of his lips to hers, really, but as he pulled away, he looked as stunned as she felt. Then she was reaching for him, her fingers tangling in the silky, cool strands of his hair as she pulled his face to hers. If they were going to do this, then she wanted a real kiss from Lucas. Even more, she wanted the real Lucas, not the one he usually showed to the women he dated.

It only took a moment before his lips opened against hers, moving in a gentle sucking motion that had her trembling and her hands grasping at his shoulders for support. He laughed a little and wrapped an arm around her waist to ground her. But as his tongue darted out to lick gently at the corners of her mouth, she acknowledged that it was going to take a lot more than a supporting arm to keep her steady.

But, as she pressed her body against his, she realized she wasn't the only one trembling. Lucas was as shaky as she was. Somehow, that realization made what they were doing so much more real—and so much more delicious.

He sucked her lower lip between his teeth and her mouth opened on a gasp. It was the invitation he was waiting for, his tongue darting inside her mouth to tease and tangle with her own.

There was a strange ringing in her ears, one she tried to ignore as she lost herself in Lucas. It was probably her subconscious's way of telling her that this whole thing was a really bad idea. But she ignored it—or at least, she tried to. All of this was overwhelming enough without facing the consequences of her actions at the same moment she was acting. Besides, for these few minutes when she was in Lucas's arms, she wanted to forget what she was doing out here. Forget all the pain and ugliness and devastation she'd seen, and all that was to come because she wasn't strong enough to find a way past the bureaucracy.

She wanted to lose herself in Lucas, to immerse herself in the desire whipping between them. He must have felt the same way, because his arms tightened around her, pulling her up to her knees so that their bodies were flush against each other, chest to chest, thigh to thigh. It was his turn to delve his hands into her hair, to pull on her curls until her head tilted at an angle satisfactory to him.

It alternately felt like they had been kissing for seconds, then hours. Long, luxurious kisses that made her lips burn and her head whirl. It felt good to kneel here, lost in the desire pumping through her body. She'd felt dead inside for so long, had deliberately tamped down on her emotions so that she wouldn't feel the pain of what she did on a daily basis. It felt amazing to say *to hell with it*. To toss her inhibitions and worries and anguish to the wind and just feel.

But Lucas broke the kisses off abruptly, pulling back and staring at her. She whimpered, tried to cling to him and he cursed even as he fumbled for her purse. "Your phone's ringing," he told her breathlessly as he handed it to her.

She felt pretty breathless herself, and also pretty stupid, as she realized the bells she'd been hearing hadn't been coming from inside her at all.

"Whoever it is has called three or four times," Lucas told her, his voice a few shades deeper than normal. "It must be important."

She checked the call log. Her heart sank as she saw that her worst fear was true—her boss's private number. *Already?* she wanted to scream. Couldn't she have just one day, one night, to herself before they came for her? Before she had to hurry down and try to contain an epidemic when they refused to give her the tools— and the time—that she needed?

She gestured to call him back, but the hand holding the phone was shaking so badly that she couldn't even punch the call button. Seeing her dilemma, Lucas wrapped his own hand under hers, held her steady. "It's okay, Kara," he murmured to her, his thumb stroking across the back of her hand. His touch soothed her like nothing else could.

Her boss picked up on the first ring, grim and to the point. He didn't even say hello, simply, "They have an outbreak of Ebola in Eritrea."

"Ebola?" she asked, a little stunned. Beside her, Lucas stiffened, made a sound of protest, but she turned her head, focused on the tree right in front of her. She couldn't afford to let him distract her right now. Until she made a decision one way or the other, this was her job—whether she liked it or not.

"How long since the outbreak started?"

"Three weeks."

"Three weeks? And it hasn't burned itself out? Did it start in a major city?" Ebola was a disease that sounded, and looked, incredibly frightening, but it wasn't something that usually created long-term epidemics. It was an awful way to die, but it was fast and it wasn't airborne—it could only spread through contact with bodily fluids. Which usually made it pretty easy to contain. Plus, with a high mortality rate, it usually died out—once its hosts died out—pretty quickly.

"They don't know where it started—figuring that out is your job. But right now it's in every major southern city—Om Hajer, T'io, Assab, Os Mara. It might be in the northern cities, as well, but we just don't know that yet."

"A couple of those cities are awfully close to the Sudanese and Ethiopian borders."

"That's what we're afraid of."

"Has it spread?"

"Based on the information we've been given, we don't think so. I've reached out to health organizations working in both countries and am waiting to hear back. But my gut tells me if it hasn't already jumped the borders, it's going to soon."

"But how is that possible? You can't get Ebola from sitting next to someone on the bus, and those who have it get sick so quickly that they don't have much chance to travel."

"I am well aware of that, Kara."

"I know, Paul. I'm sorry. I'm just trying to wrap my head around this. Are they sure it's Ebola? And why weren't we contacted before this? If it's been going on three weeks, that's a lot of deaths. Did they call in the World Health Organization instead?"

"WHO got the call at the same time we did."

"Why did they wait?"

"The Eritrean government isn't known for its willingness to allow outsiders in. They don't want anyone to witness what goes on inside the borders."

She knew that. But this was a disease that could kill a lot of people if it was already in the major cities. How could that not have mattered to them? Then again, it was just more of the same political bullshit she'd been struggling with for months now.

Frustrated, angry, she blew out a steady stream of air. No matter how long she was in this business, she would never understand how a government could stand by and watch its people die, simply to protect itself. The whole thing was anathema to her.

Her mind racing, she repeated her first question. "Are they sure it's Ebola?"

"Frankly, I don't think they know what the hell it is. They say it's Ebola and it has all the markers of the disease, but the growing infection rate doesn't make sense. And their labs aren't our labs. I won't be happy until we have a team in the field."

"Is this thing airborne?"

"They say no. Again—"

"I know, I know. You want a team there. When?"

"Three weeks ago."

She laughed, though the sound had no humor in it. "Right."

"I'm putting together a meeting for two o'clock tomorrow afternoon—I guess that would be this afternoon, since it's past midnight. I've scheduled a flight out at eight o'clock. You'll head up the team."

It wasn't a question, but she said "yes," anyway. There was no doubt she'd be on that airplane. From the second she'd seen his name on her caller ID, she'd known it would lead straight to this. Some mutation of Ebola? Hemorrhagic viruses were her specialty. Morbid as it sounded, she'd been waiting her whole career for something like this to happen.

"What time can you be here?"

"I'm out right now. I need to get home, repack." God, had she even gotten the last of her laundry done? "Catch a few hours' sleep if I'm going to be alert in the meeting. And I'm going to need to refill my field kit."

"I know. I'll have everything ready and waiting for you."

"Please. I'm a mess, totally jet lagged and nowhere close to organized. If you organize it then I go over it, there's less chance I'll miss something."

"So what time?" he asked again.

She turned around, grabbed Lucas's wrist to look at his watch. It was one-thirty. "If everything goes okay, I can be there by ten."

"Good. I want you up to speed before the rest of the team gets here."

Panic had her heart racing and her breath quickening but she refused to give in to it. She didn't have a choice—she had to keep it together. Lucas must have heard something in her breathing, though, because this time he reached for her free hand, threading his fingers through hers and squeezing tightly.

It wasn't much, wasn't a huge gesture of comfort, but it was enough to cut through the fear and get her focusing on what needed to be done.

"You know you can't send my team back out. We just got home from a two-month deployment. Davis's wife is having a baby in three weeks and Anna's mom is in the middle of chemotherapy—"

"We've called in Team Four to go with you."

Shock ricocheted through her. "That's Mike's team."

"Is that a problem?" Her boss's voice tightened up.

"It might be for Mike—and the rest of his team. They aren't going to want to report to me." Especially since she and Mike had a very bad, very public breakup three months before.

"Mike knows you're the best choice for this job, Steward."

"Yes, but—" Her protests died in her throat. She *was* the best choice for this outbreak—or at least she would be if she could get her head on straight. And yes, Mike and his team probably knew it. That didn't mean there wasn't going to be some hostility on their part. She and Mike ran things differently and team loyalty and cohesion was a big factor in cases like these.

Still, it was past time to put on her big-girl panties and deal. Mike's team would just have to do the same.

"I want Julian," she said, naming the CDC's top field doctor in infectious bleeding diseases.

"He's flying in from Haiti. He might actually beat you to Eritrea."

"Good. I also want Frieda and Van." They, too, were the cream of the CDC's Epidemic Intelligence Officer crop.

"I'll get them for you. Any other requests?"

"Sam and Violet." She named her two favorite microbiologists.

"Violet's in Alaska, but Sam's available."

"He'll have to do, then."

"On the plus side, you'll be meeting up with Pierre La Font's team from WHO."

Kara pursed her lips in a silent whistle, wondered what it was Paul wasn't telling her. It wasn't coincidence that they were bringing in the heaviest hitters in the industry for this job—herself included.

"You're going to have to coordinate with him,

Steward, so make sure not to step on too many of his toes, okay?"

"I'm not the one who has trouble playing nice in the sandbox. You know that and I know that. My counterpart at the WHO has a different outlook on the matter."

"Of course he does."

Even as they joked, the panic coalesced in her stomach, turning into a deep and churning sickness. Five years ago she would have leaped at the chance for this assignment. Hell, she probably would have been vibrating with excitement over it even two years ago. But right now it seemed a lot more like a punishment than a reward, a lot more like she was heading into hell rather than being given the prime assignment of her career.

If this thing was a mutated Ebola, changing its infection patterns, then this was it. This was her smallpox. Her hepatitis. Her AIDS. This was the case epidemiologists waited their whole career for and few ever got the chance to see.

So why did she feel like throwing up? She wasn't afraid. She knew how to be careful, how to protect herself. But just the idea of going into Eritrea, of dealing with all the problems there—caused by this disease as well as centuries of war, famine and neglect—made her sick. She didn't want to hurt anymore. Didn't want to get knee-deep into this thing only to be pulled out before she could help, really help.

She knew she didn't have it in her to walk away in the middle of this thing. Not again. Knowing she could help but being unable to do so would crush her completely.

Beside her Lucas stiffened, aware of her distress. Somehow it only made things worse. It was bad enough to admit to yourself you were a coward, but to have your best friend know made it different, somehow. Worse.

"You still there, Kara?"

The fact that her boss had called her by her first name told her that, not only was Lucas aware she was a basket case, Paul had a pretty good clue, as well. There wasn't much softness in Paul, so if even he was questioning her mental health…

"Yeah, I'm here, Paul."

There was another pause, this time on his side. "You okay to go, Kara?"

The sudden doubt in his voice had her straightening her spine and toughening up her own voice. She wasn't even close to being okay, but it wasn't as though she had a choice. Not if she wanted to be able to look herself in the mirror tomorrow. Those people needed help.

"I'm perfectly fine and definitely ready to go."

Lucas let go of her hand, made a sound of disgust deep in his throat. She glanced over at him and caught the disapproving look on his face before he could banish it. It made her panic worse, but she refused to let herself be swayed by it.

With Lucas looking on like that, she knew there was no way she'd be able to finish her discussion with her boss. She turned her back on him and walked a few steps away.

"I've got this," she continued, forcing steel into a reassurance that she was far from feeling. "But you have to promise me that barring a full-on revolution, you're not going to pull me out in the middle of this."

"Steward—"

"No, Paul. I mean it." She put it in terms she knew he would understand. "This is the case I've been waiting my whole career for. You can't put me down in the middle of it and then pull me out when it's convenient for you. I can't work like that. I won't work like that."

"You'll work how I tell you to work!" he snapped, but then his voice softened. "Look, I know what happened in Somalia was bullshit, but you have to get past it. Eritrea is a whole different game."

She wanted to laugh, but nothing was funny. Eritrea and Somalia, Ethiopia and Sudan, they were all the same game. All different sides of the same dice. And the Western world had spent the better part of two centuries rolling that dice just to see what number would come up. She was a fool to think this would be any different, but she had to. She had to believe it or there was no way she'd be able to get on that airplane.

Her prolonged silence must have made Paul nervous, because his voice was hesitant when he asked, "Steward? Are you still there? I didn't lose you, did I?"

For long seconds she considered not answering, just letting the call drift away. But then where would she be? Where would any of them be?

"I'm still here."

"Good. Okay, then, I'll see you at ten. In the meantime, I'm going to put pressure on the Eritrean government to give me all the stats and info they have."

"Which won't be much."

"No. But I'll try to have a decent report together for you by the time you take off."

"Thank you."

"I should be thanking you. And Steward…"

She braced herself for words of comfort she didn't know if she could handle hearing. "Yes?"

"Don't screw up out there."

She laughed. She should have known better than to think Paul had gotten in touch with his softer side.

"I'll do my best."

She hung up the phone and dropped it back into her bag. Then just stood for a minute gazing out into the night.

She wasn't ready to look at Lucas. She didn't know if it was because of that strange, magical kiss they'd shared minutes before or whether it was because he could so easily see through her. She'd thought she'd shored up her defenses pretty well before seeing him, but in one evening he'd shattered them and had her blubbering like a baby. She was afraid if she turned to face him now it would be an instant replay, and she couldn't take that. She'd already cried all over him like some kind of high-maintenance whiner. Doing it twice in one evening was just a bad idea.

Besides, if she faced him, she'd have to think of something to say and right now her mind was blank.

Lucas didn't seem to be suffering from the same affliction, though. "Ebola?" he asked. "A mutant strain of *Ebola?*"

"Maybe. We don't know yet. I probably shouldn't have had that conversation in front of you."

"Yeah, because I'm going to go blabbing to the whole medical community about this." He clasped her elbow, and when she still didn't face him, he placed his hands on her shoulders and turned her until there was no place else for her to look but into his eyes.

"You really think you're in shape to do this kind of thing?" he demanded. "This isn't a simple assignment, Kara. If you take it, you're in it for the long-term and you know it."

"It's not a choice, Lucas. I'm the one Paul assigned. I have to go."

Lucas cursed then, something low and vile and violent. "You know that's not true. You can beg off if you want to. You just got back, for God's sake. You need time to rest, to get your head back in the game. Hell, you were just talking about leaving the CDC."

"Yes, talking about it. I hadn't decided yet—and I still haven't. Until I do, I follow Paul's orders. Anyway, my head is already in the game, thank you very much. I can do this. I have to do this, and you telling me I'm not up for it only undermines me."

"You know I think you're brilliant. That's not the point—"

"It is exactly the point," she snapped. Then relented with a sigh. "Please, let's not do this. Is flying out barely forty-eight hours after I got back an ideal situation? Not at all. I know it. Paul knows it. And it actually goes against protocol. But emergencies happen and this is what I do. I'm the best suited to go. And none of us wants to be sitting here in six months, looking at a worldwide Ebola epidemic because the CDC didn't send in the right people."

She bent down, picked up her shoes. "Now, if you could take me home, I would greatly appreciate it."

For long seconds Lucas didn't answer and she was just beginning to wonder if she was going to have to catch a cab when he said, "Come on. Let's go."

He started toward the exit without waiting for her—which was a totally un-Lucas thing to do. It illustrated just how angry and frustrated he was with her. Which bothered her, but it wasn't like there was anything she could do about it. Frankly, she had other, more pressing things to worry about.

They walked back up the hill without ever finding the swings, and the trip up the large grassy knoll was a lot less fun than the one down had been. Especially with Lucas grim faced and angry beside her. She wanted to call him on it. To ask him why he was getting himself so worked up. But that strange and powerful kiss had made her shy with him, had turned the easy camaraderie they'd always shared into something stiff and awkward.

As they walked, Kara waited for him to say something to break the silence. But he didn't say a word. Not as they hiked the hill, not as they climbed the fence—though this time he gave her a boost—and not as they walked down the nearly empty streets of downtown.

It was sixty degrees out and she was still wearing his jacket, but she couldn't remember the last time she'd felt this cold.

By the time Lucas paid the valet and held the car door open for her—all without saying a word—she was fuming. And more hurt than she wanted to admit.

This was why she never opened herself up to people, she seethed. Why she never let them in. Because the first time you did, the first time you started to take for granted the fact that they would always be there for you, you did something they didn't like and they pulled away. Locked you out.

It had happened her entire life. When her mom would get angry she would shut down, withholding her affection until Kara fell into line. And after her mom died and she'd been forced to return to her dad's house during college vacations, she'd learned that her father's love was only as deep as her latest accomplishment. Why she'd expected better from Lucas, she didn't know.

Because he was her friend, a voice whispered in the back of her head. Because he'd always been there for her. But now, the second she'd broken the unwritten rules that governed their relationship—she'd kissed him and cried all over him in one night—he was pulling back. Getting angry the moment she had the nerve to do something he didn't like.

The worst part was that it hurt. A lot. Because she hadn't been expecting it. Because she'd broken her own rules over the years and had learned to trust Lucas implicitly. And yet here she was, here they were, right back where a part of her had always known they'd end up.

Once in front of her house, she barely waited for him to stop the car before she was opening the door and lunging for her front porch. "Thanks," she called over her shoulder. "I'll…call you when I get back."

She just needed to get inside. If she made it inside her front door without letting him see how hurt she was, everything would be fine. She had a lot to do and very little time to do it in. Once he was gone, she wouldn't even have time to think about him.

But she'd barely opened the door when he caught up with her. "What the hell is this?"

Her anger got the better of her. "Oh, so you do talk," she said snidely.

His teeth ground together, his eyes shooting sparks of rage straight through her. She gave as good as she got, then muttered through her own clenched jaw, "I think it's time for you to go."

"Yeah, because that's really going to happen."

"Lucas—"

"Don't start, Kara. I'm not going anywhere. We're going to talk about this. And if you still decide to go, you'll need a ride to the CDC."

"Still decide to go? I *am* going, and I can get myself to work just fine, thank you. I've been doing it for the last ten years of my life without any problems."

"Damn it, Kara. You don't always have to be so independent. Can't you see that I'm *worried* about you?"

Of course he was. St. Lucas, worried about everyone. She hurt a little inside hearing the words. Not because she was upset that he cared, but because everything had changed between them in the space of one evening.

She never should have cried. For seventeen years their friendship had been based on the fact that she didn't need him. Lucas didn't mind being needed— by his mother, his sister, his girlfriends, his patients. He thrived on it, really. But at the same time, her independence helped him put distance between himself and the demanding women in his life.

There'd never been any need for distance between Kara and Lucas—at least not before tonight. And she was smart enough to know that it wasn't the kiss—it was what had come before it. Now, here he was, feeling like he had a right to tell her what to do. Somehow she'd become just another woman who needed him to save her.

"Look," she finally told him as she stepped into the house. "I appreciate your concern, but I don't need it."

He followed her in. "You're not thinking clearly—"

She whirled on him, got in his face. "Don't tell me how I'm thinking. I was upset earlier. That doesn't make me less competent. I don't need you to save me, Lucas."

"Is that what you think I want to do? Save you?"

"It sure looks that way to me."

"Well, then, you don't know a damn thing, do you?"

CHAPTER FIVE

THEIR ANGRY WORDS ECHOED in Kara's foyer, bouncing off the walls and making him want to tear his hair out. What had gotten into her? One minute he was trying to help her deal with the fact that her job was a nightmare and the next minute she was kissing him. And the minute after that she was accepting an assignment to head right back into a hot zone. And not just any hot zone—no, not for Kara. She was heading straight into Ebola hell and wouldn't even acknowledge that it was a bad idea. He just wanted her to admit—

What? he asked himself angrily. What exactly did he want from Kara? For her to break down again and admit that the idea of going to Eritrea scared the hell out of her? God knows, it scared the shit out of him. Normally she seemed so indestructible, but listening to her heartache, holding her while she cried…it had gotten to him. Really gotten to him, in a way few things did anymore. She seemed so much more vulnerable now than she ever had before.

Add in that bizarre, mind-blowing kiss they'd just shared and he couldn't quite get his mind around any of this.

If someone had told him three hours ago that they'd

be here, nose to nose, both of them spoiling for a fight, he would have thought that person was insane. Not that he and Kara never fought—of course they did. She had a redhead's temper and he was as stubborn as they came. But none of their previous fights had this bruised quality, this resentment simmering right below the surface.

And he might not know much about what the hell was going on, but he knew this. He didn't want Kara to head out with things like this between them. Who knew how long it would be before he'd get the chance to see her again?

Blowing out a huge breath, he bit the bullet and lied to her for the first time in all the years he'd known her. "I'm sorry."

The look in her eye turned from furious to confused and for long seconds she didn't answer. "That's it?" she asked finally.

"I'm really sorry?" When she didn't immediately answer, he ran an impatient hand through his hair. "Jeez, Kara, what do you want? Blood?"

He half expected her to jump down his throat again, but she must have found what she was looking for— if not in his words, then his face—because she suddenly relaxed. "No, but if you're offering, some of your sweat should work nicely."

"My sweat?" he asked, wondering if he looked as lost as he felt.

She turned and headed down the hall to her bedroom. "I've got a couple trunks filled with gear stored at the top of my closet. Can you get them down for me?"

"Yeah, sure."

He followed her through the house feeling a shock similar to the aftermath of a car crash. It wasn't unusual for Kara to explode and then simmer down quickly, but this was fast even for her. Any second now, he expected to start feeling the symptoms of whiplash.

"The boxes are up there," she said, pointing to the large walk-in closet at the end of her bathroom.

He followed her directions, feeling a little awkward being in this most private room of hers. Which was ridiculous. It wasn't like he'd never been here before—he was the one who'd helped her move her furniture in, after all. The one who'd painted these walls their current shade of sky-blue. But that was different. That was before the room had turned into this sultan's paradise with the luxurious turquoise quilt and silver throw pillows.

Before a red lace bra-and-panty set had been draped across the foot of her bed.

Before he'd kissed her.

Studiously avoiding looking at her bed—which was more difficult said than done because the thing was huge and dominated the entire room—he headed into her closet and reached for the first trunk. It was a lot heavier than he thought it would be.

"Hey," he said as he carried it back into the bedroom. "How the hell did you get this thing up there to begin with?"

"Mike put them up for me. I haven't needed them in a while."

He stiffened at the mention of her last serious boy-friend—the one she'd almost married. He'd never liked Mike, had thought the guy was a pompous ass more concerned with his reputation in the field than he was in the actual work he did. Lucas had been thrilled when things didn't work out. Mike was nowhere near good enough for her and the idea that she would now be taking over his team was just one more thing Lucas didn't like about this trip.

Dropping the first load onto the floor, he went back into the closet and got the second trunk down. It was even heavier than the first. "What's in here, anyway?"

"My on-location biosafety suits."

Right. Of course. Because she was going to need the huge positive-pressure suit if she was heading into a situation where a disease like Ebola might have turned airborne. When she worked in the CDC labs, or any other well-equipped labs, they provided the suits for her. But who knew what she was heading into now.

His chest tightened and he walked to the window, staring blindly into the night. He knew her job was dangerous, knew she regularly dealt with things that could kill her. But she'd had every vaccination there was, so that when she went into the field after cholera or TB, there was little to no chance she would get it—especially with proper precautions.

But this, this was something totally different. There was no vaccine for Ebola and even if there had been, who knew what would happen with exposure to this strange new strain? Any tolerance built up to it would mean absolutely nothing.

A part of him was aware that Kara was still talking about something, but it was like she was far away. For the first time in his life, he wished he wasn't a doctor. Wished he didn't know exactly what it was she was heading into. Because knowing what could happen, thinking about it, had him paralyzed with fear.

"Don't go." The words came out before he knew he was going to say them, interrupting her in the middle of a sentence about something or other.

"Lucas."

He spun around and stalked across the room toward her, feeling like a crazy man. Feeling like he was going to jump out of his skin any second.

"Please," he begged, barely recognizing himself. "I have a bad feeling about this trip and I don't know what I'd do if anything happened to you, Kara. Please don't go."

He grabbed on to her shoulders and pulled her into his arms so that her heart beat steadily against his. Then he buried his face in her hair and just breathed, inhaling the sweet strawberry-and-magnolia scent deep into his lungs. He was acting like a maniac—he knew he was—but he couldn't seem to do anything to stop it. From the second he'd heard the word *Ebola,* his whole world had spun out of control.

"I'm going to be fine, Lucas." She murmured the words against his neck because she couldn't move. Couldn't pull back. He was holding her too tightly but he couldn't seem to ease up. "You know I'm careful."

"There's careful and then there's insane, Kara. This is insane."

"No. It's my job." She shoved against his chest but he wasn't budging. At that moment, he thought he could hold her forever if she'd let him. "You think I don't worry about you?" she asked. "Every day you go to work in the closest thing to a war zone that the U.S. has to offer. Less than a year ago you had a shooting in the lobby of your clinic and you ran straight into it."

"That was different. My patients—"

"I know. Your patients were out there and there was no way you were going to leave them at the hands of some coked-up teenager with a gun. But those people in Eritrea, they're my patients. If I can help them, Lucas, then I have to go."

Kara struggled against him, managing to pull back just enough to lift her soft, delicate hands to his face. As she held him, she looked deeply into his eyes and said, "I *need* to go."

He knew it, had known it all along. And still, "You're my best friend. I don't want to lose you."

"You won't."

"Promise me," he told her, knowing he sounded desperate but not giving a damn. He *was* desperate. She meant more to him than he ever could have imagined.

"Lucas—"

"Promise me!"

"I promise." She looked him straight in the eye, her green eyes shining with sincerity and compassion and something else he couldn't quite define. "Everything's going to be okay."

He shuddered, nodded. Dropped his head so that his forehead rested against hers. Then closed his eyes and just breathed.

He didn't know how long they stayed like that, locked in their own little world. Not long enough, because when she finally stepped back he was still not ready to let her go. Wrapping a hand around her long, slender neck, he pulled her face back to his and, for the second time that night, captured her lips with his own.

If he was going to have to let her go, going to have to spend the next weeks and months racked with terror that she was going to die in Africa, he was not letting her leave without having something to hang on to. He'd broken off the kiss in the park when her phone rang, and he'd regretted it ever since. No matter what happened, no matter how it shifted things between them, he was going to have this kiss untainted by fear or sorrow or regret. They owed each other that much.

But he wasn't counting on the way they both lit up the second their mouths touched. Like the Fourth of July and New Year's Eve all at the same time. It was as though her mouth had been made for his.

That was the first thought that ran through his mind as he deepened the kiss.

The second was that she tasted like she smelled. Like strawberries and caramel and rich, sweet cream.

The third was that he wouldn't mind staying right here, kissing her, for the next decade or so. He had a lot of time to make up for, after all.

But just because he was acting like an idiot didn't mean he really was one. So, despite the fact that every instinct he had was pushing at him to stay exactly where he was, he reluctantly pulled away.

Though every cell in his body screamed for another, longer taste of her, he figured he should check with Kara first. Make sure she was okay with this—or at the very least, not planning to smash her fist into the side of his head for overstepping his boundaries.

"What..." Her voice trailed off as she pressed shaky fingers to her mouth. When he didn't answer—he couldn't because he had no idea what to say—she tried again. "What was *that?*"

Any hope that she felt the same way he did dissipated under the shocked weight of her question. "I'm sorry," he said, stepping away from her. "Maybe we can chalk this up to too much champagne?"

"Neither of us has had a drink in hours."

"The stars?" He pointed toward the skylight above her bed.

"We already discussed the fact that there aren't any."

"Could you at least work with me here?" he finally asked her. "I'm grasping at straws."

"I can tell." She inched closer to him, pressing forward so that her chest brushed lightly against his. Heat streaked through him all over again. "The question is why you feel the need to?"

"I already apologized. I'm not sure what else to say." He looked down at her, tried to gauge her mood. She was looking up at him so that her full lips were a scant few inches from his own. As she exhaled, he could feel her warm breath brush over him.

His entire body tightened at the sensation, until the simple act of breathing hurt. He wanted another sample of her, wanted to delve inside her mouth and explore the taste and scent and touch of her until he'd satisfied the craving that had been years in the making.

He tightened his hands into fists, fought the desire back. His temper tantrum about her leaving for Eritrea had already put them on shaky ground. Kissing her had made things even less stable. Doing it again might send her running. After all, she'd done her level best to ignore the kiss they'd shared in the park. For her to run from him was the absolute last thing he wanted. He'd rather have Kara's friendship than nothing at all.

"Who says you have to say anything? It was just a kiss, right?"

"Yeah." He forced the words out between clenched teeth. "Just a kiss."

"I mean, it's not like you really laid one on me or anything." She leaned in even closer.

He couldn't help wondering what kind of kisses she was used to if she qualified what had passed between them as *just a kiss*. Maybe he'd underestimated old Mike.

The thought of Mike made him angry and he stepped back from her. Tried to turn away. The last thing he needed right now was to hear about other, better kisses she'd received from men she was more sexually attracted to than him.

She moved with him, though, as he retreated one step, two, until his back was—literally—against her bedroom wall. The warning bells he'd heard in the park had returned and they were clanging at top volume. But the fact that all the blood in his body had rushed about three feet south of his head made it impossible to pay any attention to them at all.

"It's not," she continued her earlier train of thought, "like you did this."

And then *she* was kissing *him,* her lips soft and warm and open against his own.

For a full five seconds, he did nothing, just stood there like a total loser as her lips moved slowly against his. And then reality dawned and he caught fire. Slipping a hand behind her head, he tangled his fingers in her heavy curls and pressed her mouth more firmly against him. Then he pulled her lower lip into his mouth and nibbled softly.

She gasped, laughed a little, then wrapped her arms around his neck and returned the kiss with an exuberance that delighted him.

He ran his tongue over her lips, exploring the bow-shaped indention in her upper lip that had driven him crazy for more years than he wanted to admit. Then he moved on to the full curve of her lower lip and the tender corners of her mouth. She tasted so good, felt so good, that he wanted to go on kissing her forever.

He nudged her lips with his tongue, waited for her to open for him so he could explore all of her. She didn't immediately comply. Instead, she smiled against his lips—that same tender, lopsided smile of hers that captured his attention—and his heart trembled a little in his chest.

Which was stupid, he told himself. This was just a kiss. Just an experiment on her part, nothing to get himself all worked up about. But this was Kara, and he'd waited so long to touch her like this, to kiss her and hold her and feel her like this. No matter what happened later, he would take these few moments and savor them.

And then, with a flick of her fingers, she changed everything.

SHE WAS ON FIRE, HER entire body aflame as Lucas kissed her and kissed her and kissed her. And still it wasn't enough. Frantic, frenzied, she moved her hands to the buttons of his tuxedo shirt. She wanted more. She wanted everything. She wanted…him.

She flicked at the buttons with fingers made clumsy with need and frustration. The first two gave way pretty easily under her onslaught, but the third one was more stubborn. She moaned a little, yanked at it and still it wouldn't give. Frustration ripped through her. She wanted to see Lucas, to touch him, to feel him.

He must have felt the same way, because with a muffled roar, he pushed her fingers away and ripped the shirt straight down the middle, sending buttons flying everywhere. She might have found it funny any other time but right then it was perfect, necessary, exactly what she needed.

Part of her couldn't believe they were doing this, but she was past paying attention to it. She'd spent her

entire adult life denying herself things she wanted—
it was hard to lose what you cared about if you didn't
care too much about anything. If you didn't claim anything, or anyone, as your own. But she wanted this,
wanted Lucas more than she'd ever wanted anything
in her life. She was heading back into a nightmare in
a few hours. Damn it, for once in her life she would
take this. Take Lucas. She was burning for him and
the sweet abandon that being touched by him promised. This time she would not deny herself.

Sliding her hands up Lucas's chest, she hooked her
fingers in the shoulders of his now-open shirt and
flicked it off. Watched with satisfaction as the shirt
tumbled down his arms and onto the floor. And then
she was touching him, her fingers sliding over his
warm, taut flesh as she forgot each and every worry
she had about this. About him.

She wanted to taste him, to smell him, to immerse
herself in the experience of loving Lucas. She looked
down at where her hands rested on his chest, small
against the massive bronze expanse of skin. They
trembled a little—from desire or trepidation, she
wasn't sure. She tucked them behind her to hide their
shaking and replaced them with her lips and tongue.

But Lucas must have seen the fine trembling, because he pushed her away. Just an inch or two, enough
so that he could put one long finger under her chin
and tilt her head so that she was looking him straight
in those crazy, beautiful eyes of his.

"Are you sure about this?" he asked, his voice tight
with both need and restraint. Desire was plain on his

face and she knew it cost him to ask, knew it would cost him more if she changed her mind. The fact that he asked anyway dissolved her last remaining inhibitions and she launched herself at him, wrapping her arms around his neck and pulling his warm, sexy mouth down to meet her own.

"Damn straight," she murmured against his lips, and when she did, felt his tenuous grip on control vanish along with her own. Her hands tangled in the cool silk of his hair, holding his head to her as his tongue gently parted her lips. But she didn't want gentleness now, didn't want him to hold back when everything she felt for him, everything they were to each other, was welling up inside of her. She wanted all of Lucas, his power as well as his concern, his passion as well as his tenderness.

Her tongue met his, touched, tangled, tantalized, as she explored his mouth the way she had wanted to for far too long. She sucked his lower lip between her own, nipped softly and laughed at his groan of arousal. Her hands slipped between them, slid over his hard abdomen and toyed with the beginning of the happy trail that started just beneath his belly button.

"We need to slow down," he gasped, his hand capturing hers and bringing it to his lips where he pressed kisses over her palm and at the tip of each of her fingers.

She melted at his tenderness, his sweetness. But that sweetness wasn't what she wanted. The aching emotion it brought to her was exactly what she was trying to escape from with this act of total impulsiveness. If she got swayed by it, if she let it in, she didn't know what would happen to her. To them.

"I don't want to go slow," she told him, hooking two fingers over the waistband of his dress pants and yanking him away from the wall before spinning him toward the center of the room.

His eyes widened and he grinned in a way that was both familiar and yet completely new. She could see in his eyes that he felt the same about her and it made her feel wicked, wild. Wonderful.

She walked him backward until the back of his knees hit her bed, and then she gave him a shove. He landed on the bed and she followed him, straddling his thighs as she skimmed her lips hotly over his mouth, across his cheek, up to his ear. "I want you," she whispered. "Now."

Her tongue darted out, licked his right nipple, darted back in. She did the same to his left, to his collarbone and rib cage and navel even as her fingers fumbled frantically with the hook in the waistband of his pants. But she was too aroused, was going too fast, and she couldn't get it to release. "Help me," she pleaded as her body spun more and more out of her control. She was nearly sobbing with frustrated desire.

"Kara, sweetheart. It's okay." He squeezed her hands gently, then laid them on the bed on either side of him. "We don't need to rush."

He didn't understand. She was desperate. Determined. She didn't want to think or analyze or worry. She just wanted to feel. Just wanted to hold him in her arms and pretend, for this one, perfect moment, that everything was fine. If she slowed down, if she gave herself time to think, she would remember that this was just a one-off for both of them and it would ruin everything.

"What if I want to rush?" she asked him teasingly, her hand dipping down to stroke the hard length of him through his pants.

AT THE FIRST TOUCH OF HER hand, Lucas's eyes rolled back in his head. Lust—hot, demanding, all-consuming—roared through him and he forgot the source of his caution. He cupped her face in his hands and pulled it down so that he could ravage her lips with his as he explored every centimeter of that sexy, sultry mouth.

He reached for her breasts and was frustrated to find them still covered by the silk and sequins of her dress. He wanted to touch her, to feel every inch of her lush curves pressed against his. He *had* to feel her. He grabbed the bottom of Kara's dress and yanked it over her head in one fluid motion. He tossed it behind him, not paying any attention to where it landed as his eyes fastened on her nipple through the pale pink lace of her bra.

He felt like he'd die if he didn't work his way inside her soon, but at the same time he wanted to touch her everywhere, kiss her everywhere. He had held back long enough. With a groan he wrapped his arms around Kara and flipped her onto her back.

Desperate for a taste of her, he lowered his mouth to her nipple, sucked it gently through the lace, rolled it between his teeth and lips and tongue. She went wild, bucking as she reached for his pants and shoved them halfway down his legs, her breathing ragged as she finally succeeded in freeing him.

He groaned as her fingers fastened on him. He thrust against her hand, once, twice, then did his best to slow down. It would be months before he saw her again, months before he could be with her like this again and he wanted to savor every second of their time together. But Kara's passion was a powerful aphrodisiac, as infectious as it was out of control. Suddenly, he was desperate to feel her, to taste her, with nothing between them. He worked feverishly on her bra even as he continued to lick and suck her through the fragile lace.

When finally, finally, the clasp gave way beneath his unusually clumsy fingers, Kara shuddered beneath him. Her hands tangled in his hair as she pulled his mouth down to her, even as she arched up to reach him.

He played with her for long seconds, his tongue and fingers roaming over every inch of her breasts, driving both of them completely insane. When he paused, lifting his head to look at her body, she cried out. The sharp little sound ratcheted his tension up higher. And when she reached between them, circled the hard silky length of him once again and slowly, slowly, began to stroke, he thought he would lose his mind.

Groaning, he arched against her as she rubbed her thumb over his head, and nearly lost it completely when she brought her thumb to her mouth and licked up the drop of wetness she'd taken from him. If she kept this up, he was going to go off before he ever got inside her.

In self-defense, he captured her hands and held them above her head as he kissed his way down her body, praying that he wouldn't lose it completely. He hadn't been this unsure of his ability to hold on since high school and he wanted—needed—this to last. For this to be as good for Kara as it was for him.

Her eyes blazed up at him, and he felt their verdant green could see all the way to his soul. For long seconds, he just stayed there, looking into her eyes. But eventually he had to look away—the connection he felt with her was too powerful to bear. Everything there was between them—everything that came before and everything that was still to come—seemed to be right there for him to see. He wondered, and worried, if she was experiencing the same thing.

He licked his way slowly down her rib cage to her belly button. His tongue darted out, teased the slight indentation of her navel before moving over to her right hip and the tattoo of a small pink-and-white magnolia that rested there. He'd been at the tattoo shop fifteen years before when she'd gotten it. The girl who had gone before her had cried and whimpered her way through, but not Kara. She'd cracked jokes the whole time until the tattoo artist had to tell her to stop for fear he'd mess up because he was laughing too hard.

He took a moment, traced the petals with his tongue. Fifteen years ago he could never have imagined that one day he'd be here, doing this. As he stroked his tongue against the very center of the flower, she giggled, twisted left and right, and he smiled as he moved even lower and pressed his face against her mons. She was ticklish. He'd never known that about her, but somehow it fit.

It was strange, making love to his best friend for the first time. In some ways, he knew everything about her and in others, she was brand-new to him. He liked the dichotomy more than he ever would have imagined possible.

She squirmed a little, bringing her sex to rest against his mouth and he couldn't resist. He flicked his tongue out, ran it over and around her clit before sweeping down to explore her sweet folds. She was sweet here, too, and he spent a few minutes savoring the taste and feel of her against his lips.

Soon, too soon for him, she fisted her hands in his hair. "Now," she breathed, her entire body taut with desire. "Please, Lucas. I need you now."

He wanted to put her off, to spend more time exploring her glorious, giving body, but he knew he was as close as she was. If he waited much longer, it would be over before he ever got inside her.

After giving her one last lingering kiss, he licked his way up her body, paying particular attention to the sensitive spots he'd found on his way down—the curve of her hip, the bend of her elbow, the hollow of her throat.

"Lucas!" The hands in his hair grew rough as she moaned his name, her hips bucking frantically beneath him. Her voice was high, sharp, and he knew that he had pushed her as far as she could go. He wanted to do so much more, and it killed him that he wasn't going to be able to. That in a couple hours he was going to have to say goodbye to her for God-only-knows how many months.

The thought darkened his mood, but she didn't give him time to think, to brood. Her hands clutched at his shoulders as she pulled him up and over her. "Kiss me," she whispered, gently resting her hands on his face and pulling him closer.

This kiss was different than those that came before—hungrier, but also more tender, and he gave himself over completely to the feel, the scent, the taste of her. She turned her head, exhaled, and he entered her in one smooth stroke.

She called his name again and he had started to move before it hit him that he'd forgotten to wear a condom. He started to pull out, but she clutched at him, begged him to stay.

"I need to protect you," he whispered, cursing the fact that his pants were across the room.

"I'm on the pill."

He sent a swift word of thanks to fate, the heavens, whatever was responsible for this fortuitous turn of events and then he plunged into her, hard and fast.

She screamed, orgasmed, and as her body clutched at him in a sweet, powerful rhythm, she almost took him with her. He gritted his teeth, fought his back and kept moving as her legs wrapped around his hips, her heels digging into the small of her back.

"More," she murmured, her hands twisting in the

bedsheets. He grinned down at her despite the freight train of sensation roaring through him. She looked amazing, felt amazing. And he loved it. Loved knowing she wanted him as much as he did her, loved knowing even more that it was he who had made her look like that. Who had satisfied her.

And still, he wanted to give her more. Leaning down, he drew her nipple into his mouth, rolled it under his tongue as he continued moving inside of her. He was close, so close, that he was sure he'd explode any second. But he wanted her to come again before he did. He needed to see her face as it ripped through her, feel her body as satisfaction roared through both of them.

She was moaning, pleading, her hands grabbing onto his as her body shuddered over and over again. "Please, Lucas. Please."

"That's it, sweetheart. Come for me again. I have to feel you." His voice was low, deep, as he moved faster inside of her and he could barely get the words out with the way his breath was sawing in and out of his chest.

Kara let out a low, keening cry, her body arching beneath his as a second orgasm ripped through her. He rode her through it, took her higher and higher until nothing existed but the intense, rolling pleasure that existed between them. He grabbed her hips, tilted them until she was fully open to him. And then, with a groan of ecstasy, he let himself go.

Satisfaction swept through him, powerful, intense,

never ending. For long moments, the world around him went black and he was lost, totally, to the crazy pleasure of making love to Kara.

CHAPTER SIX

WHEN IT WAS OVER, WHEN the storm that had wrapped itself around them had finally passed, Kara and Lucas lay sprawled on their backs in the center of her bed. Her head was cushioned by his biceps, her left leg tangled with his right.

Her body was limp, satisfied, overloaded with pleasure. And her head? Her head was swimming. When they'd been in college, she'd heard a few girls in the dorm talk about making love with Lucas. They'd made it sound like the most amazing thing in the world. She'd thought they were exaggerating—how great could sex with an eighteen-year-old guy be? But now she thought that the girls hadn't been effusive enough. Sex with Lucas had been…intense. Body numbing. Earth-shattering. All encompassing.

It scared her even as it thrilled her. For the first time in years, she didn't know what came next. It was a strange, exhilarating feeling.

Beside her, Lucas finally stirred. "Did we really just do that?" There was a dazed look in his eyes, as if he were waking from a dream. Or an all-out amnesiac fugue. Kara wasn't sure which, but she knew exactly how he felt.

"I think we did." She licked her lips, which felt cracked and swollen, in an effort to get some moisture into the desert that was her mouth. She could still taste him there and maybe she would have lingered over that fact if she wasn't so thirsty. For a moment, she contemplated getting up and getting a glass of water. In the end she didn't move, deciding it was too much effort. Then again, at that moment, breathing was almost too much effort.

Lucas chose that moment to groan. It was a low, hoarse sound and though it was inarticulate, still somehow managed to sum up much of what she was feeling. She wondered dazedly how he'd managed to do that.

There was a part of her that wanted to stay here—right here—forever, basking in the afterglow of Lucas's lovemaking. But the practical, organized part of her was already making plans.

Going over everything she had to pack.

Running through all the known causes of Ebola.

Trying to figure out everything she could possibly need while in Eritrea.

Too bad she didn't know why she was doing it. Whether it was because she really needed to get started packing or if she wanted to find a way to distance herself from Lucas. Not that she wanted distance, exactly. It was just that she was afraid he would—

"That was..." Lucas stopped, blew out a long breath.

She froze, her mind spinning as she waited for him to say something, anything, about what had happened.

How was it? she wanted to demand. *Did the world shake for you, too, or was this just a chance for you to get your rocks off?*

She winced at the vulgar thought, knowing it was completely unfair. After all, she was the one who had practically attacked him, who had used him to keep her mind off everything she didn't want to think about. How could she blame him for going along for the ride? Besides, Lucas wasn't the kind of guy to sleep and run. He was too much of a gentleman for that.

But what had happened between them? How had they ended up ripping each other's clothes off and having the best sex of her entire life?

Lucas was her friend. Her best friend. And now, suddenly, he'd become her lover. She didn't know what that meant or how she felt about it. She didn't know if it was going to change things, or even if she wanted it to change things.

But she couldn't help looking at him differently, as he lay there twisting a strand of her hair around his finger. She felt different, strange, but also comfortable with him in a way she'd never felt with her lovers before. Like this was something she'd been waiting for without ever realizing it.

Had she been waiting for it? Had she felt more for him than friendship all along or was this a new development? Or was she just imagining things that weren't there?

It didn't feel like that. Being with Lucas had felt real, more real than anything had in a long time. And frankly, that scared the hell out of her in a way that Eritrea never could.

So, instead of rolling over and kissing him as she wanted to, she lay there, silent, and waited for him to say something that might give her a clue as to what he was thinking.

She couldn't say how long they lay there, still and silent, their bodies resting intimately against each other and yet separate in a way they hadn't been before tonight. She knew it was a long time, was conscious of the precious minutes ticking by as she waited for him to reach some profound conclusion.

He never did. Or if he did, he didn't bother to share it with her.

Eventually, though, she couldn't put it off any longer. Five o'clock was growing ever closer and with it the next phase of her career. She had to get up, get going—whether she wanted to or not. There was laundry that needed to be done, bags that needed to be packed. And Lucas still hadn't said anything, his silence hurting her more than she would have thought possible.

Determined to brazen it out, she rolled over onto her side and dropped a quick kiss on his cheek. "I need to get going."

She started to roll away from him, but he smiled lazily, tangled a hand in her hair. Pulled her back to him and down so that her lips met his in a kiss so tender it brought tears to her eyes. Which was ridiculous. She hardly ever cried and yet, tonight, she'd done more than her fair share—which she hated. It made her feel weak and pathetic when she'd always vowed to be neither.

"I'll miss you," he told her.

"Oh, yeah?" She arched an eyebrow and shot him a sassy smile she was far from feeling

"Yeah." He reached up, traced an index finger over her right breast and then her left, stopping to lightly circle her nipple a few time. It was an absent caress, almost sweet, and still it had her breathing quickening. However this thing between them was going to end, neither of them could deny that the chemistry was powerful stuff.

Had it been there all along on his side, as well? Or had something about tonight set it off in him? She thought about it for a second and then decided she didn't want to know.

And yet, no matter how many times she'd told herself to play it cool, in the end, she had to ask. "What are we doing here, Lucas?"

He shook his head, his eyes suddenly serious. "I have no idea."

Even though she'd had much the same thought a few minutes before, it still stung. Like a sucker punch right between the ribs. "Right. Of course." She rolled off the bed and practically ran for the bathroom.

He beat her there. "That didn't come out right," he told her as he wrapped his hands around her upper arms and turned her to face him.

"I'm not sure how many other ways it could have come out."

She waited for him to say something else, but he

didn't. He just stared at her, his beautiful, blue eyes frustrated and wary and just a little disbelieving, telling her that he still hadn't wrapped his mind around what had happened between them.

Which, she reminded herself viciously, she couldn't exactly hold against him. After all, wasn't she feeling the same way?

But that was different. Lucas was always the one with the plan. The one who knew what to do when nobody else did. And if he wasn't laying out a plan now that things had changed, then it had to be because he didn't want to make one—at least not with her.

Which was fine. Better than fine, really. After all, she had more than enough on her plate without adding a long-distance quasi-relationship to the mix. Especially when that relationship would be with a control freak with mommy issues.

No, she was better off going it alone, like she always did. No one to depend on but herself. No one to hurt her when she wasn't paying attention. How could she have forgotten, even for a second, that going it alone was the best thing to do?

Even when it didn't necessarily feel like it was.

FEELING MORE AWKWARD than he could ever remember feeling, Lucas stared down at Kara.

His best friend, Kara.

The woman he had just slept with, Kara.

The doctor who was about to leave for a multimonth stint in a developing nation, Kara.

He had absolutely no idea what to say to her. Especially when her posture screamed, *Get the hell away from me, loser,* while her eyes showed just enough vulnerability to make him feel like a total heel. Even if he didn't know why he felt that way. After all, it wasn't like he'd plotted and schemed to sleep with her. She was the one who had thrown him across the bed, after all. "What can I do to help you get ready?" he asked.

The vulnerability disappeared and she shrugged. "I need to take a shower. Pack. Probably eat something, though I'm not sure what's in the house. I didn't even have time to go grocery shopping."

"Why don't you start with the shower and I'll go see what you've got in the pantry. Then we'll get you packed."

"Yeah, okay." She walked into the bathroom, then glanced at him over her shoulder as she turned the water on. The smile she gave him as she did was both shy and remote, neither emotions he was used to seeing in her. It made him feel even weirder than he already did.

Once she stepped under the hot spray, he put on his boxers and walked down the hall to the kitchen. A quick glance in the fridge told him she'd been right— there was almost nothing to work with. The pantry proved a little more interesting, but just barely.

In the end, he managed to fix two bowls of steel-cut oatmeal topped with brown sugar, cut-up dried fruit and evaporated milk. It wasn't exactly a culinary feast, but it would fill her up and give her some much-needed energy. She was starting a full day of work, jet lagged and with very little sleep.

It almost made him feel bad about what they'd spent the past hour and a half doing. Almost. Because it was hard to feel bad about sex with a beautiful woman. Especially unbelievable, amazing, earth-shattering sex that came with the added benefit of being with someone he truly cared about. He wasn't in love with Kara or anything, but he cared about her a great deal. He'd even go so far as to say he loved her as his closest friend.

But that only made this new—and wholly unexpected—development between them even more awkward. He wished he'd been able to glean an idea of what this had meant to Kara, but she'd shut down pretty quickly in the bedroom. Not that he blamed her. He hadn't exactly been forthcoming himself.

But what was he supposed to do? Never, in seventeen years, had he really imagined having sex with Kara. Sure, when they'd first met, he might have thought about her in that context—he'd been an eighteen-year-old guy. But that had only been at the very beginning. They'd become friends so quickly that he'd shoved those thoughts away and hadn't gone there again. At least not before tonight.

And now that he had gone there, what the hell was he supposed to do? He didn't have a clue, especially when he had no idea how he had got himself in this situation to begin with. It was pretty obvious that he hadn't been thinking. Just reacting to Kara's lead. So what did this mean? Was he trying to channel years of friendship into something else? Was she? Did this, *tonight,* mean that they were suddenly a couple?

The thought sent a shiver of unease through him. He didn't want to be part of a couple, wasn't interested in that kind of relationship right now. He'd spent the past year watching Amanda and Simon get back together and then Jack and Sophie fall in love, and while he was happy for both couples, he had no interest in having what they did. Romantic relationships came with all kinds of strings attached, all kinds of responsibilities that he just didn't have time for.

He winced at the thought. He didn't mean to sound callous, but between the clinic and his family, he had all the responsibility he could manage. If he wasn't finding solutions for one problem after another with his mother, then he was bailing his younger sisters out of trouble. Adding a serious girlfriend to that mix was just asking for burnout.

But then, where did that leave Kara and him? If she had no more interest in being a couple than he did, had they simply crossed the line from best friends to friends with benefits? No, his entire being rejected that description—his friendship with Kara was too important to him to be classified in such a casual way.

God, he wished he knew what Kara was thinking. Feeling. Maybe then he could get a grasp on the strange emotions rocketing around inside of him. But Kara was good at hiding her feelings—almost as good as he was—which meant he wouldn't have a clue what was up with her unless they actually had a discussion about this. And judging by everything she had left to do tonight, it might be months before they actually got the chance to have that discussion face-to-face.

Which was completely unacceptable, he decided as he slid the bowls of oatmeal onto the table and went to fetch her. She had to take a few minutes to eat, after all. He'd just catch her when her mouth was full and she had to listen.

Which proved to be easier thought than done. Because once Kara was in the kitchen with him, he found it a million times harder to voice his concerns than he had imagined. Strange that he would suddenly be tongue-tied by her. Stranger still that a look from her emerald-colored eyes would throw him for such a loop. Suddenly everything he'd planned to say sounded stupid and callow.

In the end, he decided to just ask her, however much he stumbled over the words like a teenager. "So, what are you thinking? About us? About this. I mean about…" He trailed off lamely. Seriously? It was humiliating. Had he somehow reverted to being eighteen again?

She lifted an eyebrow. "About?"

"Us. About us. Are we just—"

"Just?"

He sighed heavily, tried to find a description she wouldn't find offensive. And then narrowed his eyes when he realized she'd been laughing at him all along. "Great. I'm trying to have an adult discussion here and you're laughing your ass off. That's terrific."

She actually did laugh then, until he pushed away from the table, annoyed. She shut up, but when he looked back at her she was pressing her lips together to hide a smile.

He made a sound of disgust deep in his throat and she held a hand up, as if she was trying to placate him. "I'm sorry. You were so earnest sitting there, trying to figure out if the sex changed anything without actually coming right out and saying it."

"Okay, well, now that you've said it, *does* it change anything?"

Her smile faded. "It doesn't have to," she said quietly.

Those were the words he'd been waiting to hear, but now that she'd said them, he felt strangely unsettled. Like he was missing something obvious.

"I'm not so sure about that. I think it already has."

"For the better or the worse?"

"I don't think anyone could describe what just went on between us as worse."

She laughed, as he'd intended her to, but then grew really quiet. He'd just about given up hope that she would say anything else when she murmured, "We could just wait and see."

"Wait and see?" He didn't like the sound of that and he knew his disdain could be heard in his voice.

"Yes, Mr. Always-Has-A-Plan-And-Must-Have-Everything-Spelled-Out-For-Him. We could just wait and see what happens. I have this trip to go on, you have a clinic to run. Neither of us knows how long I'll be gone or what will happen in the interim. We could just call this a one-time thing for now and then see what happens when I get back, if anything happens."

"And if nothing happens?" Although he really couldn't see that happening. He was already hard again, already plotting how he could get her back into bed. Which, in turn, made him feel like a total sleaze. This was Kara. He shouldn't be thinking about her like that.

"Then we'll know this was just a weird confluence of factors that led to an unprecedented event."

When he just looked at her, eyebrows raised, she demanded, "What? I was trying to do Lucas-speak."

"That was not Lucas-speak. It was Kara the epidemiologist. I kind of want to hear Kara the woman speak right now, if you don't mind."

"Okay, fine. If when I come back, either of us is dating someone else or the spark is gone or whatever, it'll be no harm, no foul."

He didn't like her words, suddenly couldn't stand the idea of her dating someone else even though he didn't want to date her. Which was ridiculous. He'd never been possessive of a woman in his life and Kara was certainly not the one he should start having those feelings for. And yet they were there, right under his skin, irritating him beyond measure as he imagined her dating some nonprofit do-gooder in Africa.

It was probably biological, he assured himself. He was still warm from her, could still turn his head and catch her scent on his skin, and yet she was talking about dating someone else as if it were the most normal thing in the world. Was it any wonder he was getting his back up?

Frustrated, as much by his sudden inability to say what he meant as by his inability to understand his own emotions, he walked back to the table. But instead of taking the seat he'd set for himself, he crossed to where she was sitting. Leaned against the table right next to her, crowding her in a way he didn't normally do, just to see how she'd react. He didn't know what made him do it, didn't know what he was hoping to see. But when she glanced up, startled, he saw that hint of vulnerability again. She scrambled to cover it up, but it was too late. He'd already seen it and it proved to him that she was just as shaken up by what had happened tonight as he was. Somehow, that knowledge made this whole thing just a little bit easier to wrap his head around.

"Is that what you want to do, Kara? Just wait and see what happens?"

She started to look away, but he reached down and cupped her chin, forcing her to meet his eyes. Kara meant too much to him for him to just go along with her suggestion—unless it was what she really wanted. He might not know what he wanted, but he did know that he would never willingly hurt her.

She didn't answer for long seconds, and he grew edgy, nervous. Which was ridiculous considering he couldn't even remember the last time he'd been nervous before tonight. But then she smiled, clear-eyed, and said, "Absolutely. After all, three months is a long time. Anything could happen."

"Right." He nodded. "Anything." He moved back to his seat and dug into his breakfast, trying to ignore the fact that he was completely unsettled, partially because Kara had said exactly what he'd wanted to hear.

CHAPTER SEVEN

May

Hey Lucas,

Sorry this is going to be quick. I'm leaving for Sudan in ten minutes but you sounded so worried I wanted to answer ASAP. I'm not sure when I'll have another chance for a while. Yes, things are bad here—from what my microbiologists have figured out, we are indeed dealing with a new strain of Ebola. Even worse, it's jumped the border, which is why I'm on the way to Sudan. The cases there are similar, but different enough to have me curious. How quickly is it mutating? Is it becoming more or less deadly? Where was the first mutant strain discovered? You know the drill.

Anyway, please don't worry (I know, easier said than done). But I'm being careful as always and, so far, the rebels are behaving themselves, although I think that's just because they're rightfully terrified of catching this virus.

How are you? Everything okay at the clinic? With your family? With you?

There's so much I want to— Oops, gotta go. I

can hear the trucks starting up downstairs and I still haven't carried my bag down. I'll write again when I get the chance.

Take care,

Kara

"HEY, LUCAS, YOU GOT A MINUTE?"

Lucas looked up from reading Kara's email for the third time and did his best to pretend he wasn't freaking out. He'd been trying to read between the lines, to figure out exactly how much danger she was in. He knew from obsessively watching the news—something he'd been doing ever since Kara flew out five weeks before—that Eritrea was in a constant state of turmoil. According to CNN, the rebels *had* been active, but maybe that was somewhere far away from where Kara was. He could only hope. Not that he would put it past her to lie to him if she thought it would keep him from worrying....

Damn it! Now he was second-guessing his second guesses. Could he get any more insane? This was why he didn't do this, why he didn't sleep with women he had lasting emotional connections with. Because it made him crazy.

He was a control freak. He knew that about himself—hell, everyone who met him knew it—and it killed him that Kara was locked into an untenable situation, one that he could not do anything about.

In some ways, this trip was no different than any other she'd been on. Since she'd joined the CDC straight out of med school, worrying about her had

been par for the course. When she was in India studying malaria for her postgrad work, or in the Andes
studying the effects of AIDS on indigenous popula-
tions, or in Africa working with epidemics of cholera, dengue hemorrhagic fever, tuberculosis, polio,
measles, he'd spent many sleepless nights stressed-
out about the million and one things that could go
wrong for her.

But this time, it was different. He tried to tell himself it was because of what she'd told him, about the
lack of true support from the CDC. And while that
might be true to a certain extent, he knew there was
more to it than that.

Maybe it was because she'd hauled herself into the
middle of the biggest hellhole on earth?

Maybe it was because he spent every day worried
about her getting caught in the middle of the rebel
conflict—like Jack had the year before—and getting
maimed or injured.

Or maybe it was simply because things were so
unsettled between them.

Usually he could count on her to tell him what was
really going on. With work, with her, with the people
she saw day in and day out. But these days a couple
of inane paragraphs was all he could count on getting
from her. Was there any doubt, then, why he was scrutinizing her email like it was a letter from the IRS?

And since he *was* scrutinizing it—what was up
with that crappy closing? "Take care"? Since when did
she close an email with "Take care"? Usually he got
x's and o's, or at least a quick "Love, Kara," but ever

since they'd slept together her emails had been getting more and more impersonal. This one could have been sent to any of a couple dozen people and no one would have known the difference.

He tried to tell himself he was overreacting, that Kara had obviously been dashing the note off in a hurry. It wasn't like she'd had time to write an opus or anything. But still, "Take care"? It was like they'd gone backward seventeen years, to when they'd first become friends and were still tiptoeing around each other. It was ridiculous, maddening, especially when he knew that his emails to her weren't any better.

Somehow, despite all their reassurances, sleeping together had totally messed with their friendship. She'd suggested they wait and see, but right now, it didn't seem like there was much to wait and see about. Things were going downhill fast and there was nothing he could do about it.

It was driving the control freak in him insane. If he could just talk to her for a few minutes, if he could just hear her voice and figure out what she was thinking, things would get better. If he could just reassure her, get her to listen when he told her…what? What was it he wanted to tell her? Maybe the big problem wasn't with her, after all. Maybe it was that he didn't have a clue.

Not that it really mattered, he supposed. It wasn't like she was answering her phone, anyway. Or calling him back when he left messages.

At least she was still answering his emails, he consoled himself. Making sure to let him know that she was okay. That was something. Even if she left a maddening line dangling like "There's so much I want to…" What did she want? *What did she want?* He had a feeling he was in for a whole new batch of sleepless nights—like the ones he was already having hadn't stretched his patience to the breaking point.

"Lucas?" The knock came again, this time with a turn of the doorknob, as well.

"Sure, Jack," he said, cursing the other doctor's timing as he poked his head in. "Sorry. I guess I was lost in thought."

"No problem." Jack stepped into the room in a very un-Jack-like fashion. The former Bostonian was a fast walker and a fast talker—he did everything like it was a race. Today, though, he looked hesitant as he crossed the glorified storage closet that functioned as Lucas's office.

"What's up?" Lucas asked, concerned enough to climb to his feet.

"Just a case I want to talk to you about." Jack motioned for him to sit back down, so Lucas did, but with a feeling of extreme trepidation. There was a note in Jack's voice he didn't like, one that told him something bad was coming.

He waited impatiently while Jack settled himself in the only other chair in the room. "Do you remember examining a Taryn Washington?"

For a moment, Lucas drew a blank, but then a face came to him. "Little girl, right? About six or seven? Big brown eyes and a beautiful smile with the front two teeth missing?"

"One of them has grown in, but yeah, that description seems about right."

"I saw her for a broken arm and a black eye a couple of months ago, right? An accident on her brand-new bike, if I remember correctly."

"That's what it says."

He didn't like the odd note in Jack's voice. "You don't think that's what it was?"

"I don't have anything concrete. Just a feeling." He slid the chart across the desk to Lucas. "She came in again today."

Lucas's stomach clenched sickly. "What for?"

"I think a broken rib. I'm waiting to look at the X-rays. She's got a bunch of bruises, including the beginnings of what promises to be one hell of a shiner."

"How'd she get them?"

"Playing basketball with her older brother and his friends."

"Who do they play for? The NBA?"

"That's what I asked her mom."

"Oh, yeah? What'd she say?" Anger was beginning to blaze inside him.

"She fell all over herself trying to come up with an explanation. But it didn't make much sense to me."

Lucas nodded, flipping through the chart. "Amanda saw her three months before I did—for a sprained ankle and various bumps and bruises. Taryn told her she'd gotten them jumping off the front porch. She had thought she would fly."

Jack didn't say anything, just nodded, and Lucas's

anger turned inward. "I missed it. How the hell did I miss it?"

"Two incidents isn't unheard-of."

"No, but it should have at least struck my radar." He flipped through his case notes, looking for any hint that he'd been suspicious. But there was nothing there. "Taryn seemed fine, happy, even, when I talked to her. She laughed when I made a *Speed Racer* joke. I bought the dad's act, hook, line and sinker."

"Don't beat yourself up. I might have missed it myself if the mom had been a better liar."

"I don't believe that. You did good, Jack," he said. And he meant it. But God, it made him insane that he'd missed it. That he had sent that little girl home for more abuse. They knew about three times, but that didn't mean there weren't more. Didn't mean she hadn't been hurt, only that they hadn't brought her in for medical attention at this clinic. There was still Grady Memorial if they needed free or reduced cost care, and if nothing else, they could have paid to have her seen somewhere, as well.

"Did the girl's brother come in with her?" he asked Jack as he reached for the phone.

"No."

"Do you think he even exists? Did they mention a name?"

"Taryn called him Bobby."

"Good." He glanced at the clock as the phone on the other end of the line started to ring. It was only three o'clock, so hopefully he'd catch her.

"Hey, stranger. Haven't heard from you in a while."

The female voice that answered was somehow both sultry and teasing.

"Hi, Roni. How are you?"

"Pretty good, thanks." She paused. "So, to what do I owe this honor?"

He heard the note of interest in her voice and couldn't help wincing. A couple of months ago he might have taken her up on it, might have been interested in picking up where they'd left off a couple of years before. Roni was smart, sexy and great with the no-strings thing. But things had changed for him and he knew that he had no interest in Roni whatsoever. Somehow, he thought that was going to be the case for all the women he knew, at least until he and Kara settled things between them once and for all.

"Actually, I was hoping you could do me a favor. Off the record?"

"Oh, yeah?" Her voice had cooled considerably. "How off the record are you talking?"

"You still at Grady?"

"Yes."

"I have a case over here at the clinic that I'm thinking is child abuse. We've seen her for broken bones and numerous other bangs three times in the last six months or so, and I'm just wondering, before I call Child Protective Services…"

"If we have any cases for over here, as well?"

"Exactly."

Roni sighed. "I'm not supposed to do this, you know."

"I know, and I appreciate it. I just don't want to

have to send that girl home tonight if I don't have to. If there are enough incidents, I would suspect imminent harm and call the police instead of just CPS."

"You can't tell them if I find anything."

"Of course not. But I can tell them that I suspect they'll find a case file for her over at Grady, as well."

"Give me a minute. I'm almost at my office."

"You're the best, Roni."

"That's what all the guys say." He heard a door close and then the sound of fingers typing on a keyboard. "Okay, what's her name?"

"Taryn Washington."

He waited impatiently as Roni scrolled through the hospital database. After a couple minutes, she asked, "Six years old?"

He glanced at the birth date on the front of her chart. "Yep."

"We've got her. It looks like she's been seen in the E.R. four times in the last year."

Lucas slammed a hand down on his desk, nodded when Jack looked at him sharply. "All for falls or injuries?"

"Three times for that. Once for accidental poisoning."

That was all he needed to hear. "Thanks, Roni. I think that's more than enough to get her taken out of the home tonight."

"Glad I could help."

Lucas started to say goodbye, when something else occurred to him. "Actually, could you do one more thing for me? Can you check and see if a Robert Washington has ever been treated there, as well?"

"The father?"

"Possible older brother." He caught Jack's eyes, started to gesture, but the other doctor was already on it. He left the room and came back with another chart a couple minutes later.

"He's eleven," he said when he realized Lucas was off the phone. "We've seen him twice for skateboarding injuries and twice for bad falls on the basketball court."

"Grady's seen him seven times in the last three years." It was more than enough. "Do me a favor. Stall them while I call the police."

"Already on it," Jack said as he walked out of the room, both files clutched in his capable hands.

Lucas was pissed off at himself for missing the signs that would have spared Taryn this latest injury and at the world for being the kind of place where this happened far too often. He made the call and was assured someone would be right there. Forty minutes later, he was still waiting. And fuming because of it.

Abused children were his hot button, the one thing he saw in this clinic that guaranteed to make him crazy in ten seconds flat. When he'd been a kid, he'd had a friend whose father was a drunk. Usually he was too intoxicated to do any damage, but some nights— some nights his aim was perfect. Those were the nights Mark would limp over to spend the night at Lucas's house. Oh, he'd pretend nothing was wrong, that he had gotten hurt skateboarding like Bobby Washington. But by the time Lucas was ten, he knew what those late-night trips to his house were about. Knew what the bruises meant.

He'd told his father and his dad had called CPS, but Mark's family was as rich and respected as Lucas's. Plus, they had years of experience hiding both the senior Mark Robertson's alcoholism as well as the abuse. In the end, nothing had been done, except that Mark spent more and more time over at Lucas's house. Things had been fine for a while, or at least as fine as they could be when his friend was getting the shit beat out of him on a regular basis.

More than once Lucas had wanted to confront Mark's dad, but Mark swore things would only get worse for him at home if Lucas said anything. So he'd kept silent, and when Mark was sixteen and acting out, he'd gotten high—something he did a lot to escape his screwed-up family life—and then wrapped his car around a telephone pole.

Lucas had never backed away from a fight since and he sure as hell wasn't going to back away from this one.

Even though he was technically off—and had been for close to three hours—he'd stuck around finishing paperwork, taking overload patients to keep things moving and, now, waiting for the police to come.

He was just walking out of an exam room—a little boy with the worst case of Hand, Foot and Mouth disease he had ever seen—when he heard loud voices coming from the waiting area. He glanced at Maria, one of his nurses, to see if she knew what was going on, but she just shrugged, eyes wide.

Dropping his patient's chart on the nearest counter, he headed for the front of the clinic at a fast walk. Before he got there, he heard a loud crash followed by a string of obscenities in a deep, male voice.

Amanda, eight-and-a-half months pregnant, poked her head out of an exam room to see what was going on and he shouted, "Get back in there and close the damn door. Don't you dare walk out here right now."

Trusting Amanda to stay out of the way—for the sake of her unborn child if not her own sake—he ran the last fifty feet or so, bursting through the door into the waiting room just in time to see a huge man pick up a chair and hurl it against the wall. "You have no right to keep her from me!" he bellowed at Tawanda, the clinic's receptionist and the toughest woman he knew.

As he glanced at her out of the corner of his eye, he realized that the crash he'd heard had been the glass breaking in the window that separated her from the patients who came to check in. A chair was upside down on the counter, half resting on the computer and Tawanda herself was standing there yelling right back at the man even as blood dripped down her face from numerous cuts.

"Jesus," Jack breathed behind him. "What's he on?"

"PCP?" Lucas guessed before calling to Maria over his shoulder, "Call nine-one-one. Tell them what's going on and that we need someone here, now." They might not come quickly for an abused child, but destruction of property was another thing altogether. He ground his teeth together in annoyance. The world they lived in sucked.

As the man picked up yet another chair, Lucas started forward into a waiting room gone mad, Jack right at his heels. The room had been full when this guy had started his rampage and now was filled with people shoving and pushing in an effort to get out the door. More than a few people had been knocked down and Lucas paused to help a girl of about thirteen back to her feet. Beside him, Jack lifted a screaming toddler into his arms then helped the boy's mother to her feet, as well.

"There's an emergency exit around the corner," Lucas shouted, pointing behind him. "Go out that way." Then he turned to Jack. "Get people out of here, okay? And then get me a syringe of thioridazine. We're going to tranq this bastard."

Jack nodded grimly, started funneling as many people as he could toward the emergency door. Seconds later, a shrill alarm sounded, indicating people were getting to safety.

The sound only enraged the man more and he leaned his head back and hollered in anger. Which was fine with Lucas—he was beyond pissed himself.

Striding across the large waiting room, he put himself between the man and Tawanda, who was screaming back at him and using every obscenity in the book as she did.

"That's enough," Lucas told her, not taking his eyes off the other man—who he now recognized as Taryn's father, who he'd been hoping wouldn't show up until after his wife and child were gone. "Go get cleaned up. I've got this."

Sam Washington reached out and slammed a huge, beefy fist straight into Lucas's chest. Lucas stood his ground, refusing to back up an inch, even though he knew it was going to cost him in the morning. But there was no way in hell he was going to give this guy any kind of satisfaction—he'd already gotten more than enough of that beating the shit out of his kids.

When Lucas didn't even stumble, the guy let out another enraged scream and picked up a chair, hurling it across the room straight at the head of one of Lucas's oldest patients. If Jack hadn't gotten in the middle of it, taking the brunt of the hit, the old woman would probably be laid out cold right now.

"Hey!" Lucas said, firmly enough to get Sam's attention. "You want to tell me why you're wrecking my clinic?" Though he already had a pretty good idea.

"This bitch won't let me go back and see my wife and kid. They've been here for hours. I want to see them."

"Yeah, well, this isn't exactly the way to convince us you should be anywhere near them."

Sam threw back his head and screamed again, muscles bulging in his throat and upper arms. Lucas's stomach twisted sickly as he watched. This was what he'd sent Taryn back into because he hadn't been sharp enough to figure out what was going on when he'd seen her three months before. This was what that little girl and her brother faced on a regular basis. It was a wonder they weren't both dead.

The thought enraged him. "Get the hell out of here," he snapped. "We've already called the police and CPS. There's no way you're getting anywhere near Taryn again." Lucas wouldn't allow it, even if it meant he had to beat the hell out of the bastard himself.

"You have no right! That's my kid—"

"I have every right and I should have called on you three months ago."

"Let me see them! Let me see that bitch I'm married to! What did she tell you?" Sam picked up another chair and used every ounce of strength he had to fling it straight at Lucas.

Lucas caught it, though the impact sent shock waves of pain shooting straight up his arms. As he set the chair aside, he taunted, "Is that the best you've got?"

The waiting area was almost empty—between the two exits and Jack directing traffic, the crowd had almost completely dispersed. If he could keep this bastard's attention on him just a little longer the last of his patients would have a chance to get to safety.

Lucas moved a little then, shifted to his right just to see if the guy's eyes would track him. They did, but the pupils were dilated to hell and back. He was obviously on something, though Lucas didn't know what. He doubted it was PCP, as he'd originally thought, simply because—though enraged—Sam was still following the conversation. Still participating in it.

Out of the corner of his eye, he saw Jack walking back into the waiting room, a syringe in his hand. He must have stared at him a second too long, though, because Sam started to turn to see what he was looking at. If he spotted the tranq, all hell was going to break loose in a way it hadn't yet.

Deliberately drawing Sam's attention back to him, he sneered, "The only way you're getting back there to see your wife and daughter is through me. And frankly, I don't think you've got what it takes to beat up on a guy who can hold his own with you. You like to pick on little girls. Does it make you feel like a man every time one of her bones break?"

"I'm going to kill you, you son of a bitch!" Sam roared. His entire focus was now on Lucas. *Good.* If the guy was busy trying to kill him, he was leaving everyone else—including his wife and child—alone.

Sam raced straight at him, but Lucas stood his ground, waiting for a chance to put the guy on his ass. It came as Sam barreled full force into him. Lucas twisted at the last second, absorbing only part of the blow before he reached around and shoved Sam forward as hard as he could.

The other man stumbled, from surprise as much as the blow, and the momentum he'd already gathered put him face-first on the floor. Furious, raging, he rolled over and started climbing to his feet. But Lucas was ready and he kicked him in the chest, sent him sprawling back to the floor. Then Jack was there, sliding the syringe into the bastard's arm and depressing the plunger. Fifteen seconds later, it was lights out for Sam.

"Jesus, Lucas," Jack said as he stood back up.

"Didn't they teach you in med school not to taunt guys tripping on stimulants?"

"He was heading straight for you and your magic syringe. Should I have let him take you down on his way to the back to beat up on his wife and daughter?"

Jack held up his hands. "By all means, taunt away."

Lucas smiled a little grimly. "Somehow, that's what I thought you'd say." He rubbed a hand over his aching chest. He hoped the bastard hadn't cracked his sternum with that punch.

Fifteen seconds later, he forgot his discomfort as three armed policemen burst through the doors, guns drawn.

Fifteen seconds after that, Maria called from the back, "Hey, Lucas. Your mom's on the phone. She wants to know if you're still on for dinner tonight. Oh, and Amanda's water just broke."

For long moments, her words didn't sink in. When they finally did, he threw his head back and laughed. A couple heartbeats later, Jack joined in. Who needed war-torn Africa? They had their own crisis center right here in the middle of Atlanta. Though he wasn't sure what it said about him that of everything he'd faced that day, dinner with his mother was what scared him the most.

CHAPTER EIGHT

June

Kara,

Glad you're back from Sudan. The news is reporting that conditions there are worsening. Then again, I don't suppose things are much better in Eritrea. How is everything going? I was talking to Steve up at Johns Hopkins the other day. I guess he's been following what's going on down there pretty closely, and he says you and the team from the WHO are making great strides containing the epidemic. I'm really glad to hear that. I assume, no word from the CDC on when they're going to bring you home? Maybe they'll actually let you finish this one out.

Not much is going on here. I'm starting to use the money from the benefit for upgrades at the clinic. Better X-ray machine, new nebulizers and a bunch of other stuff I won't bore you with. Amanda and the baby are doing well, though the clinic is pretty crazed without her. Nothing compared to what you're going through, but it keeps me busy.

Take care of yourself and I'll see you soon.
Lucas
P.S. I've attached a picture of John Matthew.

Hey Lucas,
Glad to hear Amanda is doing well! Congratulate
her for me—you look great holding little John
Matthew. Very natural—especially the spit-up
on your shirt.

Yeah, we're finally seeing results here. The rate
of infection has dropped about four percent in
the last week but we're hoping for a much bigger
drop in the month to come. And yes, I'm going
to be here a while longer. The CDC and WHO
are too scared of a worldwide epidemic to pull
us out now. Just between you and me, they're
right to worry. This bug is really nasty.

I've got to go—my rounds start in a few. I'll
write again soon.
Kara

KARA'S FINGER HOVERED over the mouse as she contemplated sending her latest email to Lucas. She wasn't
sure what the point was—there was almost nothing in
it he couldn't get from watching the news. Part of her
wanted to erase the whole thing, to start over and tell
him about what was really going on with her. To tell
him that she thought about him more than she should,
especially late at night when she lay in the dark and
remembered what it had felt like to be loved by Lucas.

But that was the problem, wasn't it? She hadn't

actually been loved by Lucas—they'd only slept together. And the fact that she was feeling all these
weird things for him, that she was missing him more
this time than she ever had before, was completely on
her. He hadn't promised her anything—had in fact
bent over backward not to. Which was fine, really.

It wasn't like she hadn't known going in how things
were going to be. She'd spent the past seventeen years
watching Lucas date woman after woman and then
move on as soon as it looked like his girlfriend was
going to fall for him. Which meant he was constantly
moving on, because they *all* fell for him. How could
they not? He was gorgeous, funny, smart, kind, rich
and a doctor who helped the underprivileged. Land-
ing him was like winning the lottery. The only problem was, Lucas didn't want to be landed.

He said it was because he had enough on his plate
with work and family, but she knew the truth. He was
scared. Scared of committing to a woman and finding out that she wanted him only so that he could take
care of her. And it wasn't that Kara blamed him. She'd
been around long enough to see Lucas bail his mother
and sister out of jam after jam. She knew it exhausted
him, just as she knew he was never going to stop. Not
as long as they needed him.

Kara would wonder how she'd managed to stick
around this long, except that she'd always been careful.
Always made sure not to think about him as anything
but a friend. Always made sure not to cross the very
definite boundaries that lay between them.

She could cry on his shoulder, but not actually expect him to make things better.

She could listen to his problems, but not actually do anything to make them better, either.

And, most importantly, she could hang out with him as long as he never suspected things might turn sexual between them. In Lucas's world there were friends and then there were women he dated and never the twain shall meet.

She'd always done a pretty good job of walking the line until that last night in Atlanta when she'd totally blown it with a trifecta of rule breaking. And now... She sighed and fought the urge to bang her head on the desk. Now they were forced to communicate in these absurd, stilted emails that didn't say anything about anything. It was driving her mad.

There was so much she wanted to tell him, about what she'd seen and what she'd learned. About what was going on down here and why she thought these months were going to end up being the most important of her career. Instead, she wrote to him about the infection rate dropping. With such scintillating news she couldn't imagine how he'd manage to keep himself awake until the end.

She wished she could turn back the clock, wished that she could go back to that moment in her house when she'd shoved him onto the bed and ripped his clothes off. If none of that had happened, things would still be okay between them. She needed things to be okay. Lucas was the only person she really had in the whole world. Sure, she had friends at the CDC and at

WHO, but that was different. They weren't who she went to when she wanted to talk through a problem and they weren't who she thought about at strange times during the day, just because she saw something or heard something she thought they might like.

No, that position had been reserved for Lucas for as long as she could remember and she didn't like that things were changing.

She glanced back at the screen and thought about changing the whole email. She could erase the drivel and tell him the joke she'd heard the day before. Then she could write about Samira, the young village girl who had stood by, stoic, as Ebola wiped out her entire family. She could tell him about—

Her thought was cut off by an explosion, followed by a series of high-pitched screams. Her whole body froze at the sound, long seconds ticking by as she tried to assimilate what she'd heard. And then she was dropping the computer's mouse, running straight out the door of her makeshift research tent and into the street. She tripped on rocks and broken asphalt as she scrambled toward the main clinic.

"Julian!" She screamed the name of her team's top doctor as she crashed through the door. They didn't have time to stand on ceremony, not if what she thought had just happened really had.

He was already on his way down the hall, his small, black medical bag clutched in his hand. "Land mine?" he asked her as they headed outside as one.

"That's my guess."

He swore bitterly as they ran. "I can't believe this is still happening."

She didn't answer, but then she didn't have to. They'd had this same discussion numerous times since coming to Teseney. The war was over, but some of the cities—Teseney being the most notable, because of its location—were still surrounded by land mines that had never been disarmed, never been recovered. And still people walked through the areas where the land mines were. Still they let their children scamper through the minefield like it was nothing. And neither the government, nor the organizations that had come here to help through the months and years, had ever bothered to bring in a tank to sweep for the damn things.

Just another type of injury that could be prevented if anyone actually gave a damn.

They'd only been in Teseney three weeks and this was the second land mine that had been detonated. The first one had killed the child who had stepped on it, ripping him into so many pieces that there'd been nothing she and her team could do for him. As she ran, Kara prayed that this wasn't going to be a repeat of that first experience, prayed that whoever had set it off had managed to survive with only the loss of a limb or—

She paused when she caught sight of a woman running toward them, her long Eritrean-style dress flowing around her legs as she carried a small child in her arms. She was crying and covered in blood but she was moving fast. Kara laid on the speed, but she was exhausted from working twenty-hour days and just wasn't as fast as Julian. By the time she caught up to him, he had the unconscious child in his arms and he was working on stemming the blood coming from where her leg used to be.

"Please," the woman gasped in broken English, clutching at Julian's arm. "Please, save my daughter."

He shrugged her off even as he applied a tourniquet to what was left of the girl's leg. "We're trying. But you need to leave us alone to do our job." His voice was harsh, his face determined, as he worked to stanch the bleeding.

The woman didn't seem to understand what he was saying, her eyes filled with fear as she continued to grasp at him. Kara pulled her gently away and handed her off to Freida, who—like the rest of her team—had come running at the sound of the explosion.

Then she dropped to the ground next to Julian. "What can I do?" she asked the other doctor. He might specialize in infectious disease instead of trauma, but he was still one of the best doctors she'd ever met. If the little girl in front of them had a chance at survival, Julian would grab on to it with both hands and keep her safe. Or at least as safe as a small child allowed to run through fields of landmines could be.

"I've just about got the leg under control," he told her grimly. "But check those gashes on her arm. Make sure none of them are too deep. Then check her vitals—I think she's going into shock. We've got to get her into surgery in the next few minutes or we're going to lose her."

Kara sprang into action, checking the little girl's wounds, two of which needed stitches. The little girl screamed when she touched her, but then fell quiet. Too quiet. Kara started to talk to her, only to find that she had passed out. Which was as much a blessing as it was a horror.

After wrapping gauze around the wounds to stanch the bleeding, Kara checked the girl's vitals. "We need to get her to the clinic now!" she told Julian, who nodded but didn't move as he shoved the little girl's shirt up to check out a huge tear in her side. The blood oozing from it was dark red, nearly black.

Kara closed her eyes as nausea welled inside of her. She swallowed quickly, fought it back. Exhausted or not, she was absolutely *not* going to fall apart now. "Can you pack it?" she asked, keeping her voice deliberately low as the mother wailed a few feet away.

"No time. We've got to get her on the table."

Kara waved Van, another one of her team members, forward. The woman had a stretcher under her arm, and within seconds they had the little girl laid out on it. Then she and Julian each grabbed a side and ran toward the clinic as fast as they could. The little girl was still out of it, though her mother was running next to them, sobbing. Begging them to help her daughter.

Terror rippled through Kara as she thought of what waited for her, for them, in the operating room. Neither she nor Julian were surgeons. Though they had both done a surgical rotation in medical school, that was a long time ago and far away from here. She needed Pierre, from the WHO team, but he was hundreds of miles away in Nakfa. Or Lucas or, barring that, his partner, Jack Alexander. Any of them would know what to do here, how to help this girl.

But none of them were here, she acknowledged grimly, her eyes meeting Julian's forbidding ones. It was obvious that the same doubts running through her head were also running in his.

The knowledge gave her strength. They might not be the best shot this little girl had of surviving, but at the moment they were her only shot. It was going to have to be enough, because there was no way Kara was going to let her die. She'd already lost too many Eritrean children in the time she'd been here. She refused to lose this one, too.

"Get the mother out of here," she shouted to Van, who'd come in right behind them. As her team member hustled the woman outside, she called after her, "And get us a nurse in here, pronto."

Then she was at the portable sink, scrubbing up at lightning speed while Julian prepped to go in. As soon as she was done, they switched places. Then the nurse was there, helping her thread the needle and prepare the instruments they would need to repair the girl's torn artery.

"I want to check out her side first," Julian told her. "I can't tell what damage has been done."

"Sure." She wished longingly for an X-ray machine, was certain Julian did the same.

And then everything faded—all the background noise, all the fear clanging around inside of her, all the wishes for better equipment, better conditions, better surgeons. It all faded away, even the little voice deep inside that told her a three-month surgical rotation wasn't enough to tackle something like this. And all that was left was the patient and the slow and steady rhythm she and Julian established between them.

He started by cutting into the girl's side, and her first look at the child's ribs had Kara unsure if she wanted to cry or celebrate. Two of the ribs were shattered beyond the ability to fix, but they had slowed the shrapnel down so much that it looked like her organs were still intact. Her spleen was bleeding a little, but Julian was able to get in there and stitch it up. One of the ribs they ended up removing, while the other Kara pinned as best she could. Then, together, they got started working on her shorn femoral artery.

All together, they spent six hours operating on the girl. Two skilled surgeons could probably have done things in half the time, but both she and Julian were amateurs, though absolutely concerned with getting things right—or as right as they possibly could. It wasn't until it was all over and Julian had ordered an aggressive round of antibiotics as well as heavy-duty painkillers, that Kara let herself sag. Let herself give in to the fear and horror that had plagued her since she'd heard the land mine detonate.

"Good job," Julian told her, clapping her on the back.

"I think that's my line," she answered. "I'm glad you were here."

"I'm glad we both were. You've got the steadiest hands I've seen outside of a surgeon."

"I didn't feel steady."

"Yeah, but you were steady. Sometimes that's all we can hope for." He glanced through the door behind him, shrugged out of his bloody shirt. "You want me to talk to the mother?"

Since she knew he'd rather eat slugs than deal with their patient's mother—even to tell her the cautiously optimistic diagnosis—she told him, "Go take a shower. I've got it."

The fact that he didn't even feign reluctance as he shot out the door told her everything she needed to know about his state of mind. Maybe she wasn't the only one who'd been faking steadiness in there.

After pausing a minute to change out of her own blood-spattered shirt, Kara headed down the hallway toward the mother. There was no reason to keep the woman in agony one second longer than she had to be.

She snagged Linda on the way, a nurse who could translate. They found the girl's mother huddled on the floor of the ill-equipped waiting room, her arms wrapped around her knees as she rocked back and forth. Her face was ravaged by pain, tears falling unchecked down her cheeks.

Kara rushed across the room, crouching down on the floor next to her. "Your daughter made it through the surgery well," she said, trying to infuse her voice with confidence. "We will be monitoring her closely over the next few days and it will be a long road back, but we think she will recover."

She waited as the nurse translated her message. Then continued, "It will be hard for her. She's lost a leg and one rib, has numerous other injuries. But if we can control the infection and keep her from succumbing to shock, we'll be able to tell you more in a couple of days."

Which wasn't to say that the little girl wasn't in for a terrible time. Losing a leg was horrible in a place like America, where there was good medical care and advancements to help with lost limbs, as well as physical and occupational therapy. Here in Eritrea, there was none of that. The little girl's life was going to be very tough for a very long time. But Kara refrained from telling the mother that. One, because she figured the woman already knew. And two, because at least the little girl still had a life.

The mother sprang to her feet and hugged Kara, as she chattered away in Tigrinya. Kara nodded politely though she only caught every third or fourth word, then smiled as the nurse translated the woman's thanks.

"You're very welcome," she answered.

"Her daughter's name is Maia," the nurse informed her with a musical accent. "She is six years old."

Kara nodded. "That's a beautiful name, for a beautiful girl."

The mother nodded, still sobbing a little. In relief this time, Kara thought. She said her goodbyes and had turned to go, when the mother gasped and fell to the floor.

Kara crouched down next to her, felt for a pulse. The woman was pale and clammy—symptoms Kara

had originally taken for fear or relief but now wasn't
so sure.

"Ask her what hurts?" she instructed the nurse urgently.

The nurse did, then responded with, "Her belly.
She is pregnant."

"Okay, okay. Let's get her into an exam room so I
can take a look at her." Kara slipped one of the woman's
arms over her shoulders, waited impatiently as the
nurse did the same. Then they stood as one, taking as
much of the woman's weight on their own shoulders
as they could.

It didn't take them long to get down the hall to an
open exam room, and once there, took her even less
time to ascertain that the woman was having a miscarriage—probably brought on by the fear, terror and
strain of running with her daughter's body.

The pregnancy was early and—it turned out—not
the woman's first miscarriage. But it was still horrible to tell her what was happening, to watch her cry
as she realized she'd saved one of her children only to
lose another. After they had done all they could to help
Maia's mother and make her comfortable, Kara decided that privacy was what her patient needed most,
at least for a little while. She'd been to hell and back
twice today and it would take anyone time to recover.
Because she was stable and the bleeding had stopped,
there was no reason not to leave her alone to do just
that.

After changing out of blood-soaked clothes for the
second time in a little over an hour, Kara headed back

down the hall to check on Maia. Julian, having already changed clothes, was already with her when Kara stepped into the room.

"How's she doing?" she asked as he checked the still unconscious girl's vitals.

He didn't look up. "Better than she was."

"I guess that's something, then."

"Something." He snorted. "Yeah, I guess it's something."

Concerned at his tone—and the fact that he still hadn't looked her in the eye—Kara asked, "Everything okay?"

"Linda told me the girl's mother is pregnant."

"Was pregnant. She miscarried."

"Shitty day for her, then, huh?"

She recoiled at his callousness and almost called him on it. But when she looked closer, she realized he was just as upset as she was. More than upset, really. Sick at heart.

"Tomorrow will be better." She knew she sounded like Ms. Mary Sunshine, but she couldn't help it. If she didn't think that, didn't believe it, there was no way she could do her job. The sadness, the grief of it all, would cripple her.

He snorted again. "Yeah, sure. We're in a country where children are allowed to play near landmines, where ten percent of the population has been ravaged by Ebola, where the government cares more about how it looks than it does about saving its citizens' lives. How the hell can you think, for even a second, that tomorrow is going to be better than today?"

Julian whirled on her then, his dark eyes angry in his pale face. "Why would she get pregnant again? Knowing this is the world she is bringing her children into, knowing that she can't keep the ones she has safe, why would she want to bring another child into this hell? I don't get it."

"It's none of our business."

"Why isn't it our business?" he demanded fiercely. "I just spent six hours working on her daughter, trying to save her from something that never should have happened. Why the hell isn't it our business?"

She tried again, spouted words she wasn't even sure she believed anymore. "Accidents happen—"

"Do you really believe that bullshit? Do you really believe that letting your daughter play in a minefield is accidental? She was right there, Kara. Right there to scoop her up and run her in. It wasn't like the girl had wandered off."

"Maia."

"What?"

"Her name is Maia. Not the girl."

He threw up his hands. "Really? You're going to lecture me about impersonalization now?"

"I didn't mean—"

"That's exactly what you meant. Don't back down now." The look he shot her was filled with rage. "I don't understand how you can criticize me but have nothing but concern for her."

She sighed, thrust her hands through her hair in an effort to gain some control of the situation. Julian was furious and dangerously close to spinning off course.

She couldn't let that happen. She was team lead. He, and his mental state, were her responsibility.

"I wasn't criticizing you, Julian. You've done—"

"Yeah, right."

"Let me finish!" She held up a hand and shot him a glare of her own. "You've done amazing work since you got here. No one doubts that. I asked for you personally and I know that we would not have gotten to the bottom of this outbreak as quickly as we did if you hadn't been a part of this team."

He dismissed her words with a wave of his hand. "I don't need ego stroking, Kara."

"It's not ego stroking if it's true."

"So you say."

"So I mean." She paused, let that sink in before continuing. "We did good today. Why can't we just concentrate on that for a while?"

His laugh was bitter. "Because there's always so much more good that needs doing."

"Yeah." She inclined her head in agreement. "But you knew that going in."

"TIA?"

"TIA." She leaned over, rubbed his back a few times. Then promptly vomited water all over his shoes—right before she took a swan dive for the floor.

"What the hell?" Julian caught her as she fell. "Jesus Christ, Kara, you're burning up."

It was the last thing she heard before the world went dark.

CHAPTER NINE

July

Dear Kara,
I haven't heard from you in a couple weeks—just want to make sure you're okay.
Lucas

Kara,
It's been three weeks since your last email. Are you all right? I'm worried.
Lucas

Damn it, Kara, I'm camping out at the CDC if I don't hear from you in the next 24 hours. Where the hell are you?
Lucas

STANDING BY HIS CAR, Lucas checked his email and text messages for what had to be the fiftieth time that day. Still nothing from Kara, though he'd been very clear in the email he'd sent the night before. She needed to contact him.

Frustrated and furious, he climbed into the car,

slamming the door behind him in a totally unsatisfactory display of temper. Then used his phone to look up the website and number for the CDC. This had gone on long enough. He was going to get answers if it killed him.

After punching in the number, he waited impatiently as the phone rang for what seemed like forever. Finally, it was picked up and "Center for Disease Control, how may I help you?" came through the phone in a voice that was sweet as syrup and twice as slow.

"May I speak with Paul Lennox, please?" Lucas closed his eyes and offered up a swift prayer that this would work. Because if it didn't he was going to lose his mind.

"I believe Paul is out of the office for the day. I can transfer you to his voice mail, if you'd like."

"Is there someone else I can speak with in his department?" He knew he sounded brusque but he was out of patience. He'd been waiting for Kara to contact him for four torturous weeks now. Four weeks of wondering if she was okay, if she was even *alive*. It was bullshit and the next time he talked to her he was going to tell her so in no uncertain terms.

Because there was going to be a next time. There had to be.

"If you can tell me what you need, sir, I can try to transfer you to the correct person in Paul's department. Or, if you can wait until tomorrow, he should be back."

Wait until tomorrow? He felt like if he waited five more minutes his head was going to explode.

"Look, a friend of mine works for Paul. She's in

the field in Eritrea and I haven't heard from her in a month. I need to make sure she's okay."

"I'm sorry, sir, even if Paul was in, we wouldn't be able to give that information to you. We have a strict privacy policy—"

"I'm a doctor. I know your damn privacy policy. But I'm her emergency contact, so—"

"Well, if that's the case, then there's nothing to worry about. If something had happened to your friend, you would have been notified. I'm sure she's fine."

Somehow that didn't make him feel any better. "Look, if I could just talk to someone, anyone—"

She sighed, and the sweetness was gone from her voice when she said, "I suppose I can transfer you to Paul's administrative assistant. She might know something. But that's the best I can do—and if nothing else, you can leave a message for Paul to call you back tomorrow."

"That'd be great, thank you."

He waited on tenterhooks while the phone rang and rang. By the time the voice mail of a perky young woman named Marisa Hardley finally picked up, he was ready to throw his phone out the car window. Not to mention more than ready to storm the CDC as he'd threatened in his last email to Kara.

He settled for leaving a terse voice mail outlining his problem and requesting a call back ASAP.

After he hung up the phone, he put the car into gear and pulled out of the parking lot, doing his best to fight off the panic that was assailing him as he drove to his mother's house. This wasn't like Kara, wasn't like her at all. Yes, things had been strained between them lately, but there was no call for her to just vanish like this. They had an agreement and this disappearing act of hers was not a part of it.

Years ago, right after he'd suffered through her first hellish trip out of the country, they'd agreed that she would contact him regularly. He didn't care how—email, phone call, text, IM, he wasn't picky—but she was supposed to contact him at least once a week, just to assure him that she was okay. If she was out in the field and away from communications, she'd tell him in advance and sometimes that week would get stretched to ten or eleven days. But never had she done this. Never had she left him waiting twenty-eight days to simply hear that she was okay.

It pissed him off that she was doing it now. Made him angry to an extent he rarely let himself reach, because it wasn't helpful. He'd learned years ago, in dealing with his mom and sisters, that he had to stay cool and not let his temper get the best of him.

But this callous disregard from Kara—he wasn't used to it and didn't like it, at all.

He pulled into the driveway and, slamming out of his car, he started up the long, windy path that led to his mother's front door. The absolute last thing he wanted to do was have lunch with his mother and sisters again today, but he didn't have a choice. It was another command performance in a summer filled with them. He didn't know what had gotten into his mother, but something obviously had. Usually she was content to see him once a month—preferably right around the time she ran out of the monthly allowance doled out by his father's trust. But lately it seemed she had to see him once a week.

Still thinking about Kara, he jogged up the steps to his mother's front door. In the old days, when his dad was still alive, he would have walked right in. After all, this was the house he'd grown up in and the house that would one day be his, passed to him as it had been to the oldest son for five generations. But since his mother had taken to moving a different lover in every few months, he thought it prudent to wait on the steps until he was invited in.

In an effort to keep calm as he waited for the door to open, he went over all the places Kara could be.

She could be out in the field, without access to electricity let alone the internet.

Her camp could be under siege by rebels, her equipment seized or destroyed.

She could have contracted Ebola, could be dying in some makeshift hospital in Eritrea right now.

She could have been kidnapped by one of the rebel factions.

She could be injured and dying of infection.

Or, he admitted grimly, she could be just fine and have simply decided not to contact him because… because why? That was what was killing him. The not knowing. And she knew that about him. She knew he was not very good at not having all the information. It made him insane. As evinced by his current craziness. If he could just hear from her—

He took out his cell phone, checked messages and email again. Still nothing.

If she was okay, if something bad hadn't happened to her and she got home safe and in one piece, he was going to kill her for putting him through this.

He was just starting to call the CDC again when the door swung open and his mother stood there, dressed in a soft-pink linen pantsuit, high heels and a double strand of pearls. It was to be a casual lunch, then. No pressure. By the time he was sixteen he'd learned that all was good as long as she was wearing pearls. It was only when the colored stones came out that there was a problem. And if she was wearing diamonds on a day she didn't have a high-society gig to go to, then look out. Because she was out for blood.

But pearls, pearls were good. Lunch should be low-key—and it probably shouldn't cost him more than a few grand to get back out the door. Now if only Kara would email, he could say that things were looking up.

"Hi, Mom," he said as she stepped back and let him into the foyer.

"Hello, Lucas. How are you?" She tilted her head to the side and he obliged her by dropping a quick kiss on her still-smooth, gardenia-scented cheek.

"Great, thanks." He fumbled his cell phone into his pocket. His mother didn't like them at her table. She put up with his because he was a doctor, but she knew today was his day off and he decided not to push it. At least not unless the CDC actually called him back.

"Is everything okay?" his mother asked as she ushered him into the dining room. "You look distracted."

"I'm fine. Just busy with work."

"You're always busy," his mom chided. "No matter what time I call."

"I'm a doctor, Mom. I've got a lot of patients."

"You don't have to work as hard as you do," she told him. "If you'd just join your uncle John's private practice—"

"I've told you before, I'm not joining anyone's practice. I like my job."

"Yes, but you'd probably like a paycheck every once in a while, too, wouldn't you?"

Impatience sizzled along his nerve endings but he refused to give in to it. This was an argument they'd had a million times—having it a million and one wasn't going to change anything. Certainly not his mother's mind about the appropriate ways in which one gave back to one's community. Benefits and charity galas were one thing, but actually getting his hands dirty with the everyday tasks it took to run the clinic—that was completely outside her realm of understanding.

He tried not to blame her much—after all, she'd raised a lot of money for his clinic through the years. The fact that she'd never be caught dead in it wasn't important. His patients were what was important. Kara was.

As he took a seat at the long cherry dinner table, he glanced surreptitiously at his phone. Still nothing.

As one of his mother's maids came forward to pour him a glass of iced tea that he was perfectly capable of pouring for himself, he said, "I get a paycheck, Mom. Every two weeks. Just like most people."

"Yes, but what you get paid is barely enough to keep a hermit crab alive, and they don't eat much."

"You have no idea what I get paid."

"No, but I know it's nowhere near what your father used to make—and he's been dead ten years. With inflation what it is, it shouldn't be too hard for you to surpass his salary. All you have to do is—"

That's when he tuned her out. She always had something to say about his dad, some way to illustrate how he wasn't living up to the old man. And maybe that was true. Hell, it probably was. God knew his father had regarded his wife and daughters with a bemused kind of indulgence, had more than put up with their idiosyncrasies and bad habits.

He'd taught his son to respond the same way to them, and for a long time Lucas had. Hell, most days he still did. But the fact of the matter was, he had more respect for his mom and sisters than his dad had. Or at least, he wanted to. He wanted to expect more from them than endless parties and other carefree social gatherings. Wanted to see them be more than hostesses at fancy parties and ornaments on their husbands' or boyfriends' arms.

Too bad his wishes didn't have much power in the grand scheme of things.

"Are you paying attention to anything I'm saying?" his mother squawked. He'd gotten so caught up in his own thoughts that he'd failed to make appropriate listening noises.

"Of course I am, Mom. I'm just tired, like I told you."

"I know, sweetheart.' She reached over and squeezed his hand. "You work so hard."

A knee-jerk part of him wanted to comment that everything looked like hard work when you weren't used to doing any. But he bit the words back. It was obvious that she was trying, so the least he could do was try to meet her halfway.

"What have you been up to?" he asked. "A new benefit?"

"Actually, yes. We're raising money for the children's hospital. Do you know how little federal funding they get? It's scandalous."

"They're a private hospital, Mom. So, yeah, no federal funding."

"Well, I think it's appalling, so I've organized a few friends and we're going to raise so much money for them they won't know what hit them." She smiled at Lucas. "You'll come, won't you?"

He smiled gently at her. This was the woman he remembered from his childhood. Flighty, yes, but with a heart of gold. She'd never been able to see something wrong and not try to fix it. Admittedly, her answer was almost always to throw money at it, but hey, in a lot of cases, money worked. And he could think of a lot worse things for her to be spending time on than raising money to help sick children.

"Yes," he told her. "And you won't even have to hunt me down and threaten me. I promise I'll go."

She gave him a disbelieving look. "We'll see about

that. But it's going to be so much fun. We're going with a Brazilian Carnival theme, since it's going to be in February. A little different than the tired old Mardi Gras theme, but still seasonally appropriate. In fact…"

She was off and running, and he just let her go off on yet another tangent. It was easier, much easier, than trying to rein her in.

When the server came in with the first course of melon soup, he asked, "Where are Jenn and Lisa? Aren't they coming?"

His mom waved an airy hand. "I thought this would be so much better if it was just the two of us. I see them all the time, but I just don't get to see enough of you."

"I was here for dinner four nights ago."

"Yes, and you let your sisters do all the talking. This time, I wanted to be able to pin you down on a few things."

"What's there to pin me down on?" he wondered. "I'm an open book."

"Oh, of course you are," his mom said with a laugh. "Just like your dad was."

"What's that supposed to mean?"

"It means I have someone I want you to meet."

He paused with his spoon halfway to his mouth. "Tell me it's not a woman."

Just the thought struck terror into his heart—his mother had the worst taste in women for him and the last thing he wanted to do was find out that she had set him up on another miserable date. Especially when Kara was missing. She was all he could think about and the idea of making small talk with some stranger seemed impossible when he was nearly insane with worry. It had been all he could do to sit here for the past fifteen minutes and not pull his phone out.

In fact, now might be a perfect time to check.... Nope, still nothing.

"Lucas." His mother glared at the phone and he slipped it back into his pocket. "Sadly, I know better than to set you up. The last time cured me of it."

Well, thank God. It made sitting through the date from hell with the Atlanta senator's daughter worth it if he never had to go on another blind date. Almost.

"No," his mother reiterated. "I want you to meet Jean-Claude."

The bite of soup he'd just taken turned bitter in his mouth. "Jean-Claude?"

"Yes! He's the most wonderful man. I met him at a party a few weeks ago and we've been spending all our free time together. Which isn't as much as I'd like since he's pursuing his acting career. But still, it's enough."

Alarm bells of every shape and size were ringing in his head now, so loudly that for a second he couldn't think around them. Jean-Claude? An actor? Met at a party?

"How old is this guy, Mom?" He said the first thing that came to mind, but he could tell from the way she flinched that he had hit a sore spot. And when she didn't immediately answer, fear crawled down his spine. "Jesus, Mom, tell me he's legal."

"Of course he's legal!" she snapped. "He's older than you are, Lucas."

"By how much?"

She looked away.

"By how much?" he repeated.

"By three years," she told him.

He threw his napkin down on the table as he felt his head explode. "He's thirty-eight, Mom? Are you serious?"

"He's a very mature thirty-eight."

"I'm a mature thirty-eight."

"You're thirty-five."

He gritted his teeth. "That's the point I'm trying to make. I'm mature for thirty-eight. This guy is playing at being an actor and living off a woman more than twenty years older than he is. How is that mature?"

"I didn't bring you here to argue with me about Jean-Claude. I just wanted to tell you about him so you weren't surprised when he comes to dinner with us on Sunday."

"He's coming to dinner with us?"

"Of course. He's part of my life now."

"How is that possible? By your own admission you met him a few weeks ago."

"Yes, well, when it's right, it's right."

"And it's right with this guy?" he asked incredulously.

"It is. After all, some of us don't have seventeen years to wait around for the perfect opportunity to speak our minds."

"Seventeen years? What's that supposed to mean?"

His mother smiled serenely at him. "You're a mature thirty-eight. You figure it out."

Lucas ran a hand over his face and tried to keep his temper in check. "I don't have time for games, Mom."

She reached over and patted his cheek. "Then it's a good thing I'm not playing, isn't it?" She paused. "Eat your soup. The rest of lunch will be here any second."

He ground his teeth together. "I don't care about the stupid soup."

"That's a shame. I had Betty make it just for you. I know how you love cold soups in the summer."

He felt like he'd fallen into an episode of *The Twilight Zone,* one where the aliens were inordinately concerned with melon soup. "Who is this guy, Mom? What do you know about him?"

"I know everything I need to."

Somehow, Lucas doubted that. But he didn't have it in him to argue anymore. Not about this. His mother was going to do whatever it was she wanted to do, and she wasn't going to listen to anything he had to say on the matter.

He pushed the bowl away. "Is the rest of lunch ready?" The sooner he ate, the sooner he could escape.

"Of course." She motioned to the server, who came in with the main course—a salade Niçoise that Lucas had absolutely no interest in eating.

Still, he went through the motions, at least until his mother said, "I have a small favor to ask of you."

His checkbook started burning a hole in his pocket even as his heart sank. "How much?"

"Well, you see, yesterday was Jean-Claude's birthday and I wanted to get him something really special. The only problem is I'm having a teensy cash flow problem."

"How much?" he asked again, trying to determine just how deeply this Jean-Claude had sunk his claws into his mother's pocketbook.

"We found this absolutely gorgeous watch. A Devon Works Tread 1. It's beautiful. So sleek and impressive looking, not clunky at all like some watches are. Anyway, I love it and though he protested at first, in the end he caved and told me I could buy it for him if I insisted. Which, of course, I did."

She paused, drew in a deep, shaky breath and Lucas braced himself for what was coming next.

"But when I went to pay for it, my credit card wouldn't work. I just don't understand. You said you'd paid them all off last month. There should have been plenty of room on my American Express. And when that didn't work, I tried my other two cards but they wouldn't go through, either." She paused dramatically. "I think it must be credit card fraud, don't you? My information must have been stolen. The girl at the store told me to report it right away. So that's why I wanted to talk to you about it. So you could report it."

As she rambled, he tried to find a way to break the news to her. He thought about explaining the whole income-debt ratio thing again. Thought about telling her that money didn't actually grow on trees. And then, finally, decided to hell with it. She was a grown-up. She could take it.

"It wasn't identity theft, Mom."

"Oh, I think you're wrong. Jean-Claude says that computer hackers can get their hands on any information they want these days. They must have gotten my credit card numbers and bought a bunch of stuff for themselves." She paused. "I'm so upset. They completely ruined Jean-Claude's birthday. I was going to take him out for a nice dinner but I was too upset. I just don't know what to do about—"

She was off and rambling again, and he decided to let her, figuring it would make her calmer later. In the meantime, he checked his messages one more time. Still nothing from Kara. Damn it.

"How much was the watch?" he asked as soon as he could get a word in edgewise.

She finally stopped talking and he could see her formulating excuses in her head. "I don't know why the cost is important. It was to be a gift."

He gritted his teeth. "Well, to begin with, it will help me determine whether you're really suffering from identity theft. How about that?"

"Oh. Well, all right, then." She cleared her throat uncomfortably. "It was—" she mumbled.

His eyes narrowed. It must have been more expensive than he thought if she couldn't even bring herself to say the words out loud to him. Damn Jean-Claude, damn his mother's flighty irresponsibility and damn his father for encouraging it in both his mother and his sisters. And double damn the universe for taking his father at fifty-seven and leaving Lucas squarely in charge of the female members of his household for pretty much his entire adult life.

"How much, Mother?" He knew he sounded impatient, but he had grown tired of the cat-and-mouse games years ago. Right now he just wanted to know if there really was a problem he needed to fix or if his mother had simply lost her marbles.

So much for a nice mother-son bonding lunch.

"Don't get huffy with me, Lucas. You know I can't stand it when you talk to me like that." Her voice trembled a little. "It makes me nervous and—"

"I'm sorry. I wasn't trying to be short with you. It's just that I have things I need to do. And this Jean-Claude guy doesn't sound all that impressive to me, if you want the truth."

"Oh, but he is. And he's so smart and nice. You're going to love him."

Somehow he doubted that. Something about despising boy toys who preyed on older women who could take care of them.

Closing his eyes, he braced himself as he asked, "The watch, Mom. How much did it cost?"

"Okay, fine! It was fifteen thousand dollars, but before you get angry—"

"Fifteen thousand—"

"It's a beautiful watch. And it looks so good on Jean-Claude. He'll remember this birthday forever."

His head exploded into a migraine of epic proportions and for a moment, Lucas indulged his latest fantasy of beating the shit out of Jean-Claude. That would definitely make it a birthday that the gold-digging, scum-sucking bastard would remember.

Gritting his teeth, praying for a patience that had

run out months, *years* before, he ground out, "Mom, you can't spend fifteen thousand dollars on a watch for a guy you barely know."

Frosty silence met his words. Followed by, "Well, Lucas, I don't think it's any of your business how I spend my money."

"How you spend *my* money, don't you mean, Mother?" The words slipped out, but once they were out there, he didn't regret them. It was past time that she faced the truth. That they both did. "You've already gone through almost all the savings Dad left for you. You have enough for day-to-day living, sure, but I've been paying your credit card bills out of my trust fund for years now." A trust fund that he would much rather have given over to the clinic when he'd first started it up. But he'd known even then that he would need it to take care of his mother. Which was insane when he considered how well-off his father had left her.

"That is not true."

"Really? Because it feels true when the money comes out of my account every month." He ran a hand through his hair in agitation. "I'm co-signer on all of your credit cards, Mom, and after the debacle last month, I asked them to lower your limits to something that wouldn't bankrupt me in a couple of years."

She gasped. "You had no right! How am I supposed to go back to Jean-Claude and tell him I can't buy that watch for him? He has his heart set on it—"

"I thought you had to convince him."

"Oh, I did," she backtracked. "Of course I did. I'm

just saying that now that I insisted he have it, it's humiliating to have to go back on my word. Surely even you can see that."

What he could see was that his mother was afraid of losing her boy toy when she couldn't keep him in the style to which he'd like to become accustomed. Which was perfectly fine with Lucas. More than fine, actually. He'd had no problem with his mother dating after his father's death, had put up with her parade of aging Lotharios for years now, but he couldn't stand to see her being taken advantage of.

"I'm sorry, Mom, but I'm not going to have this argument with you. I did what I had to do."

"You know, if you'd just get a real job, making real money like your father, none of this would be an issue," she reiterated

"I have a real job. And trust me, no matter how much money I make, this would still be an issue. Because in no world would it be okay with me for my mother to throw away my trust fund on a wannabe Gallic prostitute with delusions of grandeur." Throwing down his napkin, he stood up. "Now, if you'll excuse me, I have someplace I need to be."

CHAPTER TEN

THE RED-GOLD OF AN ERITREAN dawn was just breaking over the sky the next morning when Kara slowly
straightened from where she'd been crouched over
the trash can. She wiped her mouth and reached for
the omnipresent bottle of water she'd learned to keep
close. After rinsing her mouth out, she sank slowly
onto the ground, resting her head on her knees as she
tried to breathe through the nausea that was still twisting her stomach into knots.

She'd come down with dengue hemorrhagic fever
a few weeks ago, and while she'd managed to survive—just barely—she'd been left with this absolutely
ridiculous nausea. It swept in four or five times a day,
churning up her gut until she puked, and then level-
ing her for a good fifteen minutes afterward as she
prayed for it to pass. It was just one of the lovely side
effects of the damn virus and it was getting old fast.
Especially since it had kept Julian from putting her
back on the "fit list" until this morning.

This morning's bout seemed to be lasting longer
than usual, but she told herself to hang in there, that it
had to pass soon—if for no other reason than she had
way too much to accomplish. Other members of her

team were beginning to notice that the dengue fever hadn't gone away as it should have and she knew it was only a matter of time before one of them confronted her on it. Or worse, told her boss about it. They'd let her stay after she recovered only because all the blood work had come back fine on her liver, kidneys and heart. But if it got out that she couldn't shake the nausea, she'd be on a transport plane bound for the U.S. faster than she could blink. The CDC had very specific rules about things like this. The rules were for a reason, she knew, but she just wasn't ready to leave yet.

Not because her time in Eritrea had been such a blast—it had probably been her most difficult field experience ever. And that was saying something. But she'd also made real progress, *they'd* made real progress, and the idea of going home before the epidemic was completely under control was anathema to her—especially since the CDC was actually letting her stay to finish this one out. Dengue fever or not, this was the disease of her career and she wanted to see it through.

She pushed to her knees and was starting to stand when another wave of nausea hit her, causing her stomach to cramp up and her whole body to shudder as she dry heaved. There was nothing left to come up, but that never seemed to matter. She'd been so sick for so long that she'd lost a good ten pounds in the past couple of months. The doctor in her was concerned, even as the scientist was desperate to hang on just a little longer.

Climbing to her feet slowly—weeks of experience

had taught her that she was usually okay after she dry heaved a second time—Kara went about gathering up the files she'd dropped when the nausea had hit her. When she was finished, she threw herself back into her to-do list for the day.

They had finally managed to control the Ebola epidemic, though it had been touch and go there for a while. She'd done thousands of interviews and analyzed enough data to make her eyes cross. But she believed she'd found Patient Zero, as well as the conditions that had enabled the virus to mutate into this latest version of itself. Much like dengue fever, this new strain of Ebola could be transmitted via mosquito bite—which was both frightening and fascinating. As a result of her team's findings, along with those of Pierre's WHO team, the area had been flooded with insect repellant as well as other teams, each of whom took a city and got to work on educating the populace. Her team was still in Teseney, which was proving to be one of the most difficult places to get a handle on. It wasn't as big as some of the other cities—the population here was only a little over a hundred thousand— but the city itself was in terrible shape.

One of the major points of contention in the Eritrean War of Independence, Teseney had been repeatedly leveled by bombs in an effort to cut the rebels off from the Sudanese border where they received supplies and weapons. Add in the fact that Eritrea had been closed to outside organizations for so long. That there were various ethnic groups in the city, most of whom kept to themselves and spoke separate languages. As a result, it had been very difficult to launch a campaign to eradicate the new threat of a mosquito-born Ebola hybrid.

But they were finally beginning to make progress, finally finding a way to reach through the barriers of fear and distrust that ruled this city. Not that she blamed the natives. They'd been to hell and back these past few years—was it any wonder they had issues with outsiders?

With a sigh, she pulled up her email. She hadn't checked it in the past few days as she was too busy trying to play catch-up with what was going on in the field to waste time on emails from home. But as she scanned through her in-box she realized she'd made a huge mistake. She'd been so sick for so long that she'd forgotten to contact Lucas and he was frantic.

Reaching under her cot, she pulled out the Comsat phone she kept for important phone calls to the States. It was a hell of a lot clearer than trying to unscramble half a conversation on a regular cell phone and while it belonged to the CDC and she normally only used it for emergencies, she figured this definitely qualified.

She dialed Lucas's number with shaky fingers.

He picked up on the first ring. "Kara."

"I just got your email," she told him. "I'm fine."

For long seconds, there was silence on the other end of the line. Then, "That's it? You put me through hell and all you have to say to me is that you're fine?"

"I'm sorry. Things have been crazy here." It was a lame excuse and she knew it. Her palms were sweating so badly she could barely hold the phone.

"You're sorry?"

"Yes."

"But you're not sick? You didn't contract Ebola?"

She thought of the DHF, but he sounded so strung out she figured telling him about how sick she'd been was the last thing she should do. There'd be time to talk about it once she got back to the States. "I don't have Ebola."

"Have you been out in the field?"

"Not so much lately, no."

He paused and she could feel the anger and hurt crackling down the line at her. It made her feel like an even bigger heel. It wasn't that she felt like she had to answer to him, but she'd made him a promise years ago and it was crappy of her not to keep it. Crappy of her not to think about calling the second she started to feel better.

"I'm sorry," she told him again. "Things here have been bad and I screwed up."

"Yeah, you did. But you're okay? You swear?"

"I'm fine. Just exhausted."

"The news here is reporting on renewed rebel activity in Eritrea—a result of the widespread deaths from Ebola. That hasn't touched you?"

She thought of Maia, her little leg blown off. Thought of the thousands of patients she'd treated since she'd come to this country. Thought of the pain that lived inside of her every second of every day, for all the patients she hadn't been able to help and all those she hadn't helped enough. Then said, in a voice barely above a whisper, "Everything's fine here."

"You sure?"

"Yeah." She started to stand up but her stomach pitched and rocked wildly. She froze and took deep breaths as she waited for it to pass. She should have known better—she had a very specific routine to help keep the nausea at bay first thing in the morning.

"Okay, then. I guess I'll talk to you when you get back."

"Wait? That's it? We haven't talked in weeks and that's all you have to say to me?"

"Whose fault is it that we haven't talked? It seems to me that you got down there and got wrapped up in what you were doing and forgot all about me. Which is fine. I understand that. But I've been going crazy thinking something happened to you. Thinking you'd been kidnapped or injured or—" His voice broke and for long seconds he didn't say anything else. Neither did she.

"Look," he continued, "I know things changed between us when you were in Atlanta, but that doesn't mean you have to shut me out like this. And it sure as hell doesn't give you the right to ignore me until the mood suits you. I don't deserve that."

"It wasn't like that," she started to say. But then she stopped. After all, hadn't it been just like that? She could blame the DHF all she wanted, but she'd been bouncing back this past week and a half. She could have called Lucas any number of times, and if she'd been thinking clearly, she would have. But she'd been so busy running from the weird feelings she had for him that she'd totally blown him off. She'd hurt him and there was no excuse for that.

"What was it like, then?" His voice cut like broken glass.

"I made a mistake. I'm sorry."

He sighed and she could almost see him thrusting a hand through his hair in agitation. Long seconds passed before he finally said, "Yeah, okay. You're sorry. I'm sorry, too, for jumping down your throat."

"It's okay," she told him.

"Really? Everything's okay?" He sounded sarcastic, but before she could call him on it, he said, "Look, thanks for calling. But I have to go. I've got to get to the clinic. I'm opening."

"Oh, right. Well, then, I guess I'll talk to you later."

"Yeah, later."

"Lucas—" she started, unsure what she wanted to say to him but knowing she didn't want to leave it like this, with all this coldness between them. But he had already hung up and when she tried to call him back, the phone just rang and rang and rang.

With a sigh, she hung up the phone and put it away. She'd call him later, apologize again. He couldn't stay mad at her forever. No matter how inconsiderate she'd been.

And she had been inconsiderate. Sure, she'd spent two weeks totally out of it with DHF, but she'd been lucid for more than a week now and if she'd thought about Lucas in any context other than how to keep herself from getting hurt, she would have realized that he was probably frantic. And that she was hurting him. It was the last thing she'd wanted to do, but it was obvious from his voice that she had.

And yet, how else was she supposed to protect herself from him? From this thing between them that mattered but didn't? She'd been around long enough to know Lucas didn't do commitment and yet here she was, mooning over him and waiting for him to say that he had feelings for her outside of friendship, even though she had no idea if he did or not. All she knew was that ever since they'd slept together, she'd been having weird feelings about him. Uncertainties. She didn't know what she felt for him, only that something had shifted.

And that wasn't good.

Why not? a little voice deep inside of her asked.

Because she couldn't handle the idea of being without Lucas. She'd lost her mother when she was eighteen, her father long before that when he'd walked out on the two of them. Lucas had been the one constant in her life for nearly two decades and the idea of losing him made her physically ill.

Which meant she was going to have to get a handle on all the strange feelings that were floating around inside her. Otherwise, she was going to end up losing him. God knows, she'd already done a bang-up job of pushing him away when that was the last thing she wanted to do.

Sighing heavily, she stood up and went back to her files. There was nothing she could do about the way things were now. She'd call him back later and if he didn't answer, then she'd deal with him when she got back to America. Yes, she'd acted badly. But surely seventeen years of friendship counted for something.

Besides, who knew what the future held. There was no use worrying about what was going to happen in a future she might not even have. After all, she'd survived dengue hemorrhagic fever, but there was no guarantee she'd survive everything else this country had to offer.

Van and Julian found her attitude fatalistic, but she just considered it being realistic. There were a million things that could go wrong while she was on location like this, and she'd accepted long ago that her job might end up getting her killed. It was why she'd always insisted on living every moment to the fullest.

Except with Lucas. But that was different, she told herself. Living life to the fullest included having him in that life and going down this path with him. But if they were involved romantically, one day he would move on from her the way he'd moved on from every other woman in his life and she had no idea how she would react to that.

It probably wouldn't be good, however.

Her cell phone buzzed and, despite her best intentions, she grabbed it up, hoping it was a text message from Lucas. Some ridiculous little joke or tidbit that would make her laugh. But it wasn't one of his regular messages. Instead, it was a question from Julian about a case he was working.

As she brushed her teeth in the little sink in her cubbyhole of a bathroom, fatigue dragged at her. Weighed her down so that she wanted nothing more than to climb back into bed and pull the covers over her head for the next week or so. But there was work to be done—more work than she had a chance of doing in ten weeks, let alone the three she was guessing she had left in Eritrea—so, exhausted or not, she needed to get moving.

It was just a simple case of mind over matter, she told herself as she shook out her jeans, checking them for scorpions and other desert predators before slipping into them. Now if only her matter would catch up with her mind...

She reached for her favorite tank top and shook it out much like she had her jeans before pulling it over her head. There were a lot of things she would miss about Africa when she went home. Having to worry about nasty little bugs crawling into her clothes or her bed was not going to be one of them.

She moved in front of the small dresser mirror, pulled out the moisturizer and sunscreen that she applied religiously when in Africa or South America. And nearly gasped at her first glimpse in the makeshift mirror since getting dressed. Her tank top, which she had worn hundreds of times since she'd bought it a few years before, looked positively indecent. It had always been a little snug—she liked that because it was difficult for any creature to climb into it when she was in the wilds—but at the moment it fit her like a second skin.

She wondered if she had shrunk it the last time she'd washed it? But it had been washed innumerable times and had always maintained its shape—

something she'd always loved about it. Why would it have shrunk now, especially when she hadn't treated it any differently than she had a million times before?

She knew she hadn't gained weight, not when her ribs were more prominent than ever. Turning to the side, she checked out her silhouette. Her stomach wasn't any bigger. Neither was her butt. In fact, they both looked smaller, her stomach almost concave after all of the puking and not eating she'd been doing. But her breasts looked huge, almost twice their normal size.

Which explained everything.

She stripped off the tank top and reached for a baggy white one instead. Then pulled her suitcase out from under the bed and took out one of the three small bags of tampons that were there. Her period must be about to start.

But something about seeing those three bags of tampons just sitting there made her think. Three bags of tampons were all she'd brought with her and she'd been down here three months without using even one of them? It didn't make sense.

A fleeting thought ran through her head and she froze, started counting back. Tried to figure out when her last period had been. Which, now that she thought about it, hadn't been since she'd gotten to Eritrea. How had she missed that?

She remembered skipping the first month, and putting it down to the new birth control pill she'd begun taking a few months before—the first couple of months she'd been on them her period had been superlight. But that didn't mean it should actually stop completely, did it? Not even spotting?

She thought back to what her gynecologist had told her when she'd started on the pill. It was a milder one than she was used to, the lowest level of hormones she could take to keep her cycle regular when she was out in the field. There'd been mention of a pill that could stop her period completely, but the doctor in her had been unhappy with the possible side effects of doing so. Which was why she'd chosen this one instead. And yet, here she was, three months later with no period. Unless there was another reason her period hadn't come. Like the dengue hemorrhagic fever—which could very well be the case, she told herself. Her body had been under a lot of stress lately and that could definitely stop her cycle. Of course, she had been here close to two months when she'd contracted it, so that wouldn't account for the missing two periods.

Not liking the turn her thoughts were taking at all, Kara pressed a hand to her breast and probed a little, as if she was doing her monthly exam. And winced at the ache doing so engendered. Even worse, if she searched her memories beyond the twenty-hour days she'd been working for the past three months, she realized that this wasn't the first time she'd noticed her breasts were sore. She'd simply put it down to her period coming and then gotten so busy that she'd forgotten all about it until the next time they'd bothered her.

Unsettled and more than a little nervous—though she told herself there was no reason to be—she sank down on the edge of the bed and once again started the backward count in her head. And once again, the number she reached disturbed her. Wanting to be sure she wasn't making a mistake, she pulled up her cell phone's calendar and did the same thing with the actual dates in front of her.

The answer was no less reassuring the third time around.

The part of her that was purely female wanted to say it was impossible. She was on the pill and had always been religious about taking it on time. Plus, she'd been on no antibiotics anytime close to when she and Lucas had made love. She should be *fine*.

But the doctor understood the loopholes, knew that the strength of the pill she was on *should* protect her from pregnancy. But there were no guarantees this early in the game. There hadn't been time to test it, to see how well it worked with her body chemistry. She had assumed it would work because the other ones had…but assuming might very well have made a very big ass out of her.

She counted backward one more time, just to be certain, but this time it was with a sense of inevitability and more than a little panic. Sure enough, the night she and Lucas had made love had been an optimum time for her to conceive. Maybe all that nausea she'd been blaming on dengue hemorrhagic fever had a different root entirely.

Pregnancy.

The word echoed in her thoughts, over and over again as all the implications of it slowly began crowding her mind. And still she couldn't quite wrap her mind around it.

She was pregnant.

Was she pregnant?

Dear God. She was pregnant. With Lucas's baby.

It was a lot to take in.

Her knees trembled and she slowly sank to the edge of the bed, even as her mind raced to figure out all the implications. Her musings were not reassuring.

For her, pregnancy was a disaster of epic proportions.

She traveled regularly and often to some of the most dangerous spots on earth. Spots that were no place for a baby, even if they weren't being ravaged by disease. She thought back to the discussion she'd had the night before with Julian and suddenly understood where he was coming from a lot more. No, the places she traveled were definitely not meant for children. They really weren't meant for pregnant women, either, to tell the truth.

If she was pregnant it would mean a huge change in her lifestyle. Her career. Her future. Was she ready for that? And if she wasn't, did it really matter?

Even worse, Lucas had been clear numerous times in the years she'd known him about not wanting children, not wanting a family. Which she'd always thought was a shame because he would make an absolutely amazing father. But it wasn't like she didn't understand. With his mother and sisters, was it any wonder he really didn't want to take care of anyone else?

Besides, it wasn't like she could blame any part of

this on him. He hadn't been careless. He had checked, had started to get up to get a condom and she was the one who had said no. Who had told him she was protected…because, at the time, she'd thought that she was. Because of their work, they were both tested for diseases regularly so there had been no reason to be concerned. Except obviously there had been.

Her hand crept over her still-flat stomach, pressed a little, as if she could actually feel the life that might be—that probably *was*—growing beneath her palm. Yet she'd had blood tests and nothing had come back that said she was pregnant. Could it be that Julian simply hadn't ordered that test? Sure, it was usually standard, but there'd been no reason for him to think she would be pregnant. Not when she was out here in the middle of the desert fighting one of the most dangerous diseases on earth.

Suddenly, she couldn't stand the not knowing for one second longer.

Crossing to her personal medical kit—which she usually kept with her when out in the field—she popped it open. Took out one of the pH strips they used to test all sorts of things besides pregnancy, including protein and sugar in a person's urine.

It only took a minute or so, and then she was staring at the results. The little pregnancy square had turned purple almost the second her urine had touched it. She was going to be a mother.

Deep inside of her a fragile joy began to bloom, one she hadn't expected and wasn't sure she was ready for. And yet, it was there all the same. She was going to have a baby. No, correction, she was going to have Lucas's baby. A little black-haired tyrant who would be brilliant and difficult and beautiful. So beautiful.

Her heart thudded double time in her chest, though from fear or excitement, she wasn't sure. There were a lot of obstacles in her path, a lot of reasons this was a really bad idea. But there would be time to deal with all that later. For now…her hand crept back over her stomach slowly, oh, so slowly. Almost as if she needed permission to admit its existence—and the emotions it engendered in her.

Which was stupid. She might not know what the future would hold, but for now, she was going to give herself permission to be happy. And excited.

She was bringing another life into the world, something—at thirty-five, with no husband and no long-term romantic prospects—she hadn't been sure she would ever be able to do. But she was doing it now, she told herself, though she still lacked the husband. And probably the long-term romantic prospect, as well. But that was okay. She was going to be a mother, something she hadn't realized she wanted so badly until it was a foregone conclusion. She decided to focus on that instead of all the other stuff for a little while. Reality would come crashing in soon enough.

And it did, sooner than she ever would have imagined. Because even while joy was spilling through her, another thought rose up. It overwhelmed her, changed her joy to fear and horror from one second to the next.

She was up and out of her room before she'd even made the conscious decision to move. Was racing down the stairs to the main section of the hospital with only one goal in mind. To get to Julian.

He was with a patient when she found him, finishing up his rounds before she took over for the day, and the five minutes she had to wait to speak with him were among the longest in her life.

As he moved out from behind the curtained cubicle, she basically ran him down, her ice-cold fingers clutching at his arm as article after medical journal article ran through her head.

"Kara?" Julian turned to look at her quizzically, his eyes shadowed with a concern that was nothing compared to the fear sweeping through her. "What's wrong?"

"I need you to examine me."

"Okay." He put his hand on her elbow, guiding her away from the patients. "What's going on?"

She told him, watching his face grow more and more grim as her words tumbled over each other. His expression told her everything she needed to know. She'd been right to worry. Dengue hemorrhagic fever and pregnancy did not mix well at all.

CHAPTER ELEVEN

"HEY, BOSS." TAWANDA'S voice came over Lucas's intercom. "You've got a visitor."

"Who is it?"

"Do I look like I know every damn thing in the world?" she snapped at him. "Why don't you come out here and see for yourself?"

"Okay, I will," he said with a grin. Trust Tawanda to put him in his place.

But as he walked toward the front of the clinic, his stomach knotted in trepidation. He had the sick feeling it was his mother and the truth of the matter was, he had absolutely no desire to deal with her.

After the excruciating two hours he'd spent at dinner with her and Jean-Claude the night before—*and what Atlanta-born man actually went by the name Jean-Claude*—the last thing he wanted to do was talk to her again so soon. There hadn't been enough distance yet and he knew he was going to end up saying something he wouldn't regret but that he probably shouldn't say.

Besides, if he had to listen to any more Jean-Claude stories, he was going to put a bullet in his brain. And he wouldn't even be sorry about it later.

What was she doing here, anyway? Hadn't he done his duty last night? What more could the woman want from him barring his firstborn child? He'd already written her a large check last night to tide her over until her monthly allowance came in next week. And if she'd already spent it on Jean-Claude, then he really, really didn't want to know about it.

But when he crossed into the waiting room it wasn't his mother who was standing there. It was Kara, dressed in a sleeveless lavender blouse that accented her curves, gray pants and purple kitten heels that showed off her long, long legs to their best advantage. Her red hair was loose around her shoulders and for a second he flashed back to when they'd made love. To when her hair had been wrapped around his fist and her legs around his waist.

He got hard just thinking about it, which was not a state of events he wanted to encourage. Not now, when he was still so angry with Kara and not when she was inexplicably standing in the middle of his clinic instead of being in Eritrea where she belonged. Something was wrong, obviously, and he needed to know what it was.

"Hi, Lucas," she said, her smile little more than a tremulous curving of her lips.

"Kara. What's going on? What are you doing here?"

She glanced around and he realized they were standing in the middle of his waiting room, with his patients and staff alike looking on.

"You want to come back to my office?" he asked.

"Sure. Thanks."

She knew the way—this certainly wasn't the first time she'd been to the clinic—so he stepped back and let her pass. But as he followed behind her he realized she was a little unsteady on her feet, as if she couldn't quite find her balance.

Was it an inner-ear imbalance from the flight? he wondered. Or simply the fact that she was wearing heels again after months of shoes designed to traverse desert terrain? He didn't know, but he had every intention of finding out.

Once they made it to his office, he closed the door behind them and just stood there, looking at her. Admittedly, he couldn't see much because of the dark, oversize sunglasses she wore, but he could see enough to realize she wasn't at her best. Her face was thinner, her lush lips pressed together, and when he pulled her into his arms for a hug, he froze at what he found. She was a lot skinnier and a lot more fragile. He could feel her ribs right beneath her skin, as well as the small knobs on her spine that signified each vertebra.

Concerned, he pulled back and studied her face. It was hard to see anything with the sunglasses she wore, though, so he reached up and took them off. Then almost wished he hadn't. She looked awful. Her skin was pale and sallow while the dark purple circles beneath her eyes were so deep she looked like she was sporting two shiners. Not to mention the fact that her eyes were bloodshot and so weary-looking that he felt a jolt of real fear work its way through him.

He'd seen her in bad shape before, after particularly long assignments when she'd come back exhausted, overworked, angry. But never had he seen her look this bad, as if she was fading away right in front of him.

His anger forgotten in the face of her deterioration, he grabbed her arms. Ducked his head so that she could do nothing but stare into his eyes. "Tell me the truth," he demanded as fear ricocheted through him. "What happened to you down there?"

The fact that she didn't immediately answer told him more, much more, than he wanted to know. He gave her a few seconds to get her thoughts together, then said simply, "Whatever it is, it doesn't matter. Just tell me, so we can deal with it."

Again she didn't answer and he felt frustration growing inside of him as miserable scenario after miserable scenario bombarded him. "Are you sick?" He put a finger under her chin, pressed until she was looking him straight in the eye. "It's okay, Kara. I'll take care of you. I promise. Whatever it is—"

She shoved at his hand as anger and an emotion he couldn't identify flitted across her face. "I don't need you to take care of me."

"There's nothing wrong with asking for help. Nothing wrong with letting someone help you if they can. If they want to."

He went to hug her, but she wouldn't let him. She slapped a hand on his chest, shoved him back. "You don't understand."

"Because you won't talk to me. How am I supposed to fix things if you won't give me a chance?"

"Don't you get it? There are some things you can't fix."

"Bullshit." He was starting to get scared now. He didn't like the hopeless look in her eyes or the way she wrapped her arms around her waist and held on, like they were the only things keeping her from shattering into a million pieces. "Do you hear me? That's bullshit."

"It isn't, Lucas," she said as her eyes filled with tears. "It really isn't. Sometimes, things just happen. Sometimes you can't control them. You just have to accept the inevitable."

She began sobbing, her whole body shuddering with the strength of the agony inside of her.

He'd gone beyond scared, had shot right up to terrified. He knew she didn't want him to hold her right now, but he couldn't help it. If he didn't touch her, if he couldn't prove to himself that she was still there, still strong and whole and alive, he would lose his mind.

He strode across the room, wrapped his hands around her upper arms and shook her gently. "Tell me, damn it. Tell me the truth of what's going on with you, Kara. You owe me that much."

She closed her eyes, took a deep breath. "You're right. I do." And then she sagged against him, her arms wrapping around his waist as she pressed her face into his chest and held on tight.

SHE WAS HANDLING THIS whole thing badly. She knew it, yet could do nothing to change it. Her emotions were out of control, her fear—for her baby, and for her relationship with Lucas—was a living, breathing monster inside of her.

She knew she had to move, had to talk to him, but she stayed pressed up against him as long as she reasonably could, drawing in his forest-and-sandalwood scent. Taking comfort from his familiar strength.

Tears came to her eyes, but she blinked them away. The stupid hormones were making her crazy. Lucas's chest was tense beneath her, his heart beating wildly out of control, and she knew she was just prolonging his agony even as she staved off her own.

But that wasn't fair to him. Pulling back, she asked, "Can we sit down first?" She had a feeling the kind of news she had to deliver would come better if there was no chance that Lucas might fall down in shock.

"Sit!" he told her, all but shoving her into a chair, though, instead of sitting next to her, he propped himself on the edge of his desk. "Now tell me what the hell is wrong with you. You said you didn't contract Ebola."

"I didn't," she assured him. "I did, however, come down with dengue hemorrhagic fever."

"DHF?" He stared at her incredulously. "And you survived?"

"Obviously."

"Are you all right?"

"I'm fine. Just a little worn down."

He snorted at that, but she didn't take offense. After all, she knew better than most just how bad she looked. No matter how much time she'd spent with her makeup this morning—and she had spent a considerable amount of time—she hadn't been able to do away with the sick green tinge the pregnancy, and her never-ending nausea, had given her. The magic three-month mark had come and gone and still she felt so sick that it had been all she could do to roll out of bed that morning.

Julian had told her it was a by-product of her high-risk pregnancy, a sign—unlike most *normal* morning sickness—that her body was fighting the presence of the baby as it continued to struggle to mend itself from the dengue hemorrhagic fever. His prognosis had sent her scurrying back to the States weeks ahead of schedule, hoping for a second opinion. Well, she'd gotten it. The gynecologist she had seen just that morning, a top-rated specialist in high-risk cases, had told her essentially the same thing, though even more bluntly.

A fetus surviving dengue fever intact and with no physical or neurological damage was not uncommon. A fetus surviving dengue *hemorrhagic* fever in the same condition was another thing entirely. And with a case as severe as hers had been, the baby had an even smaller chance of surviving the pregnancy, let alone the birth.

The doctor had, in fact, expressed shock that she was still pregnant at all. Had even gone so far as to tell her that she should prepare herself to lose the baby at any time. It was nothing Kara hadn't already suspected—she'd seen a lot of cases of dengue hemorrhagic fever in her time, including ones that had transcended the placenta and caused massive bleeding in the baby—but hearing the diagnosis in reference to the baby she and Lucas had made was a shock. Or, more accurately, a nightmare.

Though she'd tried to be analytical about the whole thing, had tried to fall back on her medical training, she'd ended up begging the doctor for some thread of hope. She hadn't planned on this baby, and it in fact was a huge inconvenience, but that didn't matter. From the moment she'd really wrapped her head around the fact that she was pregnant, she had wanted the baby desperately. Had wanted this small part of Lucas more than she would ever have imagined possible.

The doctor had been discouraging, as she'd ordered a comprehensive ultrasound, an amniocentesis and enough blood work to keep a vampire happy for quite some time, but she had finally relented a little. She had told Kara that there were no guarantees in this business, especially since she hadn't seen the test results yet. Maybe, just maybe, if Kara did everything right, got plenty of rest and found a way to keep as much food down as possible—all while taking a massive daily vitamin cocktail the doctor had assembled just for her. If she was the picture of perfect pregnancy behavior, she would probably still lose the baby. But maybe, just maybe, she wouldn't.

It was a slim hope, and Kara knew it, but it was also the only thing she had to hang on to at the moment. She'd hitched her wagon up to it and planned on riding that slim chance as far as she could.

But first she had to tell Lucas. She hadn't exactly been looking forward to it before she showed up at his office, but now, with him staring at her like she was a particularly unattractive bug under a microscope, she was even less enthusiastic.

He was more worried than angry, but that didn't make her feel any better. Telling him about the baby was going to be hard enough. Telling him when he was hovering over her like she was going to die at any second seemed unbearable. Not to mention what would happen after he knew. She had a feeling he would have her home and in bed before she could so much as say the word *pregnant*.

Which was fine—after all, it was where she planned to go after she told him. She was exhausted and knew, if she had any hope of keeping the baby, she was going to have to catch up on her rest. It was all part of taking better care of herself. She'd even called Paul on the way over here to discuss taking a leave of absence from the CDC. He'd agreed, but had also told her she was welcome to work from the States for as long as it took.

She had told him she would think about it, and she would. But she took two weeks of vacation time, anyway, just to give herself some breathing room. She'd spent years of her life caring for others' medical emergencies. It was past time that she took care of her own. And, if at the end of those two weeks she was still pregnant, then she would reevaluate. Talk to her doctor and see where she stood.

In all honesty, she probably should have gone straight home after her doctor's appointment. But seeing Lucas had been imperative. He had a right to know about the baby and while she supposed she could have told him about it over the phone or via email, face-to-face seemed the right way to go about it. After all, it wasn't every day a woman told her best friend that he was the father of her child.

Just the idea was turning her into a basket case. Their relationship had worked all these years because they were on even footing. Once she told him she was pregnant, that would change. Lucas would feel he had to take care of her, that she was his responsibility. And he never shirked responsibilities. But once he took her on as one more problem that needed fixing, she knew that whatever small hope she held out for them getting together would vanish. She would move from best friend and lover to woman he needed to take care of. She'd been around long enough to know it wasn't a good move.

She hated that. Hated so much that she was about to become a burden to Lucas when she had always sworn that she would never be. He already had so much on his plate, already carried the weight of the world on his broad, sturdy shoulders. How could she knowingly add to that?

Then again, how could she not? Whatever happened in the future, at that moment she was pregnant with his child. If she knew nothing else, she knew that he deserved to know about it. Even more, she knew if she didn't tell him as soon as possible, he would never forgive her.

"When were you sick?"

"It was touch and go for the last part of June and first part of July, but I've been on the mend for a couple weeks now."

"This is on the mend?" He reached for her hand,

not even bothering to be surreptitious about it as his fingers sought out her wrist—or more accurately, her pulse.

"If you think this is bad, you should have seen me before," she joked.

He didn't laugh, just looked at her with those serious blue eyes of his. "I want to check you over."

"What? No! Believe me, I've been checked and double-checked. I'm fine."

"Organ damage?"

"No."

"They did ultrasounds of your kidneys and liver?"

"Yes, and they're fine."

"Brain damage?"

"Do I sound brain damaged?" His lips twisted and she reached out and smacked his arm. "Don't you dare say it."

"I wouldn't dream of it." He reached for his stethoscope. "Your heart's okay? The bleeding didn't damage your arterial walls?"

"They're fine. Everything's fine."

He squatted down next to her, took both her hands in his. "You don't look fine, Kara. Your skin is sallow, your hair is limp, your pulse is too fast and you can barely keep your balance. That's not fine."

"You sure know how to make a girl feel beautiful."

"You're always beautiful."

"Even with my sallow skin and limp hair?"

He slipped his hands up her arms to her neck, cupped her face in his hands while his thumbs probed her lymph nodes. "What aren't you telling me?"

Exasperated, she shoved at his hands. "This isn't how I wanted to do this part."

He grew still, his eyes watchful. "Do what? What's wrong, Kara?"

She'd wanted to ease him into things, had wanted to break the news gently. But while he was sitting there, staring at her with that immovable expression on his face, she knew that wasn't going to happen.

She'd thought she was ready for this, thought she had it all worked out. But her doctor's visit had thrown everything for a loop. It was hard to imagine telling him the truth when all she really wanted to do was to curl up in a ball and weep.

Finally, she just spit it out. "I'm three months pregnant, Lucas."

CHAPTER TWELVE

FOR LONG SECONDS, LUCAS's brain couldn't process those four little words. Instead, he just stared at Kara incomprehensibly, waiting for his brain to decipher the statement.

When it finally did, he had to grab on to his desk to keep from falling over. It was like he'd swallowed a gigantic adrenaline cocktail, with every cell in his body wigging out at the same time.

"You're…"

"Pregnant, yes. Three months."

"You said that already."

"Sorry. You look kind of shocked. I wasn't sure you were tracking everything."

"I feel kind of shocked, but I'm tracking just fine." That didn't mean he didn't feel like his head was going to explode at any second.

Kara was pregnant.

Kara was pregnant with his baby.

Kara was pregnant.

In six months, he was going to be a father.

Kara was pregnant.

He had no idea what to think, how to feel, what to say. He'd always been so careful, always made certain that he would never find himself in this position. Yet here he was, with *Kara*.

"Are you okay?" he asked again.

"I'm fine."

"When did you find out?"

"Three days ago."

"The day you called me."

"Yeah, but I didn't know then. I started putting the pieces together afterward."

"You're a doctor," he told her incredulously. "How did you not know?"

"I switched birth control pills about five months ago. I put the changes in my cycle down to that and I didn't really have any other symptoms until I was recovering from the DHF, so it really didn't occur to me until—"

"Until what?"

"Until I realized my breasts were much bigger than usual, even with the weight I'd lost." She tried to say it matter-of-factly—they were both doctors, after all— but he could feel her embarrassment, especially when his eyes focused on the body part in question. She was right. Her breasts did look much bigger.

"Okay," he said. "So, you're pregnant."

"Yes."

"You're pregnant."

"Yes. Why do you keep saying that?"

"It makes it more real." He took a deep breath. "What are you planning to do?"

Her eyes darted away from him. "Well, that's the tricky part."

He braced himself. Did she want to have an abortion? And if she did, how did he feel about that? He'd always been a proponent of a woman's right to choose, but this was *his* baby. Everything seemed different now, including his relationship with Kara.

He'd felt the trajectory of his life spin off course when she'd said she was pregnant. Now he feared that it would spin even farther off kilter if she said she didn't want to keep the baby. Not that he knew what he wanted yet—he'd only known about the baby's existence for two minutes—but he didn't think he wanted that.

Kara, on the other hand, had a career that a baby just would not fit into. She'd have to give up everything to have this baby. Case in point, she was here, in his office, when she should still be in Eritrea working on the case that would make her famous.

"Lucas? Are you listening to me?"

Her voice finally penetrated the fog that had enveloped his brain and he snapped his attention back to her. "What's kind of tricky?"

"As you know, I got pregnant that night, before Eritrea. Which meant I was pregnant when I caught dengue hemorrhagic fever. And I'm pregnant now, but—" Her voice broke. "But the doctor doesn't know for how much longer. There are complications that come with getting a hemorrhagic virus while you're pregnant and she doesn't think the baby will survive."

Just that easily, his reality adjusted itself again. This time, he did sit, because his knees felt a little weak and he wasn't sure he could take any more shocks. "You've seen an obstetrician?"

"Yes. This morning. She wants to do some tests, but based on my records from Julian she's not holding out much hope." Her voice broke, but when he looked at her there were no tears on her face. Just an expression of such utter devastation that he knew he'd judged her incorrectly. Career or not, Kara wanted this baby.

Their baby.

Now, if only he could figure out what he was feeling.

"What's your doctor's name? I'd like to talk to her."

She reached into her purse, pulled out a card and handed it to him.

"Don't you need this?"

"I picked up a couple extras. I figured you'd want to find out everything you could about her."

"The thought had crossed my mind."

"I know."

They sat there in silence for a little while. He didn't know what to say, didn't know what he was feeling, didn't know how to communicate his confusion to Kara. Part of him wanted to get up, go for a walk. He needed to be alone for a while to assimilate all this and he couldn't do it in this office, surrounded by people.

But there was Kara, sitting there with her pain naked on her face and he knew he wasn't going anywhere. He needed to take care of her, needed to hold it together for her.

"What kind of tests does Dr. Beaumont want to run?"

"More blood work. An amniocentesis. Ultra-sounds."

He nodded. "I'll take you wherever you need to go."

She sighed. "I didn't tell you because I needed you to take care of me, Lucas. I told you because you have the right to know."

"What about my right to be there when they perform tests on my best friend, tests that will determine what's wrong with my child. Don't I have the right to be there for that?"

"Of course you do. I just don't want you to feel responsible—"

"I *am* responsible. That's my baby you're carrying, right?"

She nodded.

"So I *am* responsible for you being pregnant. What's wrong with me living up to my obligations?"

She opened her mouth to answer him, but just then the intercom on his desk buzzed. "Your mama's on the phone, Lucas." Tawanda's voice came through loud and clear.

"Tell her I'm busy."

"Got it." But she was back a few seconds later, a subdued note in her voice. "She says it's an emergency."

"Damn it, I don't have time for her bull—" He bit the word off. Tawanda didn't need to hear about his issues with his mother. "Tell her I'll call her back."

"You need to take it, Lucas. It's about your sister."

There was something in the receptionist's voice that alerted him, that had his heart beating faster.

He leaned across the desk and picked up the phone. "What's going on, Mom?"

"Lucas!" His mother's voice was low and trembling, like she'd been crying—something she rarely did because it ruined her makeup and made her eyes puffy. "It's Lisa. There's been an accident."

His entire body tensed. "What kind of accident?"

"She crashed her car. She's at the hospital. She's in bad shape, Lucas. They're not sure she's going to live." Her voice broke on the last word and she started to sob.

"Which hospital is she at?"

"Piedmont."

He opened his desk drawer, pulled out his keys and wallet. "I'm leaving now. I should be there in forty minutes."

"Hurry, Lucas. We need you."

"Have you called Jenn yet?"

"No. I'll do that after I hang up with you."

"Call her now, Mom. She can get there quicker than I can."

"But I need you." Her voice quivered.

"I'm coming. But I have to hang up the phone before I can leave."

"Okay. Bye, Lucas."

He hung up the phone, turned to Kara. "Lisa—"

"Was in an accident. I heard. How bad?"

"As bad as it gets, it sounds like."

"Okay. Where are we going?"

He strode toward his office door, held it open for Kara before heading out himself. "You're going home to rest. I'm going to Piedmont. I'll call you when I know something."

"You don't actually think I'm going to let you go by yourself, do you? You're shaking."

He shrugged her off. "I'm fine."

"No. You're not." She grabbed his arm. "Let's go."

On their way through the waiting area, Kara said, "Tawanda, call—"

"Jack. Already done. He's on his way in. You just go be with your sister, Lucas. We'll take care of everything here."

He nodded, half-dazed. Lisa? Dying? His carefree, live-for-the-moment, life-of-the-party little sister? Dying? He couldn't wrap his mind around it.

KARA KNEW LUCAS DIDN'T want her to go to the hospital with him, but as they walked out to the car, she knew he was lost in his own little world. She didn't like it, or the way his eyes seemed a little glazed, a little off. Oh, he said all the right things but it was pretty obvious he wasn't firing on all cylinders. Still, she knew better than to push it with him. She made it a point not to depend on anyone but herself. Lucas had practically made it a religion.

But as he deposited her at her car and prepared to climb into his own, she couldn't let him go. Not like this, when he was so obviously lost. He'd had a hell of a morning—finding out he was going to be a dad, then finding out he might not be, now finding out his baby sister was badly injured. It was a lot for anyone to take in, let alone a control freak like Lucas. In her opinion, it was amazing he was still on his feet.

"Come on," she told him. "Get in."

"What?"

"I'll give you a ride over to Piedmont."

He looked confused for a second, then narrowed his eyes at her as he said, "I'm fine, Kara."

"I never said differently. But we both know I'm a faster driver, so come on. Get in."

"I'd prefer to arrive at the hospital alive, thank you very much." He turned, headed for his car then stopped a few feet away. "But if you wanted to ride with me, I wouldn't object too much."

Wow. He was more shaken up than she'd thought. Grabbing her purse back up off the passenger seat, she locked her car and headed over to him. Then, looping her arm through his, she let him guide her toward his car.

She felt much better going with him, not letting him face whatever was waiting for him at that hospital by himself. Because of her job, she hadn't always been around when he needed her. It felt nice to be around now. Almost like a new beginning, one where they actually worked hard to be there for each other.

Whether that was true or not, as she slid into the passenger seat of Lucas's Volvo S60, she admitted that for now, she really, really liked the feeling. Which, considering the circumstances of the next few months, was probably a very good thing.

CHAPTER THIRTEEN

THE DRIVE TO THE HOSPITAL was something of a blur for Lucas. He concentrated on the road and the traffic—damn Atlanta and its massive urban sprawl—in an effort to keep from going crazy.

When he'd gotten up this morning, things had been pretty okay. Not great, as he was worried about his relationship with Kara, but okay. Now everything had gone to hell in a handbasket and he didn't have a clue what he was supposed to do to fix any of it. Kara, the baby, Lisa. He didn't know what to do. It wasn't a feeling he was used to or one that he liked.

He knew he should have insisted that Kara go home. She needed to rest, to build up her strength, and sitting with him at the hospital wasn't going to let her do any of that. At the same time, there was a part of him that was grateful she was here. Grateful that he didn't have to do this alone. But it scared the hell out of him. He wasn't used to needing anyone.

That was another monologue for another time. Right now he had to concentrate on getting to his sister, on making sure that she and his mother and Jenn were all okay. Then he'd worry about this strange breach in his own defenses.

Forty-two minutes after he left his clinic he pulled into the emergency room parking lot of the Piedmont Hospital. Of course, there was no parking, even at one in the afternoon, and it was all he could do to keep from growling in frustration.

Once again, Kara was there placing a soothing hand on his arm. "Go on in," she told him. "I'll find a place to park the car and meet you inside."

He started to argue, but she chose that moment to glare at him and bark, "Go," in the no-nonsense voice he rarely heard from her, but which he knew meant business when he did.

Pulling over to the curb in front of the E.R., he said, "Are you sure?"

She rolled her eyes. "Go, Lucas. Your family needs you."

Because she was right, and because guilt and worry had him nearly ready to jump out of his own skin, he chose to believe her. Leaping from the car, he said, "I'll go find out what's going on and then wait for you in the E.R."

"Go be wherever you need to be. Just text me and tell me where to meet you." As she crossed to the driver's side, she nearly shoved him up the walkway.

With worry for his sister beating inside of him, he took off without looking back.

KARA BREATHED A HUGE SIGH of relief as she watched Lucas all but fly through the E.R.'s front door. On the drive here, he'd been so wired that she'd feared he would take off under his own power. Not that she blamed him. Between his sister and finding out about her own illness, big, strong protector Lucas had to have been in hell. She was glad she'd come, even though she knew she had no business being here. She'd planned on going straight home after lunch and putting her feet up and instead, here she was, jockeying for a parking spot at one of the busiest hospitals in the city. But it wasn't like she'd had a choice. Lucas was messed up, though in typical Lucas fashion he was doing his best to hide it. There was no way she could leave him alone to torture himself.

Besides, she decided as she finally found a parking spot in the very last row of the main parking lot, the waiting rooms were filled with couches. She'd just find one and use it to put her feet up while they waited. It wasn't a perfect solution, but it would have to do.

By the time she walked through the doors herself, nearly twenty minutes had passed since she'd dropped Lucas at the E.R. She glanced around, but he was nowhere to be found, and a quick check of her cell phone showed that no text had come through, either.

He must be even more shaken up than she thought. Lucas was not the kind of guy to leave a lady waiting somewhere for him, or to forget to do something he was supposed to do—even in an emergency.

She knew enough about HIPAA to know that the person at the check-in window wasn't going to give her any information on Lisa Montgomery. Still, Lucas had said she was in surgery. Maybe they could at least point her toward the surgical waiting rooms?

But she had just approached the desk when Lucas

came around a corner, looking paler and more frazzled than she had ever seen him. She rushed to his side. "What's wrong, Lucas? Has something else happened to Lisa?"

What she meant, of course, was had Lisa died, but she couldn't bring herself to say the words, not when he looked so bad.

He shook his head, but he was completely dazed, his pupils much larger than usual. It was her turn to take his wrist and check his pulse. It was way too fast.

"She's still in surgery," he finally answered.

"Okay, then, it's only a matter of time until we hear something." She wrapped an arm around his waist for support, and began propelling him down the hallway he had come from. "Where are your mom and Jenn? Let's go wait with them."

He shook his head, fumbled a small, white business card out of his pocket. "I need to make a phone call first. I have to go outside to use my cell."

"Okay. Let's go." She glanced down at the card, saw it bore the name Lt. John Russell, homicide, Atlanta Police Department.

She started to ask what was going on, but the look on Lucas's face warned her not to say anything, so she pressed her lips together and simply waited. She'd find out what was going on soon enough.

It didn't take long. John Russell must have answered on the first ring, because it was only seconds before Lucas was involved in an intense—and frightening—conversation. He didn't have the phone on speaker, so she only heard one side, but what she could hear was more than bad enough.

It appeared that Lisa had been driving under the influence. They didn't have the results back from the hospital's blood draw, but there were numerous witness reports of Lisa's erratic driving in the minutes leading up to the crash, not to mention the fact that the go-cup in her car had been filled with a mixture of cranberry and vodka.

But the worst part—the part that had Lucas trembling and her on the verge of throwing up yet again—was the fact that Lisa had crashed into another car. A car filled with a mother and her three children, two of whom were in surgery in the same hospital wing as Lisa and one of whom was in critical condition. The mother was injured but stable, as Lisa had crashed into the passenger side of the car.

Closing her eyes, Kara whispered a little prayer—for the family Lisa had hit and for the twenty-six-year-old herself. She had done a terrible thing and the consequences were going to be awful. But still, Kara prayed she lived to face them.

After ten of the longest minutes of her life, Lucas hung up the phone. His color had gone from pale to gray. She knew exactly how he felt. She was more than a little green around the gills, herself. She might not be Lisa's actual sibling, but Kara had known her since Lisa was nine years old. She'd always been selfish and impetuous—her parents had raised her to be so, despite Lucas's repeated, and unheard, objections—

so the fact that this had happened wasn't entirely unexpected.

It was still horrible, though. Both Kara and Lucas
had hoped that when Lisa was finally forced to learn
that the world didn't revolve around her, the lesson
wouldn't cost her, or anyone else. But that obviously
wasn't to be, and what happened now was going to
cost everyone involved, and especially that innocent
family, much more than they could ever pay.

Lucas turned to her, pulled her into his arms and
just held on. She let him, holding on to him as tightly
as he was holding her. Giving him as much comfort
as she could, even as she took comfort from him, as
well. Comfort for what he was going through but comfort also for everything that had happened in her life
over the past few months.

Comfort for the illness she'd seen in Eritrea and
hadn't been able to cure.

Comfort for the illness she had suffered there, as
well.

And finally, comfort for the risk her baby—their
baby—was facing.

Eventually he let her go, pulled away. "Tell me,"
she said.

"I don't even know where to start. I don't think Lisa
has a drinking problem. I mean, I've obviously missed
a lot of stuff, but I don't think I've missed that. I asked
Jenn and she says no. But what other explanation can
there be? Why would she be drunk at ten-thirty in the
morning if she *wasn't* an alcoholic?"

Kara could imagine a couple scenarios, including

one where the very irresponsible Lisa—who didn't work because she lived off her trust funds from her father and grandparents—had been out partying all night and had only then been returning home. Another possible situation was an early brunch that had included Bloody Marys, mimosas or even vodka cranberries, as they had found in her car.

She said as much to Lucas, who stiffened as anger flitted across his face. When the silence stretching between them grew uncomfortable, she asked, "What are you going to do?"

"I don't know." He slumped against the wall. "Any suggestions?" From his tone of voice, she knew it was a rhetorical question.

But she did have a suggestion. Several, in fact. "I think we should go back upstairs and wait for news."

"Yeah. I guess." He made no move to get up.

"Don't you want to go back up? I assumed your mom and Jenn were up there." And she knew Lucas would never leave them to wait and worry on their own. It wasn't in his makeup.

"They are. Jean-Claude's up there, too."

"Jean-Claude?" She wasn't familiar with the name.

"Mom broke up with Nicholas a few weeks ago. Jean-Claude is her new boy toy."

Which would explain his reluctance to go back upstairs. Still, he should be with his family. He would feel a million times worse if the doctor came out to speak with them and he wasn't there.

He sighed deeply and ran a hand over his troubled face. For the first time in all the years she'd known him, he looked defeated. Like he just couldn't imagine how he was going to find his way out of the latest mess his family had gotten themselves into.

Which meant she'd have to find a way to steer him through it, because she absolutely couldn't stand to see him like this.

"When did your mom say they expected to be done with the surgery?"

"She didn't know. I asked at the nursing station and was told that it looked like a couple more hours. They couldn't give me any more information than that— not even what was wrong with her besides internal bleeding. I guess they rushed her into surgery pretty quickly after arrival."

"So, we have a while to kill, right?" She glanced at her watch. "Let's go down to the cafeteria, get something to eat. I'm betting you skipped breakfast again and I'm under order to eat every couple of hours."

Both Julian and Dr. Beaumont had made it clear that with her weight loss she couldn't afford to skip meals. No matter how nauseous she was and even if it meant turning around and puking everything back up.

The reminder of her own precarious health was all it took to get him moving. "I think the cafeteria's in the basement here." He grabbed her hand and tugged her down the hall.

"Tell me what the detective said. We need to make a plan to help Lisa when she recovers. She's going to need it."

"If she recovers." His voice was grim, maudlin

even, but she took it as a good sign that he was taking charge again. That was the Lucas she knew.

She knew the hospital well through her work with the CDC, so it only took her a couple minutes to find the elevator that led to the cafeteria. There weren't many people around at that time of day, so within five minutes the two of them were seated at an empty table, each with a huge chef's salad and a bowl of vegetable soup with some crackers.

Her stomach turned over at the smell of the soup, but Kara ignored it as she forced down one bite and then another. Across from her, Lucas was doing the same.

"So, what did the detective say?" she finally asked when both their bowls were empty.

"Nothing good. We won't know what she'll be charged with until everyone makes it out of surgery. Besides, he wouldn't give me specifics—we're not on the same side here, technically. I can't believe I'm saying it, but there's a part of me that thinks my sister deserves to go to jail for what she's done. My God, she could have killed those kids and their mother. She might have. We don't know."

"Let's just take it slow, okay, and not borrow any more trouble than we already have. I'm guessing the basic charges are going to at least be DUI with injury, which, if I'm not mistaken, is a felony. Which means you need to get your sister a lawyer as soon as you possibly can."

He looked at her in astonishment. "A lawyer? Right now we don't even know if she's going to live."

"She's going to live, Lucas. You need to believe in that even if you can't believe in anything else right now. And when she does recover, she's going to need a lawyer. Because I can promise you, the police and the D.A. aren't hanging around the hospital, simply waiting to see what's going to happen. They're gathering evidence against Lisa, evidence they are going to use to convict her."

"Rightly so, if she really did what they say she did."

Kara nodded as she placed a hand over his where it rested on the table and squeezed. "I'm not saying otherwise. I'm just saying she's going to need an attorney who is looking out for her."

"Who was looking out for those kids?" he asked. "Who was looking out for their mother? God, Kara, I'm just sick about this."

She started to answer him when her stomach went into full-blown revolt. Knowing exactly what was coming, she jumped up from the table and made a mad dash for the cafeteria door and the bathroom she had seen when they'd gotten off the elevator.

She didn't make it and ended up getting sick in a trash can right outside the cafeteria door. She vomited over and over again, until the water and soup were long gone from her stomach and she was just dry heaving. It hurt and was embarrassing, considering the number of people walking by, and at one point she had to battle tears as well at the never-ending waves of nausea.

She fiercely battled the tears. It was a close call,

though, especially when she finally lifted her head and saw Lucas standing right behind her, a glass of water in one hand and a napkin in the other.

CHAPTER FOURTEEN

HE EXTENDED THE CUP OF water, with the simple instruction, "Rinse." Which she did, before reaching for the napkin. It had killed him to stand by and do nothing as Kara threw up, and it was killing him now that he could do nothing for her. No wonder she looked like hell—if she couldn't keep any food down how was she or the baby supposed to have a fighting chance?

"This happen a lot?" he asked, rubbing her back in what he hoped was a soothing manner

"A few times a day."

"Morning sickness?"

"I'm assuming. Except it didn't hit until after the DHF, so it could be a side effect of that."

"You said the fever didn't cause any damage."

"It didn't. Nothing major, anyway. Besides, we don't know if the vomiting is because of the pregnancy or the disease, so we just have to wait a while and see if it goes away."

"And in the meantime you starve to death?" He glared at her. "I don't think so. You need Compazine."

"I've got a prescription for it in my purse. I'm not an idiot, Lucas."

"I never meant to imply that you were." He held

out his hand. "Give it to me. We'll get it filled at the pharmacy here."

"It can wait—" She started to object, but he glared at her and she stopped. He was furious, absolutely enraged, and he wasn't sure why. He just knew that he felt he was shaking apart from the inside out. It wasn't a feeling he cared for. The anger made it better, but not by much.

"Obviously, it can't." He went back into the cafeteria and cleared off their table before buying a banana, a few packages of crackers and a ginger ale. "We'll drop off your prescription on our way upstairs. In the meantime, you can see if this will settle your stomach."

She took the food from him. "Thank you."

"For what?" He hadn't done a damn thing except get her pregnant at the worst possible time. She shouldn't be thanking him. She should be kicking his ass.

"Lucas—"

He cut her off by raising his hand. Whatever she wanted to say to make him feel better, he didn't want to hear. Not right now. But it wasn't her fault that he was so pissed off at himself and the world, so he softened his voice when he asked, "Are you sure you're okay? You can take my car home if you'd like, go get some rest. I can pick it up whenever."

"I'm fine. I just traveled halfway around the world. I think I can handle an elevator ride," she told him with a roll of her eyes.

"That's not what I meant."

"I know exactly what you meant." She smiled at

him but her eyes looked sad. It only made him feel like a bigger heel.

He smiled, tried to joke. "Here I was thinking you could handle a worldwide epidemic. But if all you've got in you is an elevator ride—"

"Ha-ha. You're *so* funny." But he saw her lips twitch as she took off down the hall. Which was a good sign, even if it was more than he deserved.

When they climbed into the elevator, he grabbed her wrist. Stroked his hand over the sensitive inner skin of her wrist. The look she shot him told him, clearer than words ever could, that she was on to him. He grinned sheepishly, then did what he'd always intended and took her pulse for the second time that day.

When he was finished, she started to pull her hand away, but he held tight and threaded his fingers through her own until they were holding hands. She shivered a little, looked startled, but he didn't let go. Neither did she, though she did look like she wanted to ask him what he was doing.

He didn't have an answer for her because he didn't know himself. He was operating on instinct and right now, he wanted to touch her. Needed to touch her. It blew him away that they had made a baby together, that she was carrying his child. And while he still didn't know how he felt about the baby—especially considering all the problems they were facing—he knew he cared about Kara. Knew he wanted to make this whole thing as easy on her as he possibly could.

The elevator came to a stop and they dropped off her prescription before heading back upstairs to the surgical wing. He took it as a particularly good sign that she kept her hand firmly in his as they stepped off and strolled down the hall. It might just be because she felt sorry for him having to deal with his mother, and Jean-Claude, again, but he was shaky enough that he didn't mind the support. Which was a surprise in and of itself, but he was finding that he could accept things from Kara that he wasn't willing to take from anyone else. She calmed him down, centered him. He hoped he did the same for her.

Of course, any peace he might have been feeling crumpled at the first sight of his mother, curled up in Jean-Claude's lap while the Frenchman softly stroked her hair. Jenn didn't seem too disturbed by the scene, but then again she'd had more time to get used to it. She spent a lot more time with their mother than he did.

But then his sister wasn't the one at risk of an aneurysm every time their mother opened her mouth.

"Any news?" he asked as he settled himself and Kara on the sofa next to Jenn, though it was little more than a glorified love seat and there wasn't enough room for the three of them to sit comfortably.

Jenn shot him a strange look, but she scooted down as far as she could, which was a good thing, because he wasn't moving and neither was Kara. The only other spots available in their little section of the waiting room were either next to Jean-Claude and his mom or across from them. And since the absolute last thing he wanted to spend the next hour doing was watching them make goo-goo eyes at each other, he'd taken the only safe spot in the place. Maybe it was immature, but he didn't care. He was going with it.

"Nothing yet," Jenn said. "I asked a few minutes ago and the nurse said she would go in and check again. See if the doctor could give us any news."

He nodded, though her words did nothing to reassure him. In his experience, if things were going well, doctors were more than willing to provide updates. It was only when everything had gone to hell that they clammed up and made people wait for the most basic report.

He could feel Kara sitting stiffly beside him, knew she was thinking the exact same thing. He glanced at her in warning—the last thing he wanted was his mother to turn on the hysterics one second before she had to. Besides, he was still holding out hope that Lisa's surgeon was just an asshole, so wrapped up in his work that he couldn't care less about his patient's family.

A few minutes passed as the group of them sat there, watching the clock and wondering when the nurse was going to come back. More than once his mother sniffled a little and Jean-Claude murmured soothing things to her in French, but other than that—and the sound of his own heart pounding in his ears—the room was absolutely silent.

Eventually, Kara got up and settled herself on the empty sofa with her feet up. He bit the bullet and moved with her, sitting on the arm of the couch as he opened her ginger ale and stroked her hair as she tried to choke down a few crackers.

No one said anything, but he could feel both his mother and Jenn staring at them. He knew what they were thinking but there was no way he was going to confirm Kara's pregnancy in the middle of this dismal waiting room.

The second hand had worked its way around the clock thirty-two-and-a-half times before a nurse came into the room and walked straight toward them. He leaped to his feet and his family did the same. As he waited for her to speak, his eyes found her name tag, clung. Sandra. Her name was Sandra. He'd dated a Sandra in high school, and had fond memories of her and the name. He hoped that wasn't about to change.

"Dr. Kovac wanted me to tell you that he'll be out to speak to you soon. He's got about forty more minutes of repairs to do and then he'll close. Soon after he'll come talk to you."

"How is she?" his mother asked, her voice trembling. Lucas looked at her—really looked at her—for the first time since he'd arrived at the hospital. She looked like she'd aged fifteen years since he'd seen her last. Gone was his flighty, irresponsible, fun-loving mother. In her place was this frail, shaky woman who looked every one of her sixty-two years. He wondered what Jean-Claude thought about that, then hated himself for being churlish at a time like this. There'd be plenty of time to hate his mother's lover after his sister was out of danger.

"There was a considerable amount of damage," Sandra admitted. "But Dr. Kovac has gotten her stabilized. Please don't worry. He's the best. He'll do everything he can for your daughter."

No, he wasn't the best. Kovac wasn't close to the best thoracic surgeon in Atlanta, let alone the country. In Atlanta, he was maybe seventh or eighth. In Georgia, maybe fifteenth. In the country…he wouldn't even make a list. Sure, he was nothing to sneeze at, but saying he was the best when he wasn't didn't exactly reassure him about the nurse's honesty. And if she was lying about this, she could also be lying about how his sister was doing. He wasn't a thoracic surgeon, but he'd been a doctor long enough to recognize the signs.

As if well aware of the direction his thoughts had taken—or maybe hers had taken the same turn, seeing as she was a doctor, too—Kara murmured softly to him. Soothing little phrases so low he could barely hear them, but when accompanied by the press of her shoulder against his own, calmed him as nothing else could have.

After the nurse left, he found he couldn't sit back down, so he paced the waiting room, back and forth. Back and forth. As he did, he barely resisted the urge to tear his hair out.

How had this happened? How had they all ended up here? What had his sister been thinking—drinking like that and then getting behind the wheel? He might keep a tight hold on her truest friend—as his father intended he do until his sister was twenty-seven—but he provided her with more than enough money to take a cab if she needed to.

Or she could have called him to pick her up.

Or she could have used a credit card and he could have paid it off later.

Or she could have chosen not to drink so much to begin with.

The scenarios were, if not endless, then at least stacked pretty heavily against his beautiful, young and irresponsible sister. He wanted to rage at her for doing this, for being so careless that she'd played Russian roulette with not just her own life but other people's lives, as well. At the same time, he wanted to pull her bruised, battered body into his arms and hold her there forever. He wanted to keep her safe. He was her big brother. That was his job.

"You let this happen." His mother's voice trembled but it still carried across the waiting room to him.

He turned to stare at her, guilt a rampaging monster inside of him.

She pushed herself off Jean-Claude and came to stand a few feet from him, her face white and lined with pain. "You're cheap with her. Cheap with us. If you'd bought her a better car, she never would have been in that tin can. She would be safe. But you don't care about things like that, don't care about anything but that damn clinic. How can you care so much for strangers and yet treat your family so badly?"

Her words struck like poison-tipped arrows, played on his own thoughts and feelings of regret until he thought he'd go crazy. In his own head, his intentions had been good—there was only so much money to go around and it had to last. But had he been too controlling, not trusting his sisters and mother enough?

But they were sitting here, weren't they? After his sister had carelessly injured herself and four other people? And hadn't it been just last week that his mom had tried to throw away more than three months of his salary on a watch for a guy who would be gone as soon as he'd cleaned her out?

What was he supposed to do? What other options did he have?

Behind him he felt, more than heard, Kara move, knew that it was her hand that was resting comfortingly on his shoulder. He wanted to shrug it off—to go hide and lick his wounds in private. Kara knew about his family, had been around them off and on since college, but she'd never seen them like this. Never seen *him* like this. For the first time since he'd gotten the call that afternoon, he wished he'd left her at the clinic. He didn't want her to see him like this.

Things were already so uncertain between them that the last thing he needed was for her to take one look at this mess and hightail it out the door. Away from him, just when he was beginning to understand that his feelings for her were a lot clearer than he'd given himself credit for. Not that he thought she'd actually run away—this was Kara he was talking about. Unlike his family, she was steady as a rock. He knew that she would be right beside him until she decided he didn't need her anymore.

But that wasn't the dynamic he wanted, wasn't the relationship with her that he wanted. If he was honest, he'd admit he didn't know what he wanted. But he knew he didn't want this. He was supposed to be the strong one, the one who took care of everything. For his mom, for his sisters. For his lover. Bad enough that Kara was not the type to let him take care of her. But to think that she needed to take care of him, to protect him from his mother's poisonous barbs and his sister's irresponsible behavior when she was sicker and more fragile than he had ever seen her, was more than he could take.

"You're not going to say anything?" his mother demanded. "You're not going to defend yourself or apologize for anything?" Her voice rose a little more with each word until she was screaming at him in the middle of the waiting room. "You're just going to stand there?"

"Come on, Mom," Jenn said, crossing the room and putting an arm around their mother's shoulders. "Being in this room is making everyone fidgety. Let's go for a walk, get a cup of coffee or something."

His mother shrugged her off. "I don't want a cup of coffee. I want an apology from my son. If Lisa dies—" Her voice broke. "If Lisa dies, it's going to be on your hands. Do you understand me? It's going to be all your fault!"

She was shrieking now, sobbing, and he wanted to comfort her. Even as he bled from the wounds she'd inflicted, he wanted to wrap his arms around her and tell her everything was going to be all right. But he couldn't do that, in part because it wasn't going to be okay and in part because he knew he was the last person she would accept comfort from.

Before he could say anything in his own defense,

Kovac walked in. His skin was pale, his eyes blood-shot and he looked like he'd been on a three-day bender himself. Or, barring that, like he'd worked himself into the ground trying to save Lucas's sister.

His whole family grew quiet at the sight of the doctor, and—despite the accusations still ringing in his ears—Lucas stepped forward to shake Kovac's hand. He felt like he had done a shitty job so far, but he was still the one these kinds of duties fell to. Unless— He glanced at his mom, who clearly thought he was one step up from the anti-Christ at the moment. Nope, she definitely didn't look like she had it in her to take over.

"Hi, Aaron," he said to the other doctor, whom he'd met numerous times through the years. "Thank you for taking care of my sister."

"I'm sorry, Lucas. I didn't realize Lisa was your sister—I guess I should have made the connection." He glanced over at Kara, the look of concern on his face morphing into a smile before he seemed to stop himself. "Hey, Kara."

"Hi, Aaron."

Lucas looked back and forth between the two of them, a little startled by the warmth in Kovac's gaze as he watched Kara. But before he could make any connections between them, the other doctor cleared his throat. "Your sister was gravely injured in the crash. She wasn't wearing her seat belt, so the airbags did some damage internally, as did the momentum from the crash. Her spleen was ruptured—we ended up having to remove it. A number of her ribs were broken on the left side, and they punctured her left lung in two places. I've got that repaired, along with a tear to her left kidney, but she's going to be in for a long recovery period. She had deep cuts in numerous places—a few of them all the way down to the bone. We stitched them up, but infection could be a problem. I've got her on a course of IV antibiotics, of course, so we'll have to wait and see."

Lucas could tell there was more, could see it in the depths of the other doctor's eyes and in the stiffness of his shoulders. He was about to ask what was up, when Aaron sighed, and looked him directly in the eye. "There were some head and facial injuries. We've done an MRI and it looks like nothing more than a severe concussion, but the neurologist wants another one done in the morning. There is a little bit of swelling and—"

"Who is her neurologist?" Kara asked, before he could.

"Jean Bradshaw," he said, naming a good friend of Lucas's from med school. He relaxed a little. She really was one of the best.

"Good," he said. "What does she think?"

"She was in the O.R. with me for quite a while, and she's optimistic, actually. There are no major indicators of brain damage, which is obviously a very good thing. But again, we're going to have to wait and see. I'm going to keep her under for the next twenty-four hours at a minimum, give her body time to begin healing before she has to deal with—" He paused, looked truly uncomfortable for the first time. "Before she has to deal with everything else going on."

"You mentioned facial injuries." Candy spoke up for the first time.

"Yes, ma'am, I did. A couple of those deep slices were on her face. One on her left cheek and one on her right temple. Again, we've stitched them up—"

"*You* stitched them up?" she asked, obviously aghast.

"Mom. Give him a chance to talk."

Aaron nodded his thanks. "Actually, the plastic surgeon on duty stitched her up—Maxwell Kingston," he said to Lucas and Kara in anticipation of their next question. "He got called into another surgery, but he asked that I tell you he'll speak to you when he's back out. Or tomorrow morning, if you'd like to go home and get some rest before she comes around."

"Can you tell us anything about how the plastic surgery went?" Candy asked, her hand fluttering at her throat in the only nervous gesture she ever allowed herself.

Though he reminded himself that her concern was legitimate, Lucas couldn't help seething a little. Lisa's surgeon had just spoken about massive internal damage, possible brain damage and all his mother seemed concerned about was whether or not her face was going to scar. He couldn't decide if it was because she really was that superficial, or because she simply couldn't face the rest and was therefore focusing on the most benign, least dangerous of the injuries.

He really wanted to believe that it was the latter, but a part of him knew better. His mother was superficial even at heart, and though he loved her, it didn't surprise him in the least that she was more concerned with Lisa scarring than she was with everything else his sister had to face—including an arrest on what promised to be heavy-duty charges.

He could tell Kovac thought the same thing, though the other doctor maintained a face of bland professionalism the entire time. They spoke for a few more minutes as Kovac outlined what they were planning here, then, after reiterating that he was going to keep her under for at least twenty-four hours, he recommended that they all go home and get some rest.

"Can I see her?" he asked as Kovac turned to leave.

The other doctor nodded. "Sure, Lucas. You can each go in for a couple of minutes, but let's leave it at that for now. ICU visiting hours are almost over, anyway, so we'll look at her tomorrow morning, reevaluate where we stand. Okay?"

"Absolutely."

After the doctor left, he turned to his mother. "Do you want to go first?"

"Of course I do. She's *my* daughter. I want her to know someone who cares about her is here for her."

Meaning, obviously, that he didn't care. For a second, anger ripped through him and he contemplated punching the nearest wall—or barring that, Jean-Claude. But that wouldn't accomplish anything except to freak Kara and Jenn out and make him look like a total ass. So he kept it together. Barely.

When it was his turn to go in and see his sister, he dragged Kara along with him. He knew it was against the rules, but after what his mother had said to him, he didn't think he would be able to face his sister alone, even if she was sleeping. Kara didn't say a word, even when he knew he squeezed her hand much too tightly. She just stood there and gave him the comfort and support he so desperately needed.

They left the hospital around eight-thirty, and Kara insisted on driving. He expected her to head back to the clinic to pick up her car, so he leaned his head against the headrest and just closed his eyes. It was a long drive across town and he just didn't have the energy to talk right then.

He didn't sleep, but he didn't open his eyes again until Kara had stopped the car and turned off the engine—much more quickly than he had anticipated. He glanced around, realizing she had brought him home. "I thought we were going to get your car?" he asked, confused.

"It can wait until tomorrow." She climbed out of the car, came around his side and opened his door like he was an invalid or something.

Her concern warmed him even as it freaked him out a little. He didn't need to be coddled. Taking care of people was his job. Abdicating it, even for a night, made him nervous in a way he couldn't explain.

And still, he wanted to ask her to stay. To sleep with him, make love with him. Not because he needed her, but because...

He didn't know why. He just knew that he wanted her, badly. And didn't have a clue what to do if she didn't feel the same.

CHAPTER FIFTEEN

KARA HUSTLED LUCAS UP the front walk to his house, then waited patiently as he fumbled for his keys. She knew he was a little confused by arriving here and not at the clinic. She'd been here a million times before, so she knew he was out of sorts because she had made the decision in an effort to take care of him.

He was even worse at allowing people to do that than she was.

Not that she cared. Not tonight, when he looked more lost and more fragile than she had ever seen him. Tonight, she would take care of him whether he liked it or not.

She knew he was in bad shape when, once they were inside, he wandered aimlessly through the foyer without bothering to turn on any lights. He kicked his shoes off in the doorway to the living room, then dropped his tie on the table in the hall. Definitely not his modus operandi.

Not knowing what else to do, she followed behind him, flicking on a lamp here and a light switch there. Lucas didn't stop until he got to the kitchen, but once there he just froze. Shoulders slumped, head bowed. Like he had no idea what he was supposed to do now.

And maybe he didn't. God knows, she was playing it by ear herself. Blowing out a deep breath, she walked up behind him and wrapped her arms around his waist. He jumped a little at the first touch, but relaxed slowly as she pressed her cheek against his back and just held him for long seconds.

He smelled good, even with the day he'd had—like lemon trees and hot coffee and warm, welcoming man. He smelled like comfort, like Lucas, like home. She closed her eyes, breathed him in. As she did, she counted the slow, steady beat of his heart beneath her ear.

It sucked, really, how she'd been all around the world—more times than she could count—and the only home she'd ever been able to count on was right here, with him. She thought of the baby inside of her, of her gynecologist's dire warnings, and wanted to weep. She might never be able to have the man, to hold on to him, but she desperately wanted a chance to cradle his baby in her arms.

He was so defeated, so unlike the Lucas she was used to. Part of her wondered if she should have waited to tell him about the baby. God knows it was one more burden he didn't need right now. And if the unthinkable happened, if she lost the baby, then it would have been one less burden for him to carry on his broad shoulders. She hated that she'd been a party to hurting him today, that she'd been a part of making him look so lost. She wished she could do something to make the pain go away.

The thought had her pulling away a little despite

the rough sound of protest he made. Knowing she was walking into dangerous waters, but not caring at that moment—wanting only to care for him—she slid her right hand up his back to his shoulders, his neck. And began to slowly rub and squeeze the tightness away.

He moaned, low in his throat, his right hand coming up to capture her left one where it rested on his shoulder. "That feels good," he rasped.

"Then just relax. Enjoy it." Her own voice was husky, shaky. Which was ridiculous. She'd given him hundreds of massages before and he had done the same for her back when he'd been seriously considering going into orthopedic medicine. Those times had been different, though. She hadn't slept with him then, hadn't known what he tasted like or what it felt like to have him inside of her. Now that she did—now that the life they had unknowingly created was nestled deep within her—it felt different. Better, and in some ways, worse.

She should probably stop, but she was too much of a masochist for that. No matter how much it might hurt later, it felt good to be here with him now. To touch him, hold him. To comfort him, and in doing so, comfort herself, as well.

It didn't last, though—not that she'd really expected it to. Not with Lucas, who could only bend so far before he cracked. He'd done a lot of bending today already.

"You need to eat," he said, turning to face her.

She looked at the ground because she needed a minute to process his rejection. Intellectually, she knew that wasn't what he'd meant to do, but emotionally it was so much harder to accept. Especially when her crazy hormones had her feelings bouncing all over the place.

She started to tell him that she was okay, but it would be a lie. And no matter how messed up things were right now, she'd never lied to Lucas and she didn't plan on starting now. "Yeah. I probably should." Her stomach was churning wildly, the nausea worse because she was so hungry.

"I can call a cab, grab something to eat on the way home." She started to move around him, expecting him to step back and let her through.

He didn't budge. Instead, he slipped a finger under her chin and tilted her face up until there was nowhere to look but into the swirling depths of his eyes. "Don't," he said.

"Don't what?"

"Don't hide from me. I can see you don't feel good. Sit down and let me make you something to eat. Let me take care of you."

She was starting to hate those six words more than anything, and part of her wanted to snap that she could take care of herself. But she could see that Lucas was lost, that he needed something to ground him. Taking care of her right now was obviously what he needed.

Still, she knew it was a bad idea. In her head, she could list the many, many reasons going down this road would only hurt her in the end. But when she looked into his face, so open and vulnerable, so unlike the Lucas she was used to, she knew she wasn't going anywhere. She couldn't leave him like this, and didn't want to, anyway.

"Okay," she told him, turning her head so that her lips brushed against his suddenly unsteady palm. Which was shocking in and of itself, as Lucas had always had incredibly steady hands. Surgeon hands, though he'd chosen to be an internist instead.

And then, because tonight was different, special, outside of the norms of their relationship—much like that night three months ago—she did what she really wanted to do. Slipped her tongue a little bit past her lips and licked her way across his warm, callused palm.

Lucas's eyes darkened and he reached for her, but she slipped away, put a little distance between them. She didn't want to start something they couldn't finish, at least not without endangering her already precarious pregnancy.

"Sit down," she murmured to him softly. "I'll find something for us to eat."

"You should rest. I'll do it." He headed for the kitchen, but he looked exhausted.

"We can do it together," she told him as she followed him. "We'll be done twice as fast."

She opened the refrigerator, conscious as she did of him watching her every move. "I'm starving." She knew the admission was all it would take for him to get with the program, and when her stomach actually growled a few seconds later—lending credence to her claim—she knew she was right. Lucas the caretaker would never let her go hungry.

His fridge was surprisingly well stocked, considering the fact that he'd never been much of a cook, but she decided on a frittata, anyway. It was fast, easy and bland enough—hopefully—that her stomach would accept it.

She pulled out an array of vegetables—mushrooms, small red peppers, tomatoes, spinach, an onion—and set him to work chopping while she cracked and seasoned the eggs. Then she took her antinausea medicine as she sautéed the vegetables in a little olive oil before pouring the eggs over the top to cook. A few minutes later she shifted the pan to the already-warm oven and turned to make some toast, only to find that Lucas had beat her to it.

He'd also cleaned some fresh strawberries and she couldn't resist popping one in her mouth. They were one of the things she'd craved desperately in Africa, where there'd been none around. Since she'd gotten back to America, she'd devoured three or four pints on her own. Most of which she'd ended up throwing back up, but the cravings were bad enough that she hadn't even cared.

They sat down to dinner about half an hour after they'd started cooking it, and it was a surprisingly relaxed meal. Oh, the sexual tension from earlier was still there, but it had eased off some, while the easy friendship was out in full force. By mutual agreement they didn't talk about her pregnancy or Lisa or the other victims of the accident or what the future was going to look like for his sister. Instead, they talked of normal things, mundane things that would seem absurd to anyone who wasn't them. But it was what Lucas needed, what they both needed after the day's emotional roller coaster, and she was more than ready to embrace it.

Still, when dinner was over and they had loaded the plates into the dishwasher, she knew the reprieve was over. She needed to talk to him about a lawyer for Lisa. She'd brought it up at the hospital, then had let it slide when it was obvious Lucas hadn't been ready to deal with it yet. But it was after ten now and the clock was ticking. First thing in the morning, even before he went to the hospital, he needed to secure legal representation for Lisa.

His shoulders slumped as soon as she brought it up and the slightly lighter mood that had arrived with dinner disappeared so completely that she almost wished she hadn't broached the subject. But that wasn't fair—to Lisa or Lucas or the rest of their family. He might not want to deal with how much trouble his sister was in, but the police wouldn't have any such qualms. Better to be prepared than to be blindsided when the charges finally came down.

"I don't know what to do," he said, grabbing a beer out of the fridge for himself and a bottle of water for her. "That's never happened to me before."

"I know. And I'm sorry. I wish I could make this whole thing just disappear."

"Yeah, me, too." He sighed heavily. "I'll call our family lawyer first thing in the morning, see if he has some suggestions."

"Paul's wife is a criminal defense attorney," she

told him quietly. "I can call my boss tomorrow, ask for her number.

He winced at the words *criminal defense attorney,* but eventually he nodded. "Yeah, okay. Thanks."

For long minutes, neither of them moved. Lucas just stared into space, his face cloudy and that fantastic mind of his racing a thousand miles a second, while she just stared at him. It wasn't often that she got that opportunity and she was going to take advantage of it, even if it wasn't the optimum time.

When he'd first seen her, at his clinic, he'd told her that she looked like hell. Which was no more than the truth. Her skin was pale, her hair was lank and lacking shape. She'd lost a bunch of weight because of her illness and the pregnancy. Now, sitting here, a lot of that same description could be applied to him. It was obvious he still hadn't gotten a haircut, and his hair had been too long before she'd left for Africa. His pallor was extreme, weariness of soul and body causing huge bags underneath his eyes. And while he hadn't actually lost weight, tension had his jaw clenched so tightly that his cheekbones stuck out in sharp prominence.

She wanted to make it all disappear for him, wanted to gather him in her arms and make all the bad things that were happening just go away—for both of them. A fear of what would happen next kept her in place, and a knowledge that none of the things that were happening to them were going to disappear for long.

But as he sat there, growing more and more distant, suddenly she didn't care. Not about tomorrow or the day after that or the day after that. Lucas needed her right now and she needed him, whether she wanted to or not.

Filled with resolve and an aching tenderness that moved her in ways that few things ever could, she stood up and held out a hand to Lucas. When he didn't immediately respond—he was too lost in his own world for that—it was her turn to thread their fingers together. Then she pulled him up and, with an arm around the waist, propelled him up the stairs to his bedroom.

Once they were in the dark room, she turned on the small lamp on the dresser and shooed him toward the bathroom. "Go take a shower," she told him.

For long seconds, he didn't move. Just looked at her as if he couldn't quite comprehend what she was saying. She could tell the day was crashing in on him and all she really wanted to do was make it easier for him to get through the next few hours.

With a sigh, and a quick wish that she was not going to regret this, she stepped into Lucas's gigantic bathroom and turned on his double-headed shower. Then she reached for his shirt, began to slowly unbutton his dark blue dress shirt. His hands rose to hers, his fingers clasping hers in a soft but unbreakable grip. "What are you doing?" he asked, his voice low and growly and so sexy that her knees actually trembled.

She made sure her arousal didn't show when she answered matter-of-factly, "Getting you ready for the shower."

"I'm not a child, Kara."

"I am well aware of that." She jiggled her hands

a little and he let go. Under his dark, watchful and aroused eyes, she finished unbuttoning the shirt and then slid it off his shoulders.

"We said it was probably a one-time thing."

The words hurt, though she knew he was just being honest about his feelings even as he tried to clarify what was going on. "That was a one-time thing."

"Then what is this?"

"A different one-time thing."

She reached for his belt, unbuckled it. Opened the clasp of his dress pants and slid the zipper down. As she did, he sprang free, as hard and long as she remembered. She paused for a moment, hands trembling, body shaking with a desire she knew she couldn't satisfy. And slowly ran her palm over the front of his black boxer briefs, relishing the hot length of him under her hand.

Lucas groaned then, reaching up to pull his undershirt over his head. She dropped to her knees in front of him and pulled off his socks before slowly sliding his boxers down his legs. Then, because she couldn't help herself, she pressed a long, lingering kiss to his abdomen, right beside his navel, even as she stroked a hand up and down the hot, silky length of him.

"Kara." Her name was barely recognizable in the growl that came from his chest, but she relished it. The proof that Lucas was on the verge of losing control.

Pushing to her feet, she kept her eyes locked on his as she slipped out of her own blouse and pants. She stood there for a moment in her red lace bra and panties—the ones she'd worn today because they gave her an extra boost of confidence—and let him look his fill. Then, when Lucas's eyes darkened even more, their pupils growing enormous in the dim light, she stripped down until she was as naked as he was.

He started to speak, but she laid a finger on his lips, afraid that whatever he said was going to ruin this perfect moment between them. She knew this couldn't last, knew it wasn't permanent, but she didn't need to hear him say it again. Not now, when she already felt so incredibly vulnerable.

Eyes locked with hers, he slowly drew the tip of her finger into the wet heat of his mouth. He sucked on it for a second, then nipped at her before laving his tongue over and around her finger in an effort to take the small sting away.

It was her turn to moan, to drop her head back and close her eyes as he did it again, and again. It felt so good, *he* felt so good, that she wanted to lose herself in him forever.

But that wasn't what this was about, and even if it was, that wasn't possible right now.

Still, she made no move to stop him, just stood there and enjoyed the heat coursing through her body. When he finally lifted his head, her stomach was quivery, her legs barely supporting her.

Wanting to make him feel as good as he did her, she took his hands in hers and pulled him into the shower with her. He stiffened as the warm water hit them, then relaxed in a rush that had his eyes going sleepy and his body turning liquid against hers.

Loving the way he looked when he was all tranquil

and loose, she ran her hands over his arms, across his chest, down his back to his waist, massaging as she went in an effort to keep him that way.

As she did, he sighed a little, lowering his head so that his brow rested against hers. She froze, barely daring to breathe in case it gave him the wrong idea, made him move. Because while they'd been friends for years, had even had sex and conceived a child together, she swore that this moment, this gesture of utter vulnerability on his part, was the most intimate they had ever been.

Emotions crashed through her in an inseparable tangle. Love and compassion, fear and joy, sadness and determination. They were all there, in a mixed-up mess that she had no idea how to deal with. All she knew was that she didn't want to lose him, didn't want to lose this indefinable closeness that they shared.

At the same time, she wanted to take care of him more than she'd wanted anything in her life—except their baby. Sliding her hands slowly up his spine, she threaded her hands through his hair and gently tilted his head back until the shower spray could wash over it.

Lucas's eyes sprang open and she smiled softly at him, reassuringly, before reaching behind him and grabbing hold of his shampoo bottle. She squirted some into her palm and then carefully rubbed her two hands together before lifting them to his hair.

She shampooed him gently, concentrating more on relaxation than cleanliness. At first, he stood stiff, watching her with careful eyes. But as she dug her thumbs into the base of his neck, he groaned a little and let his head fall back again.

That's when she knew she had him.

She massaged his scalp for another minute or so, then eased his head back under the water. She made sure to keep her fingers relaxed as she soothingly stroked his scalp and rinsed each strand of hair. Then she reached for his conditioner, and did the same thing all over again.

IT WAS ALL LUCAS COULD DO not to dissolve into a boneless mass of quivering arousal as Kara stroked her long, sexy fingers through his hair. He knew she was trying to relax him, and to a certain extent it was working—he no longer had the blinding headache that had been plaguing him for hours. But at the same time, she was making him crazy, her sweet, sensual touch setting every nerve ending in his body on fire.

When she nudged him, he obligingly tilted his head back so that the warm water could slowly stream over his head and down his body. His very aroused body that was growing harder with each touch of her talented fingers. He knew she felt his arousal nestled against her stomach, but she didn't react to it. Instead, she just kept rinsing out the conditioner, which for some reason, only made him hotter.

When, after an eternity, his hair had finally been rinsed clean, Kara grabbed a bottle of shower gel and squirted some onto her hands. She rubbed them together, worked up a nice lather and then slowly began to soap him up. He nearly lost his mind before she'd moved more than an inch or two.

Her hands slid down his neck, over the width of his shoulders and down this spine to the small of his back, where she rubbed and rubbed until he could feel the knots he'd carried there all day slowly dissolving. Then she worked her way back up his spine, kneading and massaging until he felt—conversely—more relaxed and more inflamed than he could ever remember being in his life.

She spent a long time on his shoulders and upper back. He tried to stop her, to return the favor, but she just laughed, low and sexy, and swatted his hands away. Then got more soap before trailing her talented fingers over his neck and collarbone to his chest and rib cage. She circled his nipples with her soap-slicked fingers, making him nearly insane with the need to be inside her.

And then she moved lower, tickling his navel and caressing his hips before reaching between them and wrapping her hand around his hard, aching length. His eyes nearly crossed as she stroked him, up and down, up and down. When her thumb swept over his tip, circling him again and again, he lost it completely. He pulled her against him and whispered, "Kara," right before he bent his head and took her mouth with his own.

The moment Kara's lips touched his, Lucas felt the tension in his body just melt away. The clinic, his issues with his mother, even all of Lisa's problems, just rolled off him. They didn't disappear, obviously, but the smell and taste and feel of Kara took him over, distanced him from them.

Even if it was just for a little while, he was grateful. And determined to enjoy every second of it.

His hands tightened in her crazy curls and he relished the feel of them beneath his hands. Warm and wet from the water pouring over both of them, they wrapped themselves around his fingers with a mind of their own, chaining him to Kara and, more importantly, Kara to him.

It wouldn't last. He was smart enough to know that, soon enough, Kara would be running off to some far-flung corner of the globe. But she was here, now, in his arms, and he wasn't going to let her go until he had to.

She breathed out a soft, ragged sigh that parted her lips and had every nerve ending in his body standing up and taking notice. Taking advantage of the opening, he slipped his tongue inside her mouth and tangled it around her own. She tasted sweet, like cream and tart strawberries.

He wanted more of her, needed more of her, and she must have felt the same way, because her hands went from massaging to clinging in an instant. Her nails dug into the muscles of his upper back, and lust roared through him at the sweet pain of it. Part of him wanted to lift her up, press her back against the shower wall and plunge into her again and again and again, until they were both so sated and exhausted that the rest of the world no longer mattered. But it had been so long since he'd held her, since he'd kissed her and touched her, that he also wanted to take his time. To

explore every sweet inch of her until she was screaming for him to take her.

Deciding the second option was definitely the way
to go, he backed off the kiss. Turned it slow and soft
and leisurely as he stroked his tongue over her lower
lip, lingering at the upturned corners of her mouth.

She whimpered, pressed closer, and he relished her
responsiveness as he eased them both into the shower
spray, rinsing away the last remnants of soap. They
might have been friends for seventeen years and lovers for only one night, but when he touched her she lit
up completely. It was both humbling and exhilarating.

Of course, it was also frustrating as hell. Which
was why, when Kara pulled her mouth from his and
started licking her way down his neck, he didn't put
up much of a struggle. And when her mouth skimmed
over his chest, stopping to toy with first one of his nipples and then the other, he lost all sense of restraint.
He cupped the back of her head and held her in place
as streaks of lightning sizzled through him.

Not that Kara seemed to mind. She nuzzled and
licked her way down his chest before once again dropping to her knees before him. Wrapping her arms
around his upper thighs, she pressed hot, openmouthed
kisses over his abdomen, then paused to tickle his
navel with her tongue. He gasped, tensed, and she
laughed a little before continuing her downward path,
kissing along the light dusting of hair that ran from
his belly button to his groin.

By the time she reached the end of the trail, he was
gasping, panting. His knees felt like Jell-O and he

leaned back against the tiled wall of the shower, bracing himself against it even as he tangled his fingers in her hair and yanked her forward until her mouth closed gently, hotly, around him.

There was a part of him that was horrified by the rough way he was handling her, the way he'd yanked her forward and shoved himself into her mouth. But she was making crazy, sexy sounds—like she was enjoying every second of it—and the vibration of them was working its way through them, making him crazy. Still, he tried to move so that she could pull him even deeper.

And when she moaned deep in her throat, her tongue stroking up and down the length of him, he forgot to be concerned. Forgot to be polite. Instead, he leaned his head back against the shower wall, closed his eyes and just enjoyed.

CHAPTER SIXTEEN

KARA TILTED HER HEAD SO that she could see all of Lucas as she continued to go down on him. He looked amazing, the muscles of his chest and abdomen tense and standing out in stark definition, even as his face was more relaxed than she had seen it in a very long time.

The look of him, the feel and sound and taste of him, was driving her crazy. Maybe it was the pregnancy hormones, maybe it was the joy of making love to Lucas once again, but she was on fire, her body hotter than she could ever remember it being. She wanted to stand, to wrap a leg around him and let him plunge deep inside of her until they both came. Then she wanted to do it all over again.

But that wasn't to be. The doctor hadn't prohibited sex, probably because she figured there was no more damage to be done to the baby. That it was just a matter of time. But Kara refused to believe that, and she refused to take any more chances with her baby's life than she had already. Which meant she could kneel here as long as she wanted, savoring every inch of Lucas as she brought him to orgasm, but there was no way she could let him do the same to her. She wouldn't take the chance of letting him make love to her, even though she was practically desperate for the feel of him inside of her.

Determined to make him feel good, even if she couldn't let him reciprocate, she slowly lifted and lowered her mouth along his shaft, sucking gently while her tongue flicked back and forth across the small bundle of nerves centered on the bottom of the tip.

Lucas's fingers tightened in her hair and he moaned, but she was relentless. Slowly, oh, so slowly, she took all of him in her mouth, held him there. Then pulled back before doing it a second, then a third time as she swirled her tongue around and around him, savoring the musky, masculine taste of him.

He groaned again, and she glanced up at him, met his sexy, heavy-lidded eyes that got even darker when he realized she was looking. He thrust against her, his eyes focused on the way he slid back and forth between her lips. It must have done something for him, because suddenly he began thrusting harder and deeper against her.

"I'm sorry," he gasped as he seized control of her head, bobbing it up and down in time to his thrusts. "I'm sorry, baby. I can't stop. I need—"

He broke off, gasped, as she intended him to, when she dug her nails deep into the flexing muscles of his buttocks. And when she moaned her approval deep in her throat, he went a little crazy. Which was more than fine with her. She reached between them, stroked the sensitive spot at the back of his testicles at the same

time she rubbed the bottom of her tongue along the
tender underside of his shaft.

LUCAS TRIED TO SPEAK, tried to breathe, but he couldn't
do either as Kara tormented him with her wicked, wild
mouth. He knew he was close, knew if she kept it up
he was going to lose it completely and he tried to pull
back. Tried to warn her.

"Kara, baby, I'm going to—"

She nodded her head, pulled him even more tightly
inside of her as she hummed deep in her throat. The
ensuing vibrations nearly made him blind as he
fought his release. He didn't want to come this way.
He wanted to be inside of her, her nipple in his mouth
and her warm body clenching all around him, when he
gave into his release. Again he tried to pull back, and
again Kara refused to let him go. And when she used
her tongue on him yet again, it sent him into sensory
overload, his entire body spiraling out of his control.
With a long, deep groan, he emptied himself into her
mouth in the most intense orgasm of his life.

He expected her to draw back, to let go of him, but
she held on through it all, taking all he had to give
her. His knees grew weak, his vision gray, and he
stumbled a little until he sank his ass down onto the
shower bench that was just to the right of where he'd
been standing.

Kara laughed a little as she finally let him go, and
he pulled her up until she was straddling him, her
beautiful breasts level with his mouth. He was exhausted, his body all but numb from the power of his

climax. But he'd have to be dead and buried not to enjoy the sight of Kara astride him, all hot and sexy and tousled. Her beautiful red curls were crazy, her cheeks flushed, her lips red swollen as she reached forward and ran a gentle hand down his cheek. He turned his head, nipped gently at the soft, fleshy pad beneath her thumb.

Her breath caught in her throat, her eyes growing hazy, and he slipped a hand between their bodies to rub at her clit. Then he stroked his fingers down and over the soft folds of her sex, checking to make sure that she was ready for him.

She was hot and wet, and smelled so good he couldn't resist lifting her up, so that she was standing, and burying his face against her. She moaned, tensed against his mouth as he licked his way over her mons to the very heart of her. He'd spent weeks, months, dreaming of how she'd tasted and he wanted it again. Wanted to immerse himself in her as she came all over his tongue.

But suddenly she tensed against him, started to struggle. He stared at her in confusion. "What's wrong, darlin'?"

"The baby. I can't—"

"Oh, right." He cursed himself for being an idiot, for taking all this from her when he wouldn't be able to reciprocate. He really was the selfish, unfeeling bastard his mother had named him. "I'm sorry. I wasn't thinking."

"Don't be sorry. I loved every second of it."

Lucas turned off the water and reached for one of

the towels he kept draped over the shower glass. He wrapped it around her before grabbing a second one and draping it around his own hips. Then he lifted her into his arms and carried her to his bed.

Once there, he laid her gently on the navy-blue comforter before stretching out beside her. Her lips curved softly and he reached for the towel, opening it so that her long, beautiful body was bared to him.

For long seconds, he just looked at her, admiring the way the lamplight played over sun-kissed skin, casting shadows in the most interesting places. But when he leaned forward and kissed the hollow of her throat—a place he had discovered months ago—she stiffened.

"I told you."

"I know. I'm just kissing you, Kara. I wouldn't do anything to hurt the baby, either."

She relaxed slowly, and he curved an arm over her waist, pulling her body flush against his. It had been a crappy day, one of the worst of his life, but somehow having Kara here made it all more bearable.

He lay there, holding her, playing with her hair for a long time and when she didn't say anything, he figured she had fallen asleep. Which was what he needed to do if he could ever quiet his mind enough. But as he rolled over to turn off the light, Kara murmured, "Your mom is wrong, you know."

He stiffened. "I don't want to talk about it."

"I know you don't. But I couldn't let you sleep thinking anything she said had any merit. She was scared and hurting and she lashed out at you. She'll regret it in the morning."

"I'm glad you think so."

"I know so." She rolled over and this time it was her turn to curl herself around him. "You're the best person I know, Lucas Montgomery, and anyone who says differently doesn't know what they're talking about. Okay?"

He nodded because he didn't trust himself to speak. When she rolled back over onto her back, he got up and lifted her into his arms again so that he could fold the covers back. He put her back in the center of the bed, then crossed to his dresser, where he pulled out a pair of pajama bottoms he rarely bothered with and an extra large T-shirt.

After slipping the pants on, he crossed to the bed and sat beside Kara. She looked exhausted, her skin so ghostly white that the circles beneath her eyes looked even more pronounced. Sitting her up, he slipped the shirt over her head and then slid her arms through the armholes. It was huge on her, but at least it covered all the vital areas.

"Thanks, Lucas," she murmured sleepily, already curling onto her side, her knees tucked up against her chest like a child.

"No problem, darlin'." He stretched out behind her, draping an arm around her stomach so he could mold his body to hers. "Just go to sleep."

Within minutes she had done just that, her body relaxing and her breathing evening out.

He lay there with her for about half an hour, waiting for sleep to claim him. But it never did. Not that he was exactly surprised. Despite Kara's very tender and thorough ministrations—ministrations he could kick himself for allowing when he couldn't do the same for her—his mind was still racing.

Worry over Kara warred with worry for his sister and the children she'd hit, who were, even now, in intensive care. How had this happened? Yesterday, his biggest worries had been dealing with his mother's ridiculous spending habits, his sisters' irresponsibility, finding another doctor to work for a pittance at the clinic. And Kara. He'd been worried about seeing her again, about how things would go between them. About what she would want from him when he was already so bogged down with everything else.

Today, this minute, the worries of yesterday seemed ridiculously small, especially when his sister, and those she'd injured, were in critical condition and Kara was still so sick.

Knowing he wasn't going to fall asleep anytime soon, he rolled over and grabbed his tablet off the nightstand where he kept it. After logging on to the internet, he negotiated his way through the maze of passwords to get into his favorite medical database. Once there, he researched dengue hemorrhagic fever.

It was worse, and better, than he had imagined. On the plus side, if she'd had it six weeks ago and was still alive, the disease wasn't going to kill her. At the same time, the fact that she was pregnant and still so sick meant that it could have done massive damage to the baby. According to the articles he found, the chances of the baby surviving through delivery were small. It wasn't unheard-of—healthy babies had been born to mothers with DHF, but it wasn't common, either.

He knew she trusted her doctor, but he was going to drag her into the clinic for an exam, kicking and screaming if he had to. Both Jack and Amanda had a lot more experience with DHF than some Atlanta ob-gyn could hope to have and he wanted them to check Kara over from head to toe. If they said she was recovering, that everything was fine with her, then and only then would he relax.

As for the baby…he felt a little pang deep in his heart at the thought of his child. He still didn't know how he felt about becoming a father, but he knew he wanted to give the baby the best shot at survival he could. And that meant finding an obstetrician that had dealt with cases like this before. He wasn't sure where he'd find one in Atlanta, but he wasn't going to rest until he did.

With that settled in his mind—or as settled as it could get—he logged out and started to search for DUI attorneys for his sister, then decided that could wait until the morning. It had probably been a bad move for him not to find one today, but he just hadn't been able to wrap his head around it. She was absolutely guilty and it seemed wrong—horribly wrong— to hire someone who would stand up in court and say that she wasn't.

He had to get over his aversion. He knew it. After all, the justice system was built on the accused getting his or her day in court. And still it rankled, still it drove him mad that Lisa—who had everything at her disposal—had been so selfish. So stupid. So *weak*.

He shut the tablet down with a sigh, then dropped it on the floor beside the bed. He might not be able to deal with it tonight, but he would find Lisa a lawyer tomorrow, he promised himself as he shut off the bedside lamp. He was running out of time.

WHEN KARA AWOKE AT FOUR the next morning, her stomach was churning. Whatever was left of the frittata from the night before was very definitely on its way up. Determined not to wake Lucas and get him even more upset, she made a mad dash for the guest bathroom down the hall.

She made it, but with only seconds to spare. After getting sick, she pushed herself to her feet and went to rinse her mouth out in the sink. As she did, she got a glimpse of herself in the mirror. No wonder Lucas had been so concerned yesterday. She looked like hell, nearly as bad as she had when she'd been suffering from dengue hemorrhagic fever.

She knew he was worried about her and she hated that she'd added to his stress. She wanted to tell him that she was okay, that she could handle this by herself, but she knew he wouldn't believe her. Or even if he did, he wouldn't let her. He'd already decided this was his responsibility, and nothing was going to sway him from that.

Even worse, she'd gone and complicated things last night by making love to Lucas. She'd done it partially to comfort him and partially because she'd wanted him so badly that she hadn't thought about the consequences. But it was morning now and she had no idea what last night had meant. Was it another aberration, as they'd discussed in the shower? Or was it something more?

Deep inside, she knew she wanted it to be more. Her feelings for Lucas were huge and so much more than friendship. She'd figured that out in the months she'd been without him in Africa, and in the way she felt about the unborn baby she carried. She wanted it for itself, but also because it was Lucas's.

That didn't mean he felt the same way about her. He was a responsible guy and now that he knew she was pregnant with his baby, he would consider her an obligation. Someone else he had to take care of. She hated that. She wanted him to be with her because he wanted to, not because he felt he had to. He had enough obligations in his life. She didn't want to be one more.

And yet, here she was, with no one to turn to but him. It was an untenable situation, one that could have no happy ending. For either of them.

Worried, unsure what to do about anything, she finished rinsing out her mouth and shut off the tap. Whatever the solution was, it wasn't coming to her now so she might as well go back to bed and hope the nausea abated enough to let her sleep a little more. She was so tired, more tired than she could ever remember being.

But as she stepped away from the sink, she glanced down. And froze at the drops of blood she spied on the shiny white tile where she had been standing. There were only a couple, but they were more than enough to strike terror into her heart. She checked herself, realized a couple more drops had rolled down her legs. Not much. Not enough to indicate a miscarriage. But more than enough to indicate the possibility of one.

Horrified tears filled her eyes and for long minutes she couldn't think past the fear. Dr. Beaumont was right. She was going to lose the baby. She was going to—

Her breath sawed in and out as panic took over, and she clamped a hand over her mouth to stifle the sound as she sank to the ground. She couldn't wake Lucas up, couldn't let him see this. The last thing he needed right now was to deal with this on top of everything else.

Besides, she couldn't take his pity. Bad enough she had to put up with his sense of responsibility. But his pity, too? No. She wasn't going to go there.

Wrapping her arms around herself, she started to rock back and forth. As she did, her mind raced, went over everything she knew about miscarriages—from med school and from the research she'd done the past couple of weeks, since Julian had told her how unlikely it was that the pregnancy would remain viable.

Going through it all calmed her down, especially as she realized that there wasn't enough blood for this to be a sixteen-week miscarriage. She thought of the woman in Eritrea, who had lost her baby at seventeen weeks. There had been a lot of blood, plus pain and cramping.

She had none of that, just these few drops of blood. She was spotting. Just spotting.

Serenity came to her slowly. Spotting wasn't good, especially considering the fact that she'd had a hemorrhagic illness. But it wasn't the end of the world, either. It didn't mean she was going to lose what might be her only chance at being a mother.

Once her doctor's office opened in a few hours, she would call, see what Dr. Beaumont suggested. And then she would go from there. She'd probably have to take it easy for a few days, would need to get plenty of rest. It wouldn't be easy, especially with what was going on in Lucas's life right now, but she would do it. To keep their baby safe, she would do whatever she had to.

CHAPTER SEVENTEEN

LUCAS AWOKE SLOWLY, with the sense that something was terribly wrong. It took a minute for everything from the day before to rush back into his mind, and when it did, he groaned and pulled the covers over his head—something he hadn't done since he was a child.

Not that he planned to stay like that, but surely five minutes of hiding couldn't hurt before he faced what was sure to be the day from hell.

In the end, he didn't even make it two minutes. There was too much that needed to be done, too much information he had to get. And perhaps, most importantly, he had Kara to attend to. But when he reached a hand across the bed, expecting to encounter Kara, sleep-warmed and sweet smelling, all he met was air.

Her absence galvanized him as little else could. In fact, he hit the floor running. Not bothering with a T-shirt, he called her name as he hurried down the hall. What if she'd gotten sicker during the night? What if she'd gotten up to use the restroom and the nausea had made her dizzy? She could have slipped and fallen....

He knew he was being alarmist, but in those minutes, he didn't care. He needed to find Kara, needed to make sure she was all right. He'd done a crappy job of looking after her yesterday—for God's sake, he'd all but forced her to her knees in that shower. Definitely not the act of a best friend, or even a caring lover. And now, now she was…sitting under a blanket on the couch, curled up with a cup of tea or coffee and a newspaper on her lap?

Relief slammed through him, powerful and all encompassing. It was followed quickly by anger. Surely she'd heard him calling. Why had she ignored him? She must have heard the worry in his voice.

But when he walked around the couch, intent on confronting her, he realized she was fast asleep, the newspaper dangling from her limp fingers. At the sight, his heart gave one great big kick of fear—old habits died hard—and he stood there for a few moments simply watching her, making sure that her chest really was rising and falling. Which it was, slowly and steadily. Thank God.

Figuring the past two days had probably taken five years off his life—maybe ten when all was said and done—he grumbled to himself as he headed into the kitchen. He planned to start a pot of coffee, only to pull up short when he realized she had already made a pot for him—and judging by the smell, it was pretty close to fresh. She'd done a good job of anticipating his wake-up time.

The fact that she knew him well enough to anticipate it shouldn't make him so damn happy, but for some reason it did. Almost as happy as the bowl of cut-up fruit she'd set on the counter next to a big pile of his favorite blueberry bagels.

How long had she been up before she'd fallen back asleep, anyway?

After pouring himself a cup of coffee, he snagged a bagel, then settled himself at the kitchen table with his laptop and a telephone. He had a million things to do that morning. First up, he needed to call the hospital, see how his sister was. And then he had to find that damn lawyer. He thought of calling Amanda's husband, Simon, who had connections all over Atlanta. Maybe he'd have a suggestion for a lawyer who could help Lisa.

He picked up the phone, prepared to get started despite the early hour, then froze as his gaze fell on a legal pad next to his laptop. Kara's writing was all over it and she had divided the front page into three sections.

The first section read, "Six-fifteen. Lisa made it through the night. She's still asleep but Aaron plans to ease off on the medication and wake her up around two this afternoon. Two of the children in critical condition. Mother and third child, stable." As he stared at the last couple of sentences, he couldn't help wondering what strings she'd pulled at the hospital to get the information. Must have been some pretty long ones, considering how hard it was to get news like that because of Health Insurance Portability and Accountability Act.

The second section on the legal pad listed the

names and phone numbers of three attorneys, with a
star next to the first one on the list.

And the last section reminded him to eat, and mentioned that there were bagels that she'd had delivered
on the counter.

For long seconds, he sat at the table staring at her
note, an unfamiliar emotion rushing through him. It
was so unfamiliar, in fact, that he wasn't sure what to
call it. He knew only that, for the first time in his adult
life, someone was truly taking care of him instead of
the other way around. It felt strange. Nice, but strange.

He hoped Kara would let him do the same for
her. She'd always been prickly about asking for help
no matter how many times he'd tried to offer it. So
prickly, in fact, that he'd stopped offering years ago,
though it was hard. After all, she was closer to him
than just about anyone else on earth. Why shouldn't
he want to make things easier for her if he could?

He glanced back down at the yellow pad. She obviously had no compunction about making things easier
for him. Still, he knew her determination not to accept
help was because she'd spent so much of her life on
her own, having to take care of everything, much the
same way his control freak ways were a by-product
of his own family issues. Sometimes, though, understanding the why didn't make it any easier to accept.

Especially when you were a control freak.

Lucas was on his second bagel, having already
called Jack and arranged for him to cover his shift at
the clinic that morning, when Kara came stumbling
into the kitchen, eyes half-closed.

"Not one word," she said with a grimace as she fumbled her way to the stove for the teakettle and then to the sink to fill it with water.

"There's fresh coffee," he said. "I've only had two cups."

She shook her head, grunted out, "Tea," before turning on the kettle and dropping into the chair next to his. She folded her arms on the table and then rested her head in the middle of them.

"Sleep well?" he asked, tongue-in-cheek.

Her only answer was to lift one hand and flip him off.

Lucas grinned. He couldn't help himself. This was the Kara he knew and loved, not that pale, sick creature from the day before. Still, when she finally lifted her head, she looked as hollow-eyed as she had the night before. More even.

"I want you to come to the clinic." The words slipped out, but once they did, he wasn't sorry for them. "Just to get checked out. For your own peace of mind."

"My peace of mind is just fine."

"Okay, for my peace of mind, then." He locked eyes with her, refusing to let her gaze go no matter how irritated she looked. Which was pretty irritated, if he was honest. Not that he cared. Not when her health was on the line.

"I have a doctor already, one who is giving me excellent care."

"And she has much experience with pregnancy and

DHF?" He ventured to answer his own question. "No, but Amanda and Jack do."

"I don't need you to do all this," she told him with a glare. "I'm a grown woman and a doctor, to boot. I know how to take care of myself."

He knew these were dangerous waters even without the telltale scowl marks that showed up between her eyebrows whenever she was really upset. But he wasn't ready to back down. "I know you do. But, Kara, surely even you can see that you're not at your fighting best."

"I never said I was. But I am getting good medical care, so let's just leave it at that."

He nodded in understanding, even as he said, "I'm sorry. I can't."

This time her eyebrows nearly touched her hairline. "Excuse me?"

He rubbed a frustrated hand over his face and his hair as he bought time to formulate an answer. Nothing brilliant came to him, though, so he decided to tell her the truth as he understood it. It came out all mixed up with the speech he'd prepared for lunch the day before.

"Look, I know I have no right to tell you what to do. I get that. I do," he insisted at her doubtful look. "But regardless of whatever has suddenly started between us, we've been friends a long time. Surely that counts for something."

"For something?" There was a flash of hurt she couldn't hide and he felt like a total asshole. The last thing he wanted was to hurt her.

"For a lot, I mean. And I'm worried about you. I

just want to make sure you're okay and that the baby is doing the best it can. Amanda and Jack know DHF—I talked to Jack about it for a long time this morning. I just want—"

He stopped himself abruptly. Who was this moron stumbling over words? The one who couldn't seem to string two articulate sentences together. Which was ridiculous—he'd graduated summa cum laude from Harvard Medical School. Surely he could have a simple conversation with his best friend.

Kara must have decided to have mercy on him, because she stopped his incoherent ramblings with a gentle hand on his forearm. "Thank you," she told him softly.

"For what?"

"For caring about me. I appreciate it. I really do. But all this worry on your part is unnecessary."

"You're my closest friend and that's my kid you're carrying. How can worrying about you be unnecessary?"

"You've met Julian Banks, right? You know there's no way he'd let something happen to me. From the moment I contracted the stupid bug, he was right there, hassling me. Making sure I had enough fluids and was getting enough rest. He took enough blood to feed a vampire and then gave me enough blood transfusions to make up for any I'd lost or he'd taken, and then some."

He nodded, a part of him completely relieved by what she'd said. But there was another, darker part that wasn't so sure he liked the way she spoke of

Julian with such affection. Lucas should be thrilled she'd had a partner in Africa who had taken such good care of her—and he was, he really was—but at the same time, he'd wished he'd been there. Wished it had been him she'd turned to, who had found a way to help her.

Which was completely ridiculous considering it didn't matter who had treated her, as long as she had been treated. As long as she recovered. And yet, it was still there, a peculiar shot of jealousy that made absolutely no sense, particularly when he considered that he was the one who had given up on Africa and not the other way around.

"You're telling me the truth?" he finally asked, needing to hear it one more time. "You're really okay? There's no long-term damage?"

She locked gazes with him, and her green eyes were bright with honesty and reassurance. "There's no long-term damage. I'm going to be fine."

He nodded, but he still felt uneasy. He wanted to see the test results himself, wanted to know—

She sighed. "Will it really calm you down if I go see Jack?"

He jumped on the offer. "Yes."

"You won't make me see Amanda, too, or any other doctor you can dig up?"

"I swear. Just Jack. And a high-risk pregnancy specialist."

"I already have an appointment with one of those."

"Which one? Because I'm going to ask around, see who's the best—"

"Lucas!"

"Too pushy?" he asked.

"A little bit."

"Okay. We'll take you to see Jack this morning and then you can do the appointment with the specialist your obstetrician recommends."

"Well, thank you so much for your permission."

He sighed. "I'm sorry, Kara."

"It's fine." She reached over and ruffled his hair. "I know you can't help yourself."

"I really can't."

She smiled at him, and if it wasn't as brilliant as the smiles he was used to getting from her, then at least it wasn't as bad as how she'd looked last night, curled up in his arms and fighting nausea.

But, because he could still see her like that whenever he closed his eyes, and because it made him sick to think about it, he tugged on the hand he still held. "Come here."

"What do you mean?" she asked, confusion evident on her beautiful face, even as she let him pull her out of her chair.

"I need to hold you for a minute." He settled her on his lap, wrapping his arms around her and resting his chin on the top of her head. As he did, he felt himself relax—truly relax—for the first time since he'd jumped out of bed that morning. She was fine, he told himself. She was right here with him, real and substantial and perfectly solid. It was enough. More than enough.

At least for him. At least for now.

CHAPTER EIGHTEEN

THE NEXT FEW DAYS PASSED in a blur of hospital and doctor visits, trips to the lawyer's office and the police station as he tried to make sense of what his sister was up against. And when the unthinkable happened, when one of the little kids who had been in the car died, all hell broke loose.

The press had picked up the story and run with it by the second day. Lisa was the daughter of one of Atlanta's most prominent families, and the fact that she had committed such a crime was huge news. It wasn't long before the public began calling for her head and he could see why Kara had been so insistent that he get an attorney involved as quickly as possible. He needed the guy to help spin public opinion. Not in their favor, obviously, as that would be insane. But at least to not let it skew so far against Lisa.

The police were ready to level charges of DUI, DUI with injury, DUI with death and—if the prosecutor followed through with the rumor that had been circulating—second-degree murder. They were simply waiting until Lisa was well enough to deal with the charges before they arrested her.

She was doing pretty well. She'd come out of the

medically induced coma and was beginning to heal despite the catastrophic state of her life. In typical Lisa fashion, she didn't seem to quite comprehend the seriousness of what she was facing, and he didn't tell her. Not yet. There'd be plenty of time for that after she'd recovered from surgery and the concussion.

That didn't mean, however, that he could afford the same luxury. He'd been running himself ragged for a week now. He felt like a hamster on a stationary wheel—running and running and running but getting absolutely nothing accomplished.

Kara had been wonderful, though. She'd been there for him every step of the way, making sure that whatever he needed, he got. Food, someone to bounce ideas off, advice, support. She'd been there each and every day with all of that and more.

Which had only made him feel more like a heel. After all, she was the one who was pregnant, who was recovering from a serious illness. He should be the one coddling her, not the other way around. And yet, when she wrapped an arm around his waist or shoved a cup of coffee in his hand or bullied him into going to bed before the middle of the night, he couldn't fight her. Couldn't turn the tables on her. She was too good at playing the nurturer.

Which was strange, and something he'd never realized about her before. Oh, sure, he'd known she was good at her job, but analyzing facts and figures didn't require a great bedside manner. Maybe that's why he'd never noticed before. Or maybe he'd just been too wrapped up in being the caretaker to ever give anyone else a shot.

Whatever it was, he'd never been more grateful to a person in his life. She managed to keep his life on track—keep him on track—even when it seemed everything around him was falling apart. That had to count for something. Something big.

When his mother had cornered him at the hospital ten days after Lisa's accident and apologized to him for the things she'd said while Lisa was in surgery, he'd been shocked. His mother never apologized for anything—when she was in the wrong she had a tendency to just let the incident slide away into oblivion. But that day she'd told him in no uncertain terms that she had made a mistake and that she didn't know what she would have done without him.

He'd accepted the apology, though part of him still believed everything she'd said about his failings. And later, when he'd seen her talking to Kara, their heads bent together like they were sharing a secret, he'd known Kara had put his mother up to it.

What was he supposed to do with her? She spent her days taking care of him and resting to take care of the baby, and yet she balked every time he tried to do the same for her. It was frustrating in the extreme, especially when there was so much he wanted to do for her. So many ways he wanted to care for her.

If only he could figure out how to get past her defenses to do just that.

An idea struck him and he reached for his cell phone. He hadn't seen her all day and he missed her, wanted to hear her voice if only for a couple of minutes.

"Hey, Lucas? What's up?" She sounded harried, like she was in the middle of something, which was strange because he'd thought she was at home resting.

"You okay, Kara?" he demanded. "Where are you?"

"I'm grocery shopping. I needed a few things."

"Why didn't you tell me? I could have picked them up for you."

"Because I am perfectly capable of going to the store. The doctor says running a few errands is good for the baby and me. And before you ask, yes, Jack agrees. As long as I don't overdo it, I should get some walking exercise in every day."

He smiled. "Am I that predictable?"

"Even more so," she told him.

"Okay, if you know me so well, why did I call?"

"Because you missed me," she said with a laugh. When he didn't laugh with her, she sobered quickly. "I'm just kidding. I don't know why you called."

"That's exactly why I called—and to invite you to my place for dinner. I can pick you up about seven if you're interested."

"I'd love to have dinner with you, Lucas. But I can get myself to your house on my own."

Frustration ate at him. "I know that, Kara. That doesn't mean I can't come get you, though, does it?"

"I thought you were at the clinic until six tonight?"

"I am. But I can come get you—"

"My place is totally out of the way. Go home, take a shower and I'll see you about seven-fifteen or so."

"I really don't mind—"

"It's my turn to check out. I have to go, but I'll see you later." She clicked off and he was left staring at his phone, wondering how he'd been outmaneuvered again.

On the plus side, since she was driving herself to his house, he'd have more time to plan something special for her. Originally he'd planned to take her out for a nice dinner, to wine and dine her a little bit (or at least dine her, since the wine wasn't an option). But he didn't want to share her with anyone and besides, it would be better for her to rest. So he figured that an intimate dinner on the couch at his house would be better.

He could thank her for everything she'd done for him and then tell her that he wanted to take their relationship to the next level. Since the night she'd made such tender love to him, it had been like they were going backward. Like they were so busy being friends that they weren't even giving the lover thing a try.

And while he knew that she couldn't actually have sex right now, that didn't mean they couldn't kiss or cuddle or do any of the other things that people who were dating did. And though they'd never actually talked about it—or gone on a real date—he was determined that they were indeed dating. He liked her, cared about her more than anyone else in the world, was very definitely sexually attracted to her, and she was carrying his baby. What else did they need to start building a relationship? They already had more than most people ever got.

So, while he didn't have time to cook, he had more than enough time to order from a little Italian restaurant not too far from his house. Going over the menu carefully, he ordered all of Kara's favorites, including stuffed mushrooms, bruschetta and fettuccine Alfredo. And tiramisu for dessert. If things went as planned, it would have a dual effect—one, it would give him the chance to take care of her by attempting to get a large number of much-needed calories down her throat, and two, it would give him the time to tell her how he felt about her and to figure out how she felt about him. Oh, he knew she cared about him, but what he really wanted to know was if she thought they had a chance to build something more than friendship.

After work, he rushed home and set the stage. He put a couple bottles of sparkling water on to chill, set the dining room table, lit some candles. He even changed the sheets on his bed, not because he thought the night was going to end in sex but because he would really like it if she spent the night with him again. She hadn't stayed over since the day of Lisa's accident and he'd missed her. Every night he woke up reaching for her and she was never there.

Finally, he turned on some music and raced through a shower.

He was just slipping into a black T-shirt when the doorbell rang. He met her at the door with a silly bouquet of daisies—her favorite—and couldn't help smiling when her eyes turned dreamy at the sight of them. She buried her face in the huge bunch of happy-looking flowers and for long seconds—long enough that he knew he'd gotten it exactly right—just breathed them in.

"Thank you," she finally said. "They're beautiful."

"I'm glad you like them." He wrapped an arm around her slightly thickening waist, where his baby rested—his baby!—and drew her into the kitchen where she could put them in water before he pressed a wineglass full of sparkling water into her hand.

"What's all this about?" she asked him, eyeing him warily above her glass.

"Nothing. I wanted to do something nice for you. You've done so much for me these past couple of weeks—"

"I don't need payment for being your friend, Lucas."

"Yeah, but before all this crap started I thought we were on the road to being more than friends." He decided to lay it all on the line and wrapped an arm around her waist, pulled her body flush against his. "Or at least, I'd hoped we were."

Her eyes grew wide and he had to admit it—it was gratifying to watch her get all flustered and doe-eyed. It wasn't something he saw often from Kara, so he was determined to take advantage of it.

Stepping behind her, he skimmed his hands up her arms to her shoulders, than laid a tender kiss on one of her shoulders, left bare by her pretty, turquoise-colored sundress.

Her breath hitched in her throat and she melted against him. He closed his eyes and for long seconds did nothing more than savor the feeling of her against him. When she started moving restlessly, he brushed her long curls out of his way and softly bit the sensitive spot where her shoulder met her neck.

She lit up, her body moving sensuously against his until he could barely think, barely breathe. He wanted to turn her around and get lost in her kiss, in the feel and taste and scent of her mouth against his. But he had more self-control than that, he told himself as he pulled away reluctantly and ushered her into the dining room. He wasn't going to jump on her like a hungry predator no matter how much he wanted to. Tonight was about Kara, about giving back to her. He was determined to let her set the pace.

He settled her into the place he'd set for her before moving around the table to his own spot. Then, over fresh, crisp bruschetta and soft, spicy stuffed mushrooms, he set about charming her. Really charming her, in a way he never had before. What did it say about him that he'd wooed a lot of women in his life—women who didn't matter and whose faces he couldn't remember. But this woman, who had always mattered, had gotten none of it from him?

It shamed him. The callous disregard he'd shown this woman who had been so much to him in his life. His friend, his lover, his support system, his…love? The word snuck up on him, hit him on his blind side. And yet it fit in a way nothing else did, in the way nothing else had. Ever.

"Lucas?" Kara's voice was tentative. "Are you okay?"

He realized she was staring at him. Not that he

blamed her. He had pretty much shut down there for a minute, stunned by the truth of his feelings for Kara. Unable to do anything else, now that he finally understood the mixed-up emotions that had been plaguing him for weeks, months—years, if he was being honest—he took them out for a spin. At least in his own mind. He loved Kara. *He loved her.* He. Loved. Kara.

It felt frightening and exhilarating and crazy all at the same time, as if he was out of control but that it might not be such a bad thing, after all. It was a radical thought to him, but one he latched onto with both hands. He could do nothing less, not with Kara sitting across from him, watching him with those big green eyes of hers.

"I'm good," he answered her. "Great, actually."

She nodded, though the uncertainty on her face didn't fade away. She reached for her water, took a long sip. Cleared her throat. Looked anywhere but at him.

And that's when it hit him. She was as nervous as he was, and as hyperaware of the shifting planes of their relationship. And he'd done nothing to calm her down or reassure her. That was on him.

Determined to help her find her footing now that he had found his, Lucas did his best to charm the nerves from her once and for all. He told her jokes, little anecdotes from the clinic that were both clever and amusing. As they moved on to how their days had gone, he deliberately steered things away from Lisa and her myriad list of problems. Focused instead on keeping things sweet and light.

He fed her from his own hand, delivering the choicest slivers of tomato and mushroom to her mouth and relishing the feel of her lips as they brushed against his fingers.

He flirted with her shamelessly, making sure that he was always touching her. A hand on her cheek, a finger on her palm, a foot brushing against hers under the table. As the meal wore on, her eyes grew wider and wider, her hands less and less steady. It delighted him no end.

Maybe he should feel bad. God knows, he had invited her here to put her at ease so that she would open up, let him in. Instead, he was doing the exact opposite, making her so nervous that she could barely eat. And he didn't even feel badly about it.

How could he when her cheeks were flushed, her eyes sparkling? When her breath was coming too fast, so that her breasts rose and fell with each uneven inhalation. He loved that he was arousing her, loved that her reaction to him was as powerful, as all consuming as his was to her. Because, God knows, in sitting across from her, trying to seduce her, he had seduced himself, as well. Given himself completely over to her care.

But that worked two ways. She was in his care, as well, and it was his job to take care of her. To cherish her. He glanced down at her still-full plate and realized his seduction could have more serious consequences. She had barely touched her food, and that he couldn't allow.

He twisted his fork on his plate, swirling fettuccine onto the tines before reaching across the table and holding it up to her mouth. She didn't take it right away; instead, she just looked at him as if he was a puzzle she was trying to figure out. Which nearly made him laugh—he was not the mysterious one of the two of them, and never had been.

"Go on," he said softly. "You need to eat."

Eventually, she took the bite, chewing it slowly as her gaze never wavered from his. When she'd swallowed, he scooped up another bite, held it out to her again. And again she took it. They continued on this way until his plate was half-empty. When she held her hand up to stay his, he murmured, "Had enough?"

She nodded.

"Are you feeling nauseous?"

"I'm fine. I took my medicine."

"Good." It was crazy but he couldn't stop smiling. "How about dessert on the couch, then?" he asked as he cleared the plates, refusing her help when she offered.

"I'm not sure I'm ready for dessert, to be honest." She pressed a hand to a stomach still so flat it kept him up nights, worrying about her.

"Come on," he said as he grabbed a couple of forks and the pastry box the dessert had come in. "Live a little."

Her lips twisted in wry amusement. "I used to be the one saying that."

"Well, then, you should probably listen to your own advice."

"Maybe I should." But once they were on the couch,

she let him feed her only a couple of bites of the delicious cream-filled concoction before begging off.

He started to complain, to ask how she ever planned to gain back the weight she had lost and nourish the baby if she wouldn't eat, but he bit his tongue and kept his worries to himself. That wasn't what tonight was about.

Setting the dessert aside, he reached down and pulled her foot into his lap. Then began rubbing her arch with a firm but gentle touch. Chocolate and espresso cream wasn't the only way for a man to work his way into a woman's good graces.

But he hadn't rubbed her foot for more than a few seconds when she abruptly pulled it away from him.

"What's wrong?" he asked, startled by the strange and serious look on her face.

She leaned back against the other arm of the couch and asked, "What's going on, Lucas?"

"What do you mean?"

"I guess I don't understand what we're doing here." She gestured to the dessert, to her untouched glass, to him. "This isn't us."

Again, that overwhelming sense of shame washed through him. He'd fallen for her without ever giving her romance. He'd given her friendship, laughter, ease of conversation. He'd even given her passion. But he'd never given her the breathless anticipation that came with romance, even though he'd taken her to his bed twice. How could he have been so callous? Kara deserved better than that. Better than him.

"What if I want it to be?" he finally asked.

"What do you mean?"

"The fact that you don't know means I haven't taken enough care with you."

Her eyes went wide, fearful. "I don't need you to take care of me."

"It isn't the same thing." He reached over, stroked his thumb down the center of her palm. "Just so we're clear, I have no problem taking care of you, Kara. If you need me, I promise, I'll be there."

If he hadn't been watching her so closely, he probably would have missed the way her lower lip trembled. The way she looked away from him, tears trembling on her lashes. He couldn't stand seeing her cry. Could stand even less being so close and yet so far away from her. Not sure what else to do, he reached for her, pulling her against him—her cheek pressed against his chest while he stroked her hair back from her face.

Kara was confused by this change in Lucas. She liked it—she'd have to be crazy not to enjoy being pampered by him when he was at his sexiest, most charming best—but at the same time it didn't feel right. Like he was putting the moves on her because he thought he should. Because he thought this was what he needed to do for the mother of his child.

She waited for him to say something else, but when he didn't break the silence, she finally said, "I'm confused. I don't know what you want from me."

"That's just it, Kara. Tonight isn't about what I want from you. It's about what I want to give to you."

"That's just it." She sprang up, put some distance

between them. She couldn't think when he was so close to her. "I don't want anything from you."

"I get that. I understand how self-reliant you are, Kara. I'm not trying to take that from you. It's just that I want to take care of you and the baby both."

"Why?"

Now he looked as confused as she felt. "What do you mean?"

"Why do you want to take care of us?"

"Why wouldn't I? You're my responsibility. Of course I want to take care of you."

There it was, the word she dreaded and hated in equal parts. Responsibility. Kara could almost hear her heart break. Lucas cared about her, felt responsible for her, but he didn't love her. Not the way she loved him.

Swallowing the disappointment that burned in the back of her throat—disappointment that was so much worse after the sweet, tender way he'd treated her tonight—she said, "I don't want you to feel responsible for me. I don't want you to do things like this—" she swept her hand around the room "—because she feel like you have to."

"I don't feel like I have to do anything, Kara. I did this because I wanted to."

"Why?" she asked again, her whole body taut with hope and fear.

"What do you mean, why? You're the mother of my child. Why wouldn't I want to do something nice for you?"

"That's it? I'm the mother of your child?"

"Well, you are, aren't you?"

"I thought I was also your best friend, maybe even your lover. Now I'm just the mother of your child?" No matter how hard she tried, she couldn't keep the hurt from her voice.

"You know that's not what I meant."

"Oh, I think it's exactly what you meant. I'm pregnant so suddenly you have to do everything right. Wine and dine me, charm me, make me feel special and appreciated." She kept going without waiting for him to speak, because she could tell from the look on his face that she was getting it exactly right. "How far were you going to take this, Lucas? Ask me to spend the night? Ask me to move in? Ask me to marry you? How far were you willing to go to take care of me and your child?"

"Kara, don't do this. I know I've made a mess out of things, but I wasn't trying to hurt you."

"I know that. You were trying to help me. You're always trying to help me."

"And you're always throwing my help back in my face! What's so wrong about caring about you? About wanting to make things easier for you?"

"Because I don't want you to care about me. I want you to love me." The words escaped of their own volition and the second she hurled them at Lucas she longed to take them back. She didn't need to lay that kind of guilt trip on him. It wasn't his fault that he didn't love her. You couldn't pick who you loved. Hadn't she learned that as a child when her father had walked away from her mother all those years ago?

You couldn't count on anyone to feel about you the way you felt about them.

"Jesus, Kara, is that what this is about? Of course I love you—"

"Don't you dare!" She wiped an errant tear from her cheek. "Don't you dare feel sorry for me. I don't deserve that."

"Feel sorry for you? Why would I feel sorry for you when you're the strongest person I know? Kara, I admire you. And I love you. You've been my best friend for seventeen years, the person I turn to when I would never turn to anyone else. Surely you have to know how I feel about you."

"You admire me. You care about me. That's not enough to build a life on."

"I thought we'd already built a life together," he told her, his hands fastening on her shoulders and turning her to face him. "I thought that was what the last seventeen years were about. I thought that was what this baby was about. Building a life together."

She shook her head, shrugged his hands off though it was the hardest thing she'd ever done. "I need time to think."

"Okay." He nodded. "Sure. Of course. How much time?"

"I don't know. The results of the amnio will be in in a few days. Maybe then—"

"The results of the amnio? When did you go and get that done?"

"This morning. It wasn't that bad—"

"And you didn't tell me? You didn't ask me to go with you?"

"You had work and to be with your sister. I didn't need you to be there."

"What if I needed to be there? When the woman I love, the woman who is carrying my child, has a medical procedure like that done, why wouldn't I be there?"

"You were busy?"

"I was busy?" he demanded incredulously. "No way. You don't get to pawn this off on me. I told you I wanted to go. I asked you about it. You're the one who kept it to herself because you can't stand the thought of needing anyone. It's not that you're worried about inconveniencing me, it's that you're worried about needing anyone. Your dad left your mom all those years ago, but he also left you. And then your mom left you by dying and now you don't trust anyone not to leave you. You think the issues are all on my side—that I don't want to commit to anyone or take on anyone's baggage, but the truth is, you're the one who won't commit. You're the one who pushes people away before they have the chance to walk away.

"Why else wouldn't you tell me about the DHF until you were already healed? Why else would you fight me every inch of the way when I want to be involved in this pregnancy? You're kicking me to the curb before I can do the same to you. You don't trust me."

His words were absurd. Ridiculous, and yet they landed with the power of the most forceful blows.

"It's not about trust."

"Oh, I beg to differ," he said with a sneer. "From where I'm standing, it's all about trust. Do you know I've been talking to every obstetrician I know, trying to find a miracle for you? Trying to find some way to keep our baby alive? To keep you safe? I didn't want to lose you, Kara. I know how much you want this baby and I'm terrified if something happens to it you'll be devastated. I thought I was going to lose you. But I was wrong. I lost you a long time ago. Didn't I?"

"I didn't know."

"You didn't want to know." His voice cracked like a whip. "This goes much deeper, much further back than the baby. You never wanted to know, never wanted to trust me enough."

"I was trying to protect you," she said again.

"Bullshit! You were trying to protect you!" He turned then, his face distorted by pain and rage and what looked an awful lot like hate. He started to say something, then stopped himself at the last second. "Maybe I can believe you were trying to protect me by keeping that part of yourself away from me. But, Kara, that's not what relationships are about. I've leaned on you whenever I've needed to through the years, but you have never given me that same courtesy."

"Because you already had too much responsibility. Your mother, your sisters, the clinic. You always dumped women who got too demanding, who needed too much from you."

"None of them stuck around seventeen years, did they? I wasn't in love with any of them, was I? I didn't want to build a life with any of them, did I? I didn't seek them out every chance I got just because I wanted to be near them. That was for you, Kara. That was just for you. I would never resent helping you carry whatever burden you couldn't handle. How could you be my closest friend for seventeen years and not know that about me?"

"Lucas." Her voice broke and she blinked, tried to clear the tears out of her eyes that were making him look blurry. But there was nothing there. That's when she realized—she wasn't the one crying. Lucas was.

She ran to him then, threw her arms around him and held on tight. "Don't do this, please. I was trying to protect you. I swear. Do you know what it's like to go in there for these tests, to see the baby on ultrasound and realize I'll probably never get to hold him in my arms?"

"Him? It's a boy?"

"We won't know until the results come back on Tuesday. But look at you. Look at your face. Don't you get it? We're probably going to lose this baby. No matter what I do, no matter what you do, we're probably going to lose him. Do you know how much that hurts me? Why would I want you to suffer the same pain I'm suffering? Why wouldn't I want to protect you from all this if I can?"

"Because it's not your job to protect me!" he shouted.

"But it's yours to protect me?"

He didn't have an answer, so they just stood there glaring at each other as the sudden silence echoed around them.

He started to walk away, but she wrapped her arms around him, tried to hold him in place. He started to move her gently away from him. But she clung, holding on to him as tightly as she could. And eventually, he gave up fighting and just held her for long, terror-stricken seconds. Because even though he was right there, his arms tight around her, she knew that a part of him had already gone.

"When's your next doctor's appointment?" he finally asked.

"Next Tuesday."

He nodded, stepped away. "At Beaumont's office?"

"Yeah."

"I want to be there."

"Of course. My appointment's at nine-thirty."

"Text me the details. I'll meet you there."

He crossed to the kitchen then, picked up his keys from the bowl he usually threw them in. "Come on. I'll drive you home."

She stared at him stupidly as she tried to make sense of his words. "Just like that? The discussion's over and you're kicking me out?"

"I'm not kicking you out."

"Oh, really? So I can stay?"

"I don't think that would be a good idea. We both need some space right now."

"Don't put that off on me. What you mean is you need some space."

"Okay, fine. I need some space and I'd like you to leave now."

It was the final straw, the crushing blow that mixed

fear and sorrow and anger into a Molotov cocktail inside of her. Any more and she was going to catch fire. Explode.

"Fine." She marched through to the dining room, scooped her shoes up from beneath the table and then grabbed her purse off the kitchen counter where she'd left it. "But you don't need to give me a ride. I drove my car over here, remember?"

With that parting shot, she stormed out of the house and down the driveway, her head held high. She climbed in her car, started it up and began the half-hour drive to her house, the pain locked down deep inside beneath layers of icy anger. He had kicked her out. After all that talk of being there for her, he had kicked her out at the first sign of trouble. Who the hell did he think he was?

The righteous anger lasted until she was halfway home, when she glanced in her rearview mirror and realized Lucas was right behind her. Following her to make sure she got home safely. That's when the pain broke through the layers of ice she'd buried it beneath and cracked her heart in two.

CHAPTER NINETEEN

THE NEXT FOUR DAYS PASSED in a haze of misery for
Kara. After getting home from Lucas's that Thursday night from hell, she'd crawled—fully clothed—
into her bed and pulled the covers over her head. And
she hadn't come out until late the next morning when
the nausea reared its ugly head, forcing her to make
a dash for the bathroom.

After that, she'd tried to eat, for the baby's sake.
Had done some gentle exercising, again for the baby's
sake. Had sat on the couch and gotten plenty of rest,
for the baby's sake. And had died a little more with
each minute that the phone stayed silent. Without
Lucas calling to tell her he understood why she'd said
what she'd did.

She'd started to call him twice, but both times
ended up putting the phone down before she'd finished punching in his number. He was the one who
had kicked her out, who asked for space. If he changed
his mind and wanted to talk to her, he knew where
to find her.

On Monday morning, she texted him the address
for Dr. Beaumont and had waited for hours for a reply.
When she didn't get one, she texted again to make sure

it had gone through. He replied with a three-word message, Got it. Thanks.

That was it. Seventeen years reduced to three lousy words. She didn't even know how to start trying to assimilate that.

She didn't sleep at all Monday night, sick with nausea and grief and fear over what the amniocentesis results were going to show. She wanted to call Lucas, to see if he was as frightened as she was, but after his text message there was no way she could do it. She was on her own.

Which was funny, in a sad way. She'd spent almost her entire life thinking she was on her own. From the moment her father left and her mother fell apart, she had made her own way in the world. And when her mother died and she realized her father didn't actually give a damn about her, she had thought she was completely alone. Maybe, to an extent, that was true. But what she hadn't realized, what she hadn't figured out until it was too late, was that she had never really been alone. That the reason she had never been lonely, the reason her solitude had never bothered her before, was because Lucas had been there all along.

Even when they were in different med schools or different countries, he had never been more than a phone call or email away. It had taken losing that, losing him, to make her understand just how much of a role he'd played in her life, whether she'd understood it or not.

Tuesday morning bloomed clear and bright, with the birds tweeting and the sun shining and the flowers blooming all around her. If she hadn't rolled out of bed and thrown up first thing, the day's beauty would have driven her to it.

She got dressed slowly, pressing her hand against her stomach more than once as she imagined what her baby was doing inside of her. Today was the day she would find out what kind of genetic abnormalities the virus might have engendered in her child. The day she might find out whether or not she would ever be able to hold him or her in her arms, or if her body was going to destroy that dream once and for all.

She'd never been very religious, had always been something of an agnostic when it came to considering a higher power. She'd seen way too much suffering in her day, way too much violence and pain, not to wonder sometimes whether a benign God really existed. But today, for the first time in her adult life, she felt the urge to pray. Not for herself, but so that—whatever happened—her baby wouldn't suffer.

Kara closed her eyes and made a silent appeal. She didn't get an answer, but then she hadn't really expected one.

She made the short trip to Dr. Beaumont's office without the radio on. She couldn't handle the cheerful lilt of the D.J.'s voice, not when her whole world was falling in around her.

She'd timed things just right so that she wouldn't get to the office until exactly nine-thirty. She didn't think she could handle sitting around the waiting room for very long while Lucas ignored her. With any luck, he'd have gotten stuck at the clinic and be running late.

But Lucas wasn't the most responsible person she'd ever met for no reason. When she opened the door to the doctor's office, he was sitting right there in the middle of the waiting room, a magazine about parenting on his lap and a totally blank look on his face. The only emotion he showed at all, in fact, was in the way his right index finger tapped against his leg. It was the one poker tell he'd never been able to break.

The door closed behind her with a thump and he glanced up at the sound. Their eyes met and for long seconds she forgot how to breathe. His were ablaze with so much emotion that she almost got lost in them. And then, very deliberately, he turned away.

She checked in with the receptionist and then went to choose a seat. Which brought on a whole new agony of indecision. All the other women in the room whose husbands had accompanied them were sitting right up next to them. But she was afraid if she got that close to Lucas he'd make a point of getting up and moving away from her. Besides, with as churlish as he was being, she wasn't sure she wanted to be anywhere near him, anyway.

Finally, she decided on the chair that was kitty-corner to him. Close enough that it was obvious they were sitting together, but not so close she actually had to look at him or feel his thigh rub against hers.

All her worry ended up being for naught, anyway, because as she sat, the nurse called her to the back. Lucas waited for her to pass before he got up and followed her. It was strange having him there, would have been weird even if they had been getting along.

He stood to the side while they weighed her and the nurse made a disapproving sound because she'd actually lost two pounds since her visit the week before.

"Still nauseous, even with the medicine?" she asked as she wrote Kara's name on a cup and handed it to her.

"Pretty much all the time."

She shook her head. "These babies sure do take a lot out of their mamas, don't they?" She addressed the question to Lucas because Kara was already heading into the bathroom to pee in the cup. But she couldn't help herself. She held her breath, lingering by door as she waited for his answer.

"I don't know how she does it," he finally told the nurse, who nodded.

She let her breath out slowly, took care of what she had to, and then hurried out. Lucas was in exam room two and Dr. Beaumont was inside, already chatting with him.

"I didn't realize Lucas was your baby's father," she said as soon as Kara came in the room. Which, judging by the way Lucas stiffened, was pretty much the worst thing she could have said.

Not that Kara particularly cared at that moment. Her eyes were fixated on the folder the obstetrician held in her hands. The results of the amnio were in there.

"So, what did the tests say?" she asked abruptly, absolutely unable to make small talk until she knew if her child was going to survive.

Mary Beaumont smiled in understanding. "Actually, they came back much better than I anticipated. I was going to start by examining you, but let's get this part out of the way before we get to the fun stuff."

She opened the folder, handed a copy of the amnio results to both Kara and Lucas. "I don't normally do this, but will since you're both doctors. As you can see, the main area of concern is the thrombocytopenia, which, I have to admit, I've been expecting. Low platelet counts in the fetus of a mother who has had dengue hemorrhagic fever are not uncommon. There are a couple of different treatments for it and I'll talk you both about them, as well as which course I think we should follow. But the other test results are excellent, really."

"Thrombocytopenia can be treated by giving Kara a platelet transfusion once a week," Lucas commented.

"Yes. And that's what I'd like to try first. There are no guarantees this early in the game, but on the plus side, we've caught it in plenty of time to do something about it. This will, of course, necessitate a C-section, as we don't want to risk brain damage as the baby goes through the birth canal with low platelets. But this is cause for definite optimism." She smiled at Kara. "You were right all along."

Kara's relief was so acute that the room began to spin around her. She listed to the side, probably would have passed out if Lucas hadn't grabbed her and shoved her head between her legs.

Mary gave her a few seconds to stop seeing gray and then said, "Okay, you. Up on the table. At the moment, I'm a lot more concerned about your health than I am the baby's. She's doing fine—"

"She?" Lucas interrupted.

"Didn't see that on the amnio result sheet, hmm? Yes, Kara is very definitely carrying a little girl."

THE NEXT FEW MINUTES PASSED in a blur for Lucas as he tried to assimilate the fact that he *was* going to be a father—of a little girl—while also trying to catch everything Mary had to say about Kara's health which, as he'd feared all along, was quite precarious.

"We've got to get you eating," Mary said severely as she scribbled on her prescription pad. "You are now fifteen pounds under minimum weight for your height."

"I am eating. Like six times a day."

"Yes, but you're throwing up five times a day and that is not conducive to fetal or maternal health." She handed her the sheet of paper. "Here's a prescription for metoclopramide. Let's try this since the other medicine isn't working. It's a little stronger but still safe for the baby—certainly safer than having a mother who can't nourish her. And before you start in on me, yes, there's only been one definitive study done on metoclopramide, but it was a huge one and the results were very positive. Besides, the baby is at a lot more risk if you starve to death than if you take this medication."

She kept writing. "I want you to double your iron intake, which I know, is a lot with what you're on already, but there's some research that claims it will help with the fetal platelets. I'll set up the first transfusion and call you with all the information. It will be in the dialysis center upstairs and it will take about five and a half hours each time, so be prepared for that when you come.

"I'd like to see you back in one week and if you have no other questions, then you are free to go." She looked at them both, eyebrows raised in silent inquiry.

"If we can get Kara eating, she's going to be okay?"

Mary nodded. "The baby—"

"Not the baby," he interrupted. "Kara. Kara is going to be all right?"

The other doctor smiled then, reached over and squeezed his hand. "She's strong and she was healthy when all this started. The ultrasounds of her organs look good. If we can get her on track with the nausea, she should be just fine."

Relief overwhelmed him, so acute that he suddenly understood why Kara had nearly passed out when she'd heard about the baby. His legs felt like they had turned to rubber.

As Kara went to check out and make her next appointment, he muttered, "I'll meet you in front." And then he dashed for the door, not stopping until he was outside in the late-summer sunlight.

Bracing his hands on his thighs, he bent over, drew in a series of long, shallow breaths as he tried to come to terms with everything that Mary Beaumont had said. The baby—his daughter—was probably going to be okay and Kara, thank God, Kara was fine. She was fine.

A sob welled up, deep in his chest and he tried

to cough it out. Bad enough that he felt like a total louse for how he'd treated Kara Thursday night. The last thing he needed was to feel like a wimp, as well. But the second the first sob dissolved another rose up and took its place. He leaned back against the building and gave himself a minute, just a minute, to sob out his relief.

"Lucas?"

He stiffened when Kara called his name, turned his head and wiped away the tears he hadn't been strong enough to stop.

"Are you all right?" She crept closer, put a tentative hand on his shoulder, as if she was afraid of being rejected.

He was an even bigger ass than he thought, spouting all that shit at her because he couldn't deal with the fact that he'd failed her. That all these years she hadn't felt comfortable enough with him to come to him when she needed someone. That wasn't her fault. It was his, and he'd been too big of a moron to realize it until it was too late.

"Yeah, I'm fine." He straightened up and she let her hand drop back down to her side. He felt the loss keenly.

"It's wonderful, isn't it, that the baby's going to be okay?"

"Yeah, really wonderful." And it was. But it wasn't worry for the baby that had kept him up the past few weeks. It was worry for the baby's mother.

"Well, I should get going," she said. "You probably have to get back to the clinic and—"

"Don't go." The words tumbled out at the exact same second he grabbed on to her hand in a near bone-crushing grip, and he didn't even bother trying to stop them.

"I'm sorry. I'm so sorry I said all that crap the other night. It was mean and ugly and wrong—"

"No." She pulled his hand up—the one that was still entwined with hers, and pressed it to her heart. "You were right. I didn't trust you to choose me because no one ever had before. Not my mom, not my dad. But that's my baggage. It has nothing to do with you and I should have known—"

"I should have asked more, if you needed anything. If I could help with something. You just always seemed so self-sufficient—"

"I am self-sufficient."

"I know. You're the strongest woman I've ever met and I love you, so much more than I know how to show you."

"I love you, too, Lucas. I think I always have, from that first moment you grinned at me after bonking me on the head with that stupid volleyball."

He grinned. "It got your attention, didn't it?"

"Yeah, right. You don't actually expect me to believe you threw that serve, game point, just to get my attention."

"Damn straight I did. Up until then, you'd been eyeing my roommate. I didn't like it."

"You had a girlfriend."

"I still didn't like it."

"How very dog in the manger of you."

"Yeah, well, it might have taken me seventeen years, but I finally figured out what I should have known all along. I love you."

"I love you, too."

He grinned. He couldn't hear those three words enough. "The question is, what are you going to do about it?"

"Me? Why is it up to me?"

He grinned. "Because it's always been up to you. But, because I'm feeling magnanimous, I'll give you a hint."

"Oh, yeah?" She pursed her lips in that way she had that used to make him wonder what it would be like to kiss her. Now he knew. And he still wanted to feel it again. And again.

"Yeah." He bent down, kissed her soundly, reveling in the response she no longer bothered trying to hide. "If you ask nicely enough, I'll even let you make an honest man of me."

Her eyes grew wide. "*That's* my hint?"

"That's your hint?"

"You want me to ask you…"

"I do." He grinned, kissed her again. "See, there's another hint."

"I think you should ask me."

"Why? You're a self-sufficient woman. You can handle it."

She cupped his face in her hands, looked deep into his eyes. "You mean I can handle you."

"That's exactly what I mean."

"All right, then. But you're buying the ring."

He reached into his pocket and pulled out a small, blue box. "I already did."

* * * * *

REQUEST YOUR FREE BOOKS!
2 FREE NOVELS PLUS 2 FREE GIFTS!

Harlequin®

Super Romance®

Exciting, emotional, unexpected!

Turn the page for a preview of
THE OTHER SIDE OF US

by
Sarah Mayberry,

*coming January 2013
from Harlequin® Superromance®.*

*PLUS, exciting changes are in the works!
Enjoy the same great stories in a longer format
and new look—beginning January 2013!*

Coming January 2013

THE OTHER SIDE OF US
A brand-new novel
from Harlequin® Superromance® author
Sarah Mayberry

Oliver Garrett was only trying to introduce himself to his new—and very attractive—neighbor, Mackenzie Williams. Nothing wrong with being friendly, right? But then she shut the door in his face! Read on for an exciting excerpt from THE OTHER SIDE OF US by Sarah Mayberry.

OLIVER STARED AT THE DOOR in shock. He was pretty sure no one had ever slammed a door in his face before. Not once.

He walked to his place.

Clearly, Mackenzie Williams was not interested in being friendly. From the second she'd laid eyes on him she'd been willing him gone. Well. He wouldn't make the mistake of doing the right thing again. She could take her rude self and—

He paused, aware of the hostility in his thoughts. Perhaps too high a level given his brief acquaintance with Mackenzie. They'd been talking, what? For a handful of minutes?

Six months ago this incident would have made him laugh and worry about her blood pressure. Today he had the urge to do something childish to let her know that he wasn't interested in her anyway.

But that wasn't entirely true.

Because he *was* interested. When he'd gotten that first glimpse of her, had seen her gorgeous toned body, he'd lost track of his thoughts. And it had taken a second or two to remember what he'd intended to say.

So, yeah. He did want to know his new neighbor. He wanted to think there was a good explanation for her rudeness, that it wasn't a reaction to the sight of him.

Guess that means another trip next door.

Next time, however, he'd be prepared. Next time he would give her a strong reason *not* to close the door.

What will Oliver's plan to win over Mackenzie be?
Stay tuned next month for a continuing excerpt from
THE OTHER SIDE OF US *by Sarah Mayberry,*
available January 2013 from Harlequin® Superromance®.

HARLEQUIN®

ROMANTIC
SUSPENSE

Get your heart racing this holiday season with double the pulse-pounding action.

Christmas Confidential

Featuring

Holiday Protector by **Marilyn Pappano**

Miri Duncan doesn't care that it's almost Christmas. She's got bigger worries on her mind. But surviving the trip to Georgia from Texas is going to be her biggest challenge. Days in a car with the man who broke her heart and helped send her to prison—private investigator Dean Montgomery.

A Chance Reunion by **Linda Conrad**

When the husband Elana Novak left behind five years ago shows up in her new California home she knows danger is coming her way. To protect the man she is quickly falling for Elana must convince private investigator Gage Chance that she is a different person. But Gage isn't about to let her walk away…even with the bad guys right on their heels.

Available December 2012 wherever books are sold!

www.Harlequin.com

HRS27801

When legacy commands, these Greek royals must obey!

Discover a page-turning new Harlequin Presents®
duet from *USA TODAY* bestselling author

Maisey Yates

A ROYAL WORLD APART

Desperate to escape an arranged marriage, Princess
Evangelina has tried every trick in her little black book
to dodge her security guards. But where everyone else
has failed, will her new bodyguard bend her to his
will…and steal her heart?

Available November 13, 2012.

AT HIS MAJESTY'S REQUEST

Prince Stavros Drakos rules his country like his
business—with a will of iron! And when duty demands
an heir, this resolute bachelor will turn his sole
focus to the task….

But will he finally have met his match in a world-
renowned matchmaker?

**Coming December 18, 2012,
wherever books are sold.**